*"You might be able to make my body react, but you'll never touch my heart,"* Dora said.

"Is that a challenge? Didn't I warn you about making challenges? You're destined to be defeated." Khalil pressed a kiss to her forehead.

Dora wanted to scream in frustration. How could this be happening?

"You will be mine," Khalil said confidently.

"I will never love you."

"You say that now, but I wonder if you've already fallen in love with me. Am I who you dreamed about?" Khalil asked.

She turned her back on him and made a feeble effort to gather some control. She had to be strong. She had to learn how to protect herself from him. If she didn't, his words would become prophecy. He was arrogant and selfish...and he was right.

He was the kind of man she'd dreamed about. Every cell of her body ached for his possession.

Dear Reader,

With spring in the air, there's no better way to herald the season and continue to celebrate Silhouette's 20th Anniversary year than with an exhilarating month of romance from Special Edition!

Kicking off a great lineup is *Beginning with Baby,* a heartwarming THAT'S MY BABY! story by rising star Christie Ridgway. Longtime Special Edition favorite Susan Mallery turns up the heat in *The Sheik's Kidnapped Bride,* the first book in her new DESERT ROGUES series. And popular author Laurie Paige wraps up the SO MANY BABIES miniseries with *Make Way for Babies!,* a poignant reunion romance in which a set of newborn twins unwittingly plays Cupid!

Beloved author Gina Wilkins weaves a sensuous modern love story about two career-minded people who are unexpectedly swept away by desire in *Surprise Partners.* In *Her Wildest Wedding Dreams* from veteran author Celeste Hamilton, a sheltered woman finds the passion of a lifetime in a rugged rancher's arms. And finally, Carol Finch brings every woman's fantasy to life with an irresistible millionaire hero in her compelling novel *Soul Mates.*

It's a gripping month of reading in Special Edition. Enjoy!

All the best,

Karen Taylor Richman
Senior Editor

Please address questions and book requests to:
Silhouette Reader Service
U.S.: 3010 Walden Ave., P.O. Box 1325, Buffalo, NY 14269
Canadian: P.O. Box 609, Fort Erie, Ont. L2A 5X3

# SUSAN MALLERY

## THE SHEIK'S KIDNAPPED BRIDE

Silhouette®

SPECIAL EDITION®

Published by Silhouette Books
America's Publisher of Contemporary Romance

To Christina Dodd, who has spent much of the past three
years whining, "When are you going to write a sheik
book?" And to those of you who share the fantasy of the
darkly handsome man of the desert who rides in to
sweep one off one's feet. Enjoy!

SILHOUETTE BOOKS

ISBN 0-373-24316-2

THE SHEIK'S KIDNAPPED BRIDE

Visit Silhouette at www.eHarlequin.com

**Printed in U.S.A.**

**Books by Susan Mallery**

---

### *SUSAN MALLERY*

is the bestselling author of over thirty books for
Silhouette. Always a fan of romance novels, Susan finds
herself in the unique position of living out her own personal romantic fantasy with the new man in her life.
Susan lives in sunny California with her handsome hero
husband and her two adorable-but-not-bright cats.

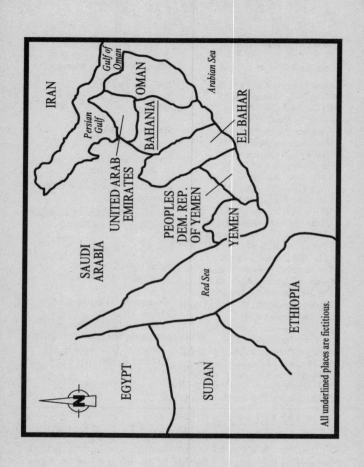

All underlined places are fictitious.

## Chapter One

A bride?

Prince Khalil Khan stared out onto the tarmac and told himself what he saw was nothing more than a mirage. He was familiar with the phenomenon, having experienced it both times he'd been stupid enough to get lost in the vast desert of El Bahar. He knew the telltale signs of shimmering heat, a wavering image, the sensation of pain pounding at the back of his eyes.

Unfortunately none of those symptoms occurred at this moment. It was January, not mid-July, and piles of dirty snow stood at the edge of the runway. So much for the shimmering heat. He had no headache—at least not one from staring at the mirage. The image in question neither wavered nor disappeared. It approached steadily in a determined fashion. There was also the small detail of this not being El Bahar. Instead, he found himself in the middle of an airfield in Kansas.

If this wasn't a mirage, then a dark-haired woman in an ill-fitting wedding gown really walked toward him.

"I've committed a grievous sin," he muttered to himself. "In a past life, if not in this one."

The woman stopped in front of him. Her eyes, a nondescript shade of brown, were red-rimmed from crying. He bit back a sigh and a curse. He loathed weak females.

"Excuse me," she said, her voice husky, most likely from her emotional outburst. "I've been stranded here." She motioned to the small airport that primarily served corporate jets. "This is going to sound a little strange, but I need a ride."

He stared down at her, giving her what his grandmother, Fatima, referred to as his imperious look, although to him it felt no different from any other expression. "You don't know where the plane is headed."

The woman swallowed. Two bright spots stained her pale skin, making her look feverish and unattractive. "I know, but it's not here. I need to get to a city." Her fingers twisted together. "I've been stranded. I don't have any luggage or regular clothes." She tugged at the waist of her wedding gown.

He was almost curious enough to ask how she came to be left at the Salina Airport in a wedding gown in the winter. She had no coat, or if she did, she wasn't wearing it. Perhaps she was unbalanced.

Just then, one of the glass doors opened and a tall, statuesque blonde came out of the terminal carrying a cup of coffee. Her short skirt exposed long, perfect legs, while her too-tight sweater outlined full breasts that jiggled with each step. When she saw Khalil, she waggled her fingers at him and smiled.

"I got some coffee," she said, as if he couldn't figure out what was in the clearly marked cup.

Again he wondered what trick of fate had brought him to this place in his life. What was supposed to have been a simple three-week business trip to the United States had turned into a hellish journey. His assistant, a pleasant and efficient young man, had been forced to return to El Bahar when his mother took ill. Both of the hotels Khalil had stayed in had lost his reservations, forcing him to sleep in a regular room instead of a suite. His jet had developed mechanical trouble, and the plane he'd chartered as a re-placement didn't have the fuel capacity to fly from Los Angeles to New York, hence the stop in this outpost of an airport. Last but certainly not least, his temporary sec-retary had an intelligence level in direct contrast to the size of her breasts. She seemed convinced that all she'd been hired to do was smile and preen. He'd made dozens of attempts to explain that he had actual work for her, but it was all beyond her capacity.

Now he stared at a lost bride who wanted his help. So ended his first week. He could only wonder what the other two would bring.

A steady throbbing began at his temples. "There are extra seats," he said at last. "We are going to New York. You may come if you'd like, but please do so silently. If you so much as sniffle, I will put you out of the plane myself, regardless of our altitude."

With that, he turned on his heel and crossed to the small corporate jet.

Dora Nelson stared after the stranger. He certainly didn't understand the meaning of the word gracious, but then she was in no position to complain. Besides, if she was going to be critical about anyone's behavior on this bright, sunny afternoon, what about her own? She was currently the reigning Queen of Stupid.

As far as she could tell, she'd only been really dumb twice in the past four or five years. Unfortunately both events had occurred within a few weeks of each other. Her first mistake had been believing that Gerald cared about her. Her second had been refusing to get back on his plane that morning. She supposed that a part of her hadn't thought that her boss and soon-to-be ex-fiancé would really fly off and leave her stranded without her luggage, her purse, or even a coat. She had no money, no wallet, and most likely, no job.

At least she had a ride, she reminded herself as she picked up the trailing skirts of her wedding gown and walked toward the waiting corporate jet. Once in New York, she could phone her bank and get them to wire her some money. Which only solved one of her problems. She didn't have identification, so flying a commercial plane was out of the question. Then there was that pesky detail of canceling her wedding. It was supposed to be in four weeks. Two days before, she'd been excited to mail out three hundred invitations. She was an idiot.

Dora climbed up the stairs of the jet. Her gown slipped off one shoulder, and she had to stop to jerk it back into place. It wasn't enough that she didn't have any regular clothes with her, but just to add to that particular humiliation, her dress was too small. The seamstress had delivered it that morning with a promise it would be perfect. Dora hadn't been able to stand waiting so she'd tried it on during the flight. The seamstress had been wrong. The cool air nipped at Dora's bare back, where the buttons couldn't be fastened.

She entered the cabin, taking in the plush leather seats, matching sets faced each other. The incredibly beautiful young blonde woman she'd noticed earlier glanced up and frowned.

"Who are you?"

Dora tried to think of a witty response, but there wasn't one. She muttered, "Nobody," as she made her way down the aisle and collapsed into a seat at the rear of the plane.

The man, the tall, dark, incredibly handsome stranger who was her rescuer, sat directly in front of her. She leaned forward and tapped him on the shoulder.

"Excuse me. I know you wanted me to be quiet, and at the risk of being asked to leave the plane, would you mind if I made some coffee?"

The man turned and stared at her. "You know your way around the galley?"

She resisted the urge to say "Well, duh." After all, it wasn't hard. But his brown-black eyes didn't contain a lick of humor, and this had not been her day. She allowed herself a simple "Yes," and waited.

He waved toward the tiny kitchenette. "Please. I would like some as well. Can you make it strong?"

"I can make it anyway you'd like." She figured she would use two of the premeasured bags, then cut hers with hot water.

"I would ask you to show my assistant, but I suspect the details of the process would be beyond her."

Dora stared at him, not sure he was kidding, yet knowing there was no way he was telling the truth. Anyone could learn to make coffee. She glanced up toward the beautiful blue-eyed blonde in her clinging clothes, and perfect makeup. Or maybe almost anyone.

Dora stood up, yanked her dress into place and made for the galley. Three minutes later, she had the coffeepot brewing. She took her seat, fastened her seat belt, and closed her eyes. Her life had taken a disastrous turn.

Somehow she was going to have to get it back on track. Easier said than done.

She drew in a deep breath and then released it. The pilot made an announcement, which she ignored, then the plane began to move toward the runway. In a couple of minutes, they were airborne. Dora didn't bother looking out the window. Flying in corporate jets had been a part of her job, and it no longer impressed her.

When they'd reached ten thousand feet, she got up and poured herself a half cup of coffee, filled the rest of it with water and popped it into the microwave. She took the man his cup. He thanked her absently. She supposed that some other time she might have been insulted to be treated like a piece of furniture, but today it suited her mood. She wanted to disappear. What she didn't want to have to do is deal with the mess that was her life.

Why hadn't she waited to mail the invitations? Why had she fallen for such a jerk? She should have known about Gerald, she told herself as she carried her steaming mug back to her seat. Maybe that was the problem, she thought sadly. Maybe some part of her had always suspected he was little more than a snake, using her to protect himself.

She continued to stare out the window, not really seeing anything, thinking and planning, wishing the next couple of weeks were already behind her. They'd been in the air nearly forty minutes when a heated exchange broke through her thoughts.

"I told you to line up these figures," a frustrated male voice said. "You're not doing it right."

"Don't be mad, Khalil," the woman purred. "I'm trying."

"Trying is not good enough. I need this report before

we land. Never mind. When we get to New York, get off this plane and get out of my sight.''

Dora glanced up in time to see Khalil wrestling a laptop computer from the blonde. At least he hadn't asked the woman to leave right now, she thought with a slight smile. She should be grateful.

Khalil turned to go back to his seat. When he saw Dora watching, he grimaced. ''I suppose you think I'm unnecessarily cruel.''

Dora shrugged. ''Not if she can't work a spreadsheet program and that's what you hired her for.''

''I was promised an efficient temporary assistant,'' he said. ''This is what I received instead.'' He pointed to the woman in question.

The blonde was about as dumb as she was pretty. She half stood and waved at Dora. ''I'm Bambi.'' She smiled at Khalil's retreat. ''He's a prince.''

Prince was not the word Dora would have used to describe the man, but he *had* given her a ride. ''What computer program are you in?'' she asked.

He glared suspiciously, then told her.

She shifted to the aisle seat and held out her hand for the computer. ''Trust me,'' she said when he hesitated. ''If you don't like my work, you can always personally escort me off the plane.''

He gave her both the laptop and a slight smile. He was amazingly good-looking, she thought, staring into deep, dark eyes. She didn't know if it was genetics or sun that had darkened his skin, but it didn't matter. The color suited him. Even the thin scar on his left cheek added to his appeal.

His chiseled features—straight nose, strong jaw, high cheekbones—made him look like an ancient statue come to life. He wore a gray suit that she guessed cost more than she'd made the entire previous quarter. With his broad shoulders and narrow hips, he was a walking, breathing cliché. She had to admit, she kind of liked that in a man.

Then she reminded herself that she was thirty, not pretty, and that every single one of the extra twenty pounds she carried were firmly planted below her waist. She was, to be slightly euphemistic, pear-shaped. Men like him did not notice women like her. Or to be a little more honest, no man noticed a woman like her. Except Gerald...and she'd discovered that morning that he'd just been pretending. It was all too much to think about right now.

She moved the cursor to the top of the spreadsheet and saw what Khalil was trying to do. "Where's the raw data?" she asked as she realigned columns.

He reached for a manila folder, then motioned for her to slide back to the window seat. He sat next to her and pulled out several sheets. "I'm doing a comparison. We're considering purchasing one of two companies. I want to do several cost analyses, then pull apart their income statements."

Dora glanced over the pages he held, then nodded. She could have done the work in her sleep. "Do you want gross sales to be net of returns or do you want to analyze returns separately?"

Dark eyebrows rose slightly, then he answered her question.

Two hours later, Dora pushed the built-in printer back between the seats and handed Khalil his report. "There are two copies there," she told him. "And you have the disk."

Bambi still sat in the front of the cabin. She flipped through a fashion magazine, apparently unconcerned about her loss of a job. Dora wished she could be as blasé about her own circumstances.

The pilot came on over the intercom and informed them they'd been cleared to land. Dora took her seat at the rear of the plane and fastened her seat belt. She glanced at her watch and stifled a moan of dismay. It was after seven in the evening, which meant it was four in Los Angeles. How was she supposed to speak to someone at her bank now? She bit her lower lip. If she'd been thinking, she could have called from the plane, catching someone before the bank closed. But she hadn't been thinking. It looked as if she was going to spend the night at the airport, sleeping on a bench. What a perfect end to her hideous day.

After they'd landed, she took her time standing up and leaving the plane. There was something especially humiliating about walking around in a wedding dress that didn't fasten up the back, and she preferred to be humiliated in private. But when she walked down the narrow staircase, onto the field, she found Khalil and Bambi still standing by the jet.

"I said you were fired," Khalil was saying.

Bambi smiled. "I know. Thank you, Khalil. It was so difficult working for you. Not just because your business stuff is, you know, so complicated, but because I could barely hold myself back." She pressed her impressive body close to his. "I want you."

Despite herself, Dora slowed to listen. She thought the only ongoing soap opera had occurred in her life. Apparently other people suffered from the same problem.

"Ms. Anderson, I have no interest in you, personally or otherwise. You are fired. Get out of my sight."

Bambi pouted. Her lips were a perfect rosebud of

bloodred. "You don't mean that. You're rich and I'm beautiful. We belong together."

He stiffened, as if insulted. "I am Prince Khalil Khan of El Bahar. You will *not* question my word."

Dora felt her mouth drop open. Bambi hadn't been kidding. He was a prince. A real prince. She frantically searched her memory for some information on El Bahar. Not much came to her, except a vague recollection that the country was somewhere on the Saudi peninsula, was ruled by a king with three sons and had long been neutral in political issues.

"But Khalil," Bambi wailed. "I was Miss July."

Dora's gaze settled on Bambi's body and didn't doubt the young woman's statement. She was incredible enough to be a centerfold. While Khalil showed admirable restraint and good taste, they would have made an impressive couple.

Khalil looked at Dora. "I don't know your name."

"That's because you didn't ask me," Dora said, stepping toward him and holding out her hand. "I'm Dora Nelson."

Khalil seemed momentarily startled by her forwardness, then took her hand in his. She'd had a split-second premonition, a voice in her mind calling out a warning, so she was nearly prepared for the jolt of pure heat that slammed through her when they touched. It was all she could do not to jump back. Khalil, of course, was completely unaffected. He released her hand and gave a slight nod.

The perfect ending to a perfect day, she thought, wishing she could laugh, or at least not break down sobbing.

"Thanks for the ride," she said, forcing lightness into her voice. "You're a real prince." She paused, pressed her fingers to her mouth. "Sorry. That came out wrong. I'm a little tired. But I am grateful." She turned to go.

"Wait! Ms. Nelson, I would like to speak to you. I am temporarily without an assistant. As I'm in your country for the next two weeks, I wondered if you would consider working for me until I leave."

"This is ridiculous," Bambi said, stamping her high-heel-shod foot. "I'm beautiful. She's not. In fact, she's—"

Dora winced and braced herself for the insult, but it wasn't forthcoming. She realized that Khalil had motioned to two men standing by the entrance to the terminal. She hadn't noticed them before, but they came over and took Bambi by the arms.

"Stop," the blonde called as she was led away. "You can't do this to me. Khalil, I know you want me. We'll be great together. Khalil, no. You're so rich and I—"

The glass door cut her off in midsentence. Dora breathed a sigh of relief. Khalil did the same.

"A most distressing woman," he said. "As I was saying, would you consider a temporary job? The pay is generous. Five thousand a week."

She blinked. "Dollars?"

"Yes, of course."

It was more than she made in a month back in Los Angeles.

She looked around the airport. Khalil's job was a gift from heaven, and miracles had been in short supply lately. She nodded. "Sure. I'll do it, on the condition that I can have an advance so I can buy myself some clothes."

He took his wallet out of his inside jacket pocket and peeled off several hundred-dollar bills. "Here." He handed her the money. "This is for you. As far as the clothes, we'll call from the car, and you can have what you need delivered to the hotel.'' He flashed her a smile. ''Consider it a signing bonus.''

Dora felt all the blood rush out of her head. It wasn't the sight of the money or the fact that her problems had been, at least temporarily, solved. It was the impact of his smile. The contrast of dark skin against white teeth, the way his lips had curved up at the corners. He'd been transformed from terrifically handsome to absolutely irresistible.

Just then, a long, dark limo pulled up next to the jet. The two men returned from their escort duties in time to hold the rear door open for Khalil and herself.

In her career as an executive secretary, Dora had found herself traveling in style a time or two, but never before in the company of a prince. She slid across the smooth leather seat to the far side of the vehicle. One of the suited men stepped in next and sat facing her. Khalil settled onto the bench seat next to her. The last suited guy—was he a bodyguard?—got in next to the driver.

They pulled away in a matter of seconds. Dora found herself fighting a smile and then laughter. Just that morning she'd been in her own apartment in Los Angeles, planning her day, expecting to be married at the end of the month. Now she was in New York, in a limo with an El Baharian prince. She'd lost her purse, her fiancé *and* her dignity. Yet all she wanted to do was laugh. Was it hysterics or simply relief that she wasn't going to be spending the night on a bench at the airport?

Khalil popped open the top of the armrest he'd lowered between them and pulled out a cellular phone. ''Here's where we're staying,'' he said, handing her both the phone and a gold-embossed business card. ''Phone the hotel, and ask them to recommend a boutique that can deliver clothing to you this evening, then get in touch with them, and order what you need. Have them bill my room at the hotel.''

He gave her a second card that proclaimed him as Khalil Khan, minister of resource development, El Bahar. She supposed the small crown in the top, center of the card made it clear he was a member of the royal family.

She glanced around the interior of the limo. The suited man stared out the rear window, but he could obviously hear everything that was being said. As could Khalil, not to mention the two men sitting up front. She swallowed. Oh, joy. She was going to have to order a week's worth of clothes, not to mention lingerie in front of four strange men. It seemed as if her good fortune was never going to end.

## Chapter Two

The lobby of the elegant hotel stretched up at least three stories. Dora tried not to gawk as she took in the fine furniture, the expensive rugs, and the chandeliers that sparkled like cut crystal…which they probably were.

She'd never been part of an entourage before, and the sensation was slightly disconcerting. Or maybe the attention they received had more to do with her attire than Khalil's wealth. Dora attempted to look casual as they crossed the marble floor and headed to the registration area, but it was tough.

They were interrupted before they could reach the clerk waiting there. A small, well-dressed man bowed low before Khalil, then introduced himself as the night manager of the hotel. They were instantly whisked into the elevator, where the manager inserted a key before pushing a button for the top floor.

So the rich didn't have to check in, Dora thought with

a slight smile. How nice. They probably got to keep the plush bathrobes as well.

When the elevator doors opened, a discreet brass plaque listed only three room numbers. Dora swallowed. Three suites took up the whole floor? That wasn't possible. Maybe there was a private club or a banquet room or something. There had to be. The hotel was huge. If there were only three suites on one floor, then they would be incredible, not to mention very large.

The manager turned left and walked a few feet before opening double doors. Khalil paused and motioned for Dora to go first. She did so, trying not to think about the fact that the sight of her bra strap and a triangle of bare flesh was anything but appealing.

She was so caught up in feeling self-conscious, she almost didn't take in the dimensions of the main room. Then she saw the floor-to-ceiling windows and a view of the city and Central Park that made her gasp in disbelief.

The living room was the size of a basketball court and decorated to befit visiting royalty. There were marble pillars and huge sofas. Original art including paintings and a nearly life-size bronze of a horse. Tucked in the corner by the window was a baby grand piano. Hallways ran both left and right. The manager pointed to the left.

"The dining room is next door, and beyond that, the full kitchen. Please let us know if you'll require the services of a chef. At the end are the offices. We've installed the office equipment you requested, along with the phone lines." He motioned to the right. "Four bedrooms, including the master suite. A light supper is set up, and several items were delivered from the boutique. We put the latter in one of the bedrooms."

Khalil nodded. "Thank you, Jacques," he said, barely paying attention to the other man. "That will be all."

The manager bowed again. "It is our great pleasure to have you as our guest, Prince Khalil. My staff is here to serve you."

"Yes. Good night."

Dora still couldn't believe she was in this room, listening to this conversation. She had to keep telling herself to press her lips together so that her mouth wouldn't fall open in shock. She hadn't known that suites like this existed, let alone ever dreamed that she might spend the night in one. Or maybe Khalil planned to give her a small room somewhere else. Who cares, she thought, suppressing a grin. Any room in this place was going to be fabulous.

Khalil spoke to the two suits, and they disappeared down the hall. Then he turned to her. "I find the bodyguards tiresome," he said. "However, my father insists my two brothers and I are protected when we travel away from El Bahar."

"It seems like a sound precaution," she offered, not sure if a comment was expected.

"I suppose. They stay in the suite and accompany me when I leave. But they are discreet and won't be in your way."

"I appreciate that," she said. How nice to know that the bodyguards wouldn't inconvenience her. And to think she'd been so darned worried about that, too.

"As you heard, your clothes are in your room. I ordered a light supper. That should be in your room, as well. I would like to begin our work day promptly at eight. The office is over that way." He pointed to the hallway on the left.

"I'll be there," she told him. "If I get lost, I'll phone for one of the maids to show me the way."

"I think you're intelligent enough to find it on your own."

As he spoke, he smiled at her. She suddenly found herself slightly breathless and had to clear her throat before she could speak.

"I'll do my best." She took a step toward the bedrooms, then paused. "What do I call you? Your Highness? Prince Khalil?"

"Khalil is fine."

She took another step, stopped and turned to face him. He was tall and forbidding in a deliciously handsome way. For a second, Dora wished that she was as beautiful as the Bambis of this world, that God hadn't been quite so generous with brains and had instead given her a pretty face or a killer body. But He hadn't, and she really didn't want to give up her intelligence. Not after she'd gotten used to it being around.

"Thank you," she said simply. "You were very kind to me today, and I appreciate it."

He waved off her words. "My act of kindness as you call it, turned into my own good fortune. I would not have survived another day with that woman tormenting me. Good night, Dora."

His final words were a dismissal, and she took the hint, heading in the direction of the bedrooms.

It wasn't hard to figure out which was hers. Two doors were already closed and a third led to a huge master suite. She had a brief impression of a four-poster bed large enough to comfortably sleep four, a sitting area, complete with fireplace, and fantasy bathroom beyond. Then she made her way to the open door at the end of the hall.

The large space had been decorated with blues and golds. The furniture looked French and highly polished. A small table in the corner contained a room service tray, and more than a half-dozen shopping bags were lined up in front of the queen-size bed.

Dora hesitated, not sure which to deal with first, then her stomach growled, and she remembered that she hadn't eaten since early that morning, back in her apartment in Los Angeles. She sat down and made quick work of the salad and roll, then moved on to the delicately flavored chicken, served with baby vegetables and saffron rice. She saved the gooey chocolate dessert for later.

Still sipping her glass of chardonnay, she moved to the bed and settled on the mattress. As she did so, the mirror on the dresser opposite reflected her image. She stared at herself and resisted the need to groan aloud.

She was a mess. Whatever makeup she put on that morning had either faded or drifted under her eyes, leaving her skin sallow and smudgy looking. Her short, dark hair had gone flat, and the ill-fitting wedding dress billowed out around her in a most unflattering way.

"My life is a mess," she told her reflection and didn't get a single argument in return.

Twelve hours earlier, she'd been happy and content, planning her wedding, preparing to travel to Boston with her boss-fiancé. Now she was alone in New York, at the mercy of a virtual stranger. Granted, the stranger was a prince, and how many people could say that about their rescuer? But he was hardly more than a temporary refuge. When her two weeks were up, she was going to have to return to the disaster that was her current circumstances. She would probably even have to face Gerald again.

The thought made her shiver, so she pushed it away. Instead of dwelling on something horrible, she bent over and pulled the first shopping bag onto the bed, then dumped the contents. She did the same with the next bag and the next until they were all empty and a huge pile of wonderfully expensive new garments surrounded her.

There were shoes and bras and nightgowns and dresses and skirts and blouses. A tissue-wrapped box contained an entire set of makeup and brushes. Another zippered case had been filled with toiletries.

She stood up and yanked off the wedding gown, tossing it into a heap in the corner, then pulled on the first dress, a soft blue silk shift that skimmed over her full hips. Delicate roses in a slightly darker shade of blue had been embroidered into the shoulder and upper bodice, drawing the eye higher on her body and actually making her looked balanced.

She looked more closely at the clothes and realized the blouses were all light or bright colors, while the skirts were more subdued. At first she marveled at the insightfulness of the boutique's manager, then she remembered that she'd given them her sizes—the top half of her body differing from the bottom by a full size less.

Dora shrugged and returned her attention to her reflection. She'd never looked better. The boutique's manager had created an attractive illusion, sight unseen. Then Dora glanced at the price tag hanging from the sleeve of the dress. Her mouth dropped open and she made an audible gasp.

Twelve hundred dollars.

She blinked. Twelve hundred dollars? For a dress she would wear to the office? She looked at the crumpled wedding gown, the one she'd bought on sale at an outlet.

She stared at the clothes she'd tossed carelessly on the bed and realized she didn't dare calculate how much all this had cost. It would make her nauseous. Instead she hung them up in her walk-in closet, then washed her face, changed into a plain cotton nightgown, which probably cost more than her wedding gown, and got into bed.

As she settled back against the fluffy pillows, she thought about her day. Which was a mistake because it forced her to think about Gerald. The man was a weasel. A walking, breathing snake of a weasel. She was better off without him. Better to live alone than to live a lie.

She believed what she was saying, even as the words broke her heart. It was one thing to find out that her fiancé had never loved her, it was another to have that information thrown in her face. She rolled onto her side and pulled her knees up to her chest. Was it her? Had she been to blame? After all, in her whole life, no one had ever wanted her.

Gerald hadn't wanted her, either, she thought as the first tears formed beneath her closed lids. He'd only pretended. He—

The sound of soft, female laughter drifted through her closed door. Dora raised her head, then relaxed as she realized her handsome prince had company for the evening. What kind of woman would Khalil Khan of El Bahar have in his bed? Someone beautiful, she thought, but the woman would have to be bright. After all, Bambi had driven him crazy.

She smiled at the memory of his encounter with the former centerfold. Who was this man who had changed her life, if only for a few days? What was he like? Was he a weasel, too, the same as Gerald? Were all men? Or was he different? Was he honorable and did he tell the truth?

She didn't want to think about him too much, preferring not to risk her temporary job by creating a fantasy world. But if she didn't think about Khalil, she would have to think about all she faced back in Los Angeles. At least she could cancel the wedding long distance. That would be humiliating enough, but better than doing it in person.

Tears came again, and she fought them. She was done crying over Gerald. He wasn't worth a single one of her tears. Except, she thought as she pulled the covers higher, she'd wanted so much for him to love her. No man ever had. But he'd only pretended. And she'd believed him. It was a sad statement about both herself and her life.

"Yes, I understand, Mr. Boulier. The restaurant's wine list is most impressive, however the prince prefers to make his own selections from his private cellar. These wines have been flown in from El Bahar. He is happy to pay the corkage fee to use his wines, but if this is too much of an insult to you and your staff, then we'll simply have to reschedule the dinner elsewhere."

Dora heard the spluttering on the other end of the phone, but she wasn't listening. Instead her attention focused on the fax coming over the second line. She caught the phrase "developments in memory chips" and knew it was the information she'd been waiting for.

"I'm sorry, Mr. Boulier, what did you say?"

"Of course I understand the prince's preference. We will be honored to accommodate his request."

Dora gave a little smile, although she kept any note of triumph out of her voice. "I'll be sure to inform him of your cooperation. The final count is thirty-five for dinner."

"But you're closing my restaurant, and we can easily accommodate twice that many. The price I quoted you was for seventy-five dinners."

"I understand. However, privacy is of the utmost importance to the prince. You'll be paid for seventy-five dinners, but you need only prepare thirty-five. Is that a problem?'' She could practically hear the man tapping on his calculator keys. He was about to make a small fortune for very little work.

"Of course not," Mr. Boulier said, his voice quivering slightly. "We'll be ready."

"Thank you so much for your help. See you tomorrow evening."

She hung up the phone, then picked it up when it rang immediately. The man identified himself. Dora checked his name against a long list, then accessed the scheduling program on her computer, made an appointment, and hung up again. Before the phone could ring a third time, she flipped the switch that sent calls to voice mail and rose from her desk. On her way out, she grabbed the waiting fax, three folders and her notebook.

Khalil's office was next to hers. He left the door open and had told her to feel free to interrupt with information or questions. In the past five days, they'd developed a rhythm in their working style, with her giving him updates once in the morning, then again in the afternoon.

She crossed the Oriental rug and took a seat in front of his desk. He gave her an acknowledging nod. "I'll just be a minute," he said.

"No problem."

She let her gaze move to the open windows behind him, through which she could see south, across the city. It was a clear but cold January morning, and from this many stories up, the city was beautiful. She'd never been a fan of New York, but the past few days had changed her mind. There was so much to do. When her temporary job with Khalil ended, she just might spend a few days here on her own...in a slightly less expensive hotel, of course, she thought with a smile.

Khalil continued to type, staring at his screen with

fierce concentration. As usual, he wore a well-tailored suit that emphasized the animal strength and grace of his body. Looking there for too long was a dangerous occupation, so she moved her gaze higher. His dark hair hung to the edge of his collar. He wore it brushed straight back, and the thick strands seemed inclined to obey his wishes. She rarely saw a hair out of place.

He had a commanding profile, all sharp edges and lines. When he at last turned to face her, she took in the uncompromising set of his mouth, the faintly stern expression that drew his eyebrows together, the narrow, pale scar on his left cheek.

Occasionally she was able to forget that she was currently employed by royalty, but most of the time it was easy to remember. Khalil held himself slightly apart. He didn't encourage familiarity and rarely responded to her humor. His keen intelligence kept her from dismissing him as pompous, and his incredible good looks gave her heart a regular workout. He was in many ways, the most complex person she'd ever met.

"How was your morning?" he asked politely as he gave her his full attention.

Dora knew him well enough to know that the question was a courtesy, not a request for information.

"Things are going well," she said, handing him the fax. "Here's the update on the new computer chips."

She paused while he scanned the document. His eyes were large and dark brown. Sometimes she would swear that he could see all the way to her soul, which was ridiculous and wishful thinking on her part. The man barely noticed she was alive. To him, she was efficient office equipment. A robot disguised as a woman.

She brushed her hand against the soft wool of her skirt and smiled at the feel of the supple fabric. As it had that first night, her new wardrobe continued to be a marvel. Today she wore a dark brown straight skirt and a fawn-colored, cropped, boxy cardigan. She would never have thought to put the two different silhouettes together, but they worked perfectly. The dark skirt created the illusion of long, lean lines, while the square-shaped sweater balanced her hips. Last Friday she'd ducked out early and had gone shopping, treating herself to a pair of riding-style boots that completed the ensemble. For the first time in her life, Dora felt vaguely attractive.

Khalil put down the fax. "What else?"

She told him about his new appointment with the scientists working on water reclamation. Khalil turned to his computer and touched a few keys, bringing up his schedule for the next day. Dora's recent entry was highlighted.

"Very good," he told her. "As a desert nation, we are especially concerned with providing enough water for our growing population and for irrigation. It is my belief that we will eventually reclaim the desert, although I'm sure she's going to be most reluctant to be tamed."

"I didn't realize the desert was considered female."

"Most definitely. All things unpredictable have that designation. Boats, planes, Mother Nature."

She wondered if he had trouble with the women in his life. As far as she could tell, he hadn't had any more company since the first night they'd arrived. Did the prince have someone special in his life? For all she knew, he was married.

The thought was vaguely disquieting. She pushed it to the back of her mind. "I've confirmed the arrangements for dinner tomorrow night," she said. "I'll have the wine shipped over in the morning."

"How much did they protest at us bringing our own?"

She smiled. ''Mr. Boulier squawked, but eventually he saw reason.''

''I'm sure you had something to do with that,'' he said, then passed her three thick envelopes. ''More invitations to charity functions. I only have time for one. Which would you recommend?''

She flipped through the elegant invitations, then shrugged. ''It's your call. Personally I would pick the one that funds Pediatric AIDS research, but there are likely to be more attractive young women at the fashion show to help the homeless.''

She glanced at him from under her lashes, but Khalil didn't crack a smile. While she wasn't expecting a knock-knock joke festival, didn't the man have a sense of humor? Still, she refused to complain. In the past five days, she'd found herself becoming an important part of his team here in the United States. She didn't just hand out papers or get coffee. Last night she'd dined with Khalil and two senators who had wanted to talk to the prince about the progress El Bahar had made in developing drought-resistant crops. While her official function had been to take notes and keep track of what information he agreed to send to the senators, when the meeting was over, Khalil had stayed up to talk with her for a few minutes, asking her opinion on the meeting.

A quiet knock at the open door broke through her thoughts. She glanced up and saw a waiter standing there with a room service cart. She and Khalil frequently shared a working lunch.

''The dining room, please,'' she said.

She picked up the folders she'd brought with her. Khalil collected a few of his own, along with a legal pad. They walked down the long hallway to the dining room, where lunch was being set up.

"Accept the invitation to the Pediatric benefit," he said. "Refuse the others."

"Sure," she said, a little surprised that he was doing as she'd suggested. But then, he frequently surprised her.

The first day, when he'd invited her to dine with him at lunch, she'd gotten all flustered and nervous. But Dora had quickly learned Khalil simply didn't like to waste time. They had much to discuss, they had to eat—why not accomplish both tasks at the same time?

She pulled out a chair and took a seat. Khalil did the same, then opened his first folder. "About the embassy party," he began.

Two hours later the table was clear, and she had enough work to keep her busy well into the night. However, she didn't mind the long hours. If nothing else, they kept her from thinking about the mess she'd left behind. Unfortunately she couldn't avoid it forever. When it was obvious their meeting was nearly over, she cleared her throat.

"Khalil, I need to take a little time off this afternoon." She hesitated. "I think an hour should do it. I have several phone calls to make to Los Angeles. I don't have a telephone credit card with me, of course. Perhaps you could deduct them…"

He was already waving away her offer. She figured he would, but she had to make the attempt.

"The calls are not an issue," he said. "Are you having problems replacing the contents of your wallet?"

"Not really. A couple of credit cards have already been delivered. Someone I know at work has express-mailed my passport to me, so I have a picture ID and can fly home when the time comes. But it's time for me to pick up the pieces of my personal life."

Until that moment it hadn't occurred to Khalil that his new assistant might *have* a personal life. She was so good at her job that he barely thought of her as a person. He frowned as he remembered the circumstances of their meeting—the airport in Kansas, her wedding dress that didn't button up the back, the lack of luggage.

"I assume this has something to do with why you were alone at the Salina airport."

Dora flushed slightly. She folded her arms over her chest and tugged at the hem of her sweater. "Yes, well, it does of course." She hesitated.

He was about to tell her that she was welcome to keep her private life to herself when he found himself wanting to know the details. "What happened?" he asked. "Are you in some kind of trouble?"

Dora looked startled. She had brown eyes, like many of the women in El Bahar, but the similarity ended there. Dora's skin was pale, her face more round than angular. She had that undeniable quality that set American women apart from women in other countries.

"I'm not in trouble the way you mean it," she said, then sighed. "The abridged version of this mess is that I was flying to Boston with my boss, who was also my fiancé. The wedding gown had been delivered that morning. I wanted to try it on and see how well it fit. Sometimes they need alterations." She pressed her lips together. "Anyway, I went into the back to try it on and when I came out, Gerald—he's my boss—had his hand up Glenda's skirt, and they were about ready to do the wild thing right there on the plane." She spoke matter-of-factly, but he could see the hurt in her brown eyes. "At least I found out before we were married."

Khalil didn't know what to address first, the fact that her fiancé had so dishonored his intended, that she'd been engaged to her employer, the identity of the mysterious Glenda, or Dora's use of the phrase "the wild thing."

He went with the most simple. "Who is Glenda?"

"One of the executives where I worked. HTS is a family-owned company. Mr. Greene does not like his employees fooling around. He actually doesn't like anyone fooling around. Glenda's married, which makes the whole thing more sleazy. I just hate it."

Usually a small, slight smile lurked at the corners of Dora's mouth, but now her lips pulled straight. Khalil felt a flicker of compassion. Dora had many fine qualities. She was intelligent and hardworking. He enjoyed her sense of humor, although that piece of news would probably surprise her. She was naturally more aggressive and less deferential than he liked his women, but that was because she was American. All in all, she was an excellent employee, and it annoyed him that her previous boss had treated her badly.

"Obviously there was a big fight," she said. She dropped her hands to her lap, then twisted her fingers together. "I was angry and hurt and humiliated. Glenda just sat there like a little female toad. Smiling her blond-girl smile. I hate her." She shrugged. "When the plane landed in Salina, I just wanted to get away from them all. I stomped off the jet and refused to get back on. I wasn't thinking."

"How unlike you," he murmured.

"Isn't it? Gerald demanded that I rejoin him, and when I refused, he told the pilot to take off. There I was, trapped with no luggage, no purse, no money. Nothing. I never thought he would leave me. But then I never thought he would bop Glenda, either." Her voice dropped to a discouraged whisper. "I guess I never knew him at all."

Whatever opinion he'd previously had of Gerald dropped even lower. Khalil thought longingly of times in ancient El Bahar when the law allowed a prince to horse-whip a man for any offense.

"Now I have a wedding to cancel," Dora said. "Three hundred invitations had gone out the previous day. Talk about timing."

"As you said, better to know now."

"Right." She gave him a quick smile, but it was as much of a lie as if she'd told him she'd long since recovered from Gerald's betrayal.

"Have you spoken with him?" he asked.

"Gerald? No, and I don't want to. He's only going to yell at me. I'm not sure how he's explained my disappearance to Mr. Greene." She swallowed. "I'm glad we're through," she said firmly. "He told me he cared about me, and he was lying. I could never have stayed with someone like that. This is all for the best."

She spoke the truth, however Khalil doubted if she believed it completely. He knew she would with time, and she would begin to get on with her life. Until then, the greatest kindness would be to keep her busy. That was, at least, something at which he could excel.

## Chapter Three

The grandfather clock in the corner of the main sitting room chimed the hour. Dora counted along, then had to hold back her surprise when she realized it was already midnight. It seemed only a few minutes had passed since she and Khalil had sat down to talk. But that had been nearly three hours before, and she knew that if she had a drop of sense in her head, she would excuse herself and head off to her own room.

Except she didn't want to go. Not only did she want to hear how the story ended, but she wanted to continue to sit here, staring at Khalil and allowing herself to pretend that he was so much more than just her boss.

"My grandmother was angry with Malik for disobeying her," he was saying. "She took his prize stallion and sold him. By the time Malik figured out what had happened, it was too late. The poor animal had been gelded. Malik was so furious he marched up to our father and demanded that Fatima be whipped for her insolence.''

"Error in judgment," Dora said, imagining an angry twelve-year-old boy whose plans to start a breeding ranch had just been thwarted by fate in the form of his grandmother and an impatient horse seller.

"Exactly," he told her. "Instead it was Malik who was severely punished. For three weeks, he was only allowed to leave his room for his lessons, and he had to apologize for 'borrowing' our grandmother's mare in the first place.''

Khalil set his brandy down on the coffee table in front of the long sofa and leaned back in his seat. "I remember speaking with him while he was being confined. He told me that when he was finally king, he would create a law that would make grandmothers answerable to their grandsons, especially when the grandsons were crown princes. When Fatima found out, she was most unimpressed. She informed Malik that first he had to grow up to be king, but at the rate he was making mistakes, that wasn't going to happen.''

Dora laughed. "Let me guess. Now Malik and his grandmother are extremely close.''

"Of course. We all adore her. Our mother died when we were quite young. She raised us. She is an extraordinary woman.''

His large, dark eyes took on a faraway expression. Dora knew that he was no longer in the large New York suite, but had instead returned to El Bahar. What was it like there, she wondered? That mysterious land of which her employer spoke. Was it as wonderful as she imagined?

"Will Malik be king?" she asked.

"When our father dies. Malik is a good leader, if a little imperious and dictatorial.''

"That must run in the family," she murmured as she took another sip of her drink.

Khalil stared at her, then raised his eyebrows. "I know you're not speaking of me."

"Of course not." But she couldn't keep the smile out of her voice.

"It is simply because you are a Western woman," he informed her gravely. "You're too used to having your way in all areas of your life. Had you been raised correctly, you would not think ill of me."

"Raised correctly?" She laughed. "I don't want to think about what that means. And while we're on the subject, I don't think ill of you. I've very much enjoyed working for you. The time has gone by very quickly." She couldn't believe there were only two more days until he returned to El Bahar. "I'll be sorry when you're gone."

She spoke the last sentence without thinking, then wondered if she'd made a mistake. In the past twelve days she'd gotten to know her employer. He *was* imperious and dictatorial, but he was also fair. At times he treated her as if she were a computer or a robot, but she didn't mind that. He was never hurtful—the way Gerald had been. Khalil didn't comment on her appearance, make snide remarks, or speak down to her. When he asked her opinion, he expected her to have one, and then he listened as she spoke. If the matter involved something strictly "American" more often than not, he took her advice.

He was also a rich, handsome prince and prime female fantasy material. She tried to ignore that information, but occasionally she forgot and found herself getting lost in his eyes, or the perfect tailoring of his suit.

"You have been most efficient," he told her. "I've been told that I expect too much of my staff, but you've never once complained. I appreciate that, along with all your hard work.''

She felt herself flush slightly at his compliment. ''You're just grateful not to have to deal with Bambi,'' she said teasingly.

He didn't return her smile. ''I believe I would have been forced to strangle her. It would have created an international incident.''

He shifted on the sofa, until he faced her. Several floor lamps cast a warm glow in the room, leaving only the corners in shadow. Despite the late hour and the fact that they were virtually alone, she wasn't the least bit concerned that Khalil would try anything. Aside from the fact that a fabulously handsome, wealthy prince wouldn't notice she was a woman rather than a piece of office furniture, she knew in her heart that he was nothing like Gerald. He wouldn't come on to her simply to relieve an itch.

She'd heard about the passions of men of the desert and watching Khalil, she could believe that he was more close to his animal nature than many Western men. But she still trusted him. He wouldn't use a woman for sport, which is what Gerald had done.

''What will you do when I leave?'' he asked. ''Not return to Gerald.''

''Never that,'' she promised, then had to clear her throat. It had tightened with a rush of disappointment.

While she'd known that he would be returning to El Bahar in the next couple of days, she'd started to hope he might want to take her with him. A foolish dream on her part. But how could she help wanting to meet his father and brothers, his grandmother, Fatima? She longed to see El Bahar and the palace. Khalil had painted a picture of a wild, untamed land entering the modern age. She found herself wanting to be a part of the transformation. Which was crazy. She was nothing more than a glorified secretary. Women like her didn't change anything.

He leaned forward and picked up his drink. "I'll make some inquiries tomorrow," he said. "I know several executives across the country. You deserve more than what you had, Dora, and I'd like to help you find that."

"Thank you."

His kind words took some of the sting out of being left behind. She told herself it was enough that he would take the time to help her. How many other men would do so after such a short acquaintance? She also told herself that she had better be careful not to make Khalil a saint in her eyes. He was very much a mortal man.

And she was very much a mortal woman, in danger of developing a huge crush on her handsome boss. So the best course of action was to remove herself from temptation.

She rose to her feet. "Good night, Khalil," she said. "What time tomorrow morning?"

"About eight," he told her. "Good night, Dora."

She smiled and left the room. A part of her wanted to believe his low, liquid chocolate voice had lingered over her name, but it was the same part of her that had been willing to believe that Gerald was a man of his word.

As she walked down the hallway toward her bedroom, she decided that despite the late hour, she still wasn't sleepy. So she would take some time to review her list of what she had left to do to cancel the wedding. If nothing else, dealing with her broken past would remind her how important it was to be sensible in matters of the heart, and that falling for one's boss was a slick, steep road to disaster.

Ten minutes later she went down the neatly printed list.

She'd already had a carefully worded notice canceling the wedding sent out to all three hundred guests. The church, the hall, the caterer, the florist, and the musicians had been canceled. She was stuck with the dress. Dora glanced toward the closet, but she couldn't see even a hint of white lace. That was because she'd shoved the garment all the way in the back. When she left the hotel, she would give it to the nearest thrift store. She never wanted to see that white gown again.

She left her desk and moved to the bed. Once there, she sank onto the firm mattress. Now, with the clarity of hindsight, it was easy to see how she'd come to be in such a mess, but at the time she'd been blind. Her own loneliness and emotional hunger had allowed her to believe that a slightly handsome, very selfish man was really a charming gentleman in disguise.

She'd worked for Gerald for nearly a year before anything romantic had happened. In that time she'd found herself daydreaming about him. Perhaps it was because she didn't have anything in her life except her work and a clean, but empty apartment. She had no hobbies, few friends, no social life. She wasn't the kind of woman men were attracted to. Some of it was her brain—she was usually smarter than the man in question and most were threatened by that. Then there was the matter of her plain face and her less-than-perfect body. And her natural reticence. She'd found herself turning thirty, living alone with no hope for a future beyond growing old by herself.

Then one night she and Gerald had been working late. She'd known he was between girlfriends. He generally dated a woman for a month or two, then dumped her for someone else. That evening she and Gerald had been together in the close confines of the copy machine room. They'd ordered in Chinese, and he'd dug up a bottle of wine somewhere. She'd been tipsy after just one glass, giggling and smiling and wishing it all could be real. Then suddenly it was—he was holding her and kissing her, and she found herself responding hungrily. All her fantasies had filled her mind until she'd convinced herself they were real. That she loved Gerald, and he'd finally recognized he cared about her, too.

Looking back she realized that a part of her had never believed, but she'd ignored the voice of reason because after thirty years of being innocent, she was finally in a man's arms.

They'd been interrupted before they'd done much more than kiss. Mr. Greene, the company president, had come across them and had been horrified. Company policy forbade casual relationships between employees, and executives had been fired for dallying with their staff. Gerald had told the older man that he and Dora were engaged.

From that moment until the fight on the airplane less than two weeks ago, Dora had existed in a blurry dreamworld. Gerald had attempted to convince her that his passion and his love were real, and she'd let him because she'd wanted it to be true. They'd pulled together a large wedding in less than two months. For the first time in her life she'd belonged to someone. But even then, she'd had her doubts. Gerald had never told her he loved her. And they'd never made love. In fact, he barely touched her.

So while she'd been devastated by what had happened on the plane, she hadn't been surprised. In that moment, she'd seen the truth in all its ugly harshness. He'd used her vulnerability because he'd wanted to keep his job. He'd never cared about her—she wasn't even sure he liked her. She was lucky to have escaped him. Except now she would always be alone.

Dora stretched out on the mattress and promised herself

she wouldn't cry. Many women were happy on their own. Perhaps she would never have a husband or children, but she could still be fulfilled. Her mistake had been to put her life on hold while waiting for a man. That's what she had to change. She would learn to be happy on her own. She was smart, and she wasn't afraid to work hard. This was the only life she had, and she'd better make the best of it.

That decided, she sat back up and reached for her notepad. She began a list. As soon as she found a job, she would start taking classes. Cooking, decorating, Italian lessons, gardening, anything until she discovered a hobby about which she could be passionate. She would search out a travel agency that catered to single women. Not to help her find a man, but to give her the opportunity to make friends with other women. She started a list of places she would like to see, then wrote down all the books she'd been telling herself she would read. She closed her eyes for a moment and earnestly promised herself she would learn to be happy by herself. Yes, she'd just suffered through a humiliating experience, but she'd been given a second chance, and she was going to grab it with both hands. She was many things, but she wasn't a quitter. If she gave up on herself, then Gerald won. She would do anything to make sure the final victory was hers.

Fifteen minutes after Dora had gone to bed, Khalil tried to concentrate on the report he held, but the technical explanation of road resurfacing could not keep his attention. Despite the late hour, the faint sound of traffic on the street below drifted into the room. It had been nearly three weeks, and he was ready to go home.

Khalil missed El Bahar. He missed the bustling city, his work at the palace, his family. While he enjoyed travel from time to time, when his trips were nearly over, he frequently found himself wishing to return home. He'd refocused his attention on the words in front of him when he heard a light tap on the door to the suite. He put down the report and frowned as he glanced at his watch. It was well after midnight, and he wasn't expecting a visitor. Perhaps Dora had ordered something from room service.

But when he walked to the door and pulled it open, he didn't see a uniform-clad waiter holding a tray. Instead a petite, dark-haired young woman with the face of an angel stared at him.

"Hello, Khalil."

Her voice was little more than a low purr. She entered the room, moving with the grace of a cat. A deep blue sequined gown outlined every perfect curve of her siren's body, makeup accentuated lovely features, especially her full, pouty mouth, and a cloud of sensual perfume settled around her. The light in the parlor flashed against the diamonds glittering at her ears, her neck, and her wrists. Her hands were small, her nails long. She was, on the outside at least, the most lovely female ever born.

She made his skin crawl.

Khalil took a step back to avoid her brushing against him. She caught the involuntary gesture and smiled at him. "Are we to play that game again?" she asked as she moved into the room and draped her fur wrap over one of the chairs. "Am I to be the hunter while you are the frightened prey?" She moved close, neatly trapping him against a pillar. "I like that game."

Sexual desire glinted in her almond-shaped eyes. She pressed her hands to his chest. "Kiss me, Khalil. Kiss me, and make love with me."

Swallowing his repugnance, he pushed her away, then stalked to the window. "Get out," he said, his voice low and controlled only by a supreme act of will. What he wanted to do was toss her out the window, or perhaps find a less violent way to keep her out of his life.

She closed the front door of the suite, then gave a low laugh. "But, darling, I'm the one who's angry with you. Not the other way around. You've been in the city for nearly two weeks, yet you've not once called me or asked me to visit. I'm quite put out." She pouted. The sexy movement of her mouth did little to arouse him.

"We have nothing to say to each other, Amber. I didn't call you because I had no desire to spend time in your company."

She waved her left hand at him. The large diamond there glittered like a dime-store bauble. But he knew the oversize solitaire was very real. He *should* know. He'd paid for it.

"You're going to have to change your mind about me, my love," she said. "After all, we *are* engaged."

Khalil turned away from her and stared out the window. As much as he wanted to ignore her words, he could not. "I don't want to marry you," he growled. "I've never wanted you."

"But you *are* a prince, and therefore marry for duty and country, rather than personal feelings. I'm your duty, Khalil. I'm your destiny."

He spun back to face her. Rage boiled inside of him. Rage and anger and frustration because there wasn't a damn thing he could do to fix the problem.

Amber leaned against the sofa and smiled at him, her lovely cat smile exposing small, white, straight teeth. Behind those perfect features and that incredible body lay the heart and soul of a snake.

He knew the truth about her—that when she was in El Bahar she played the dutiful daughter, but when she left her country and family behind, she transformed. Out in the world, Amber was a hedonist. She'd taken her first man when she was thirteen. Since then her conquests had grown in number. He'd heard her called a beautiful whore, and he wasn't sure he could find it in himself to disagree with the assessment.

She pushed away from the sofa and walked toward him. "I will have you," she whispered. "You will marry me, and then you will bed me. I will be your wife."

"Never."

She laughed. "Break the engagement? I think not. After all, you'd have to give a reason. What would you say?"

"The truth."

She laughed again. "Ah, that. You would go to my father, the prime minister of El Bahar, and offer him proof of my wild ways. You would taunt him with the facts, telling him that his favorite daughter, the very jewel of his life, was a great seducer of men? I don't think so."

Her brown eyes twinkled at the thought. "How sad he would be. That great statesman, a true leader and advocate of the people brought down by a wayward child."

Khalil ground his teeth together. He wanted to deny all that she said, but he could not. Amber was right—if he, Khalil, told her father the truth about his daughter, the man would be destroyed. Ancient El Baharian custom demanded that the father take responsibility for the sins of his children. Aleser would resign as prime minister, and El Bahar would lose a great man. The choice was simple—his silence for his country's future.

"I have money," he said.

She dismissed him with a wave. "*I* have money, too, Khalil. What I don't have is a title. I wish to be a princess."

"What about queen?" he asked. "I would have thought that was more to your liking."

She looked thoughtful. "It's something I've considered, but I'm afraid that's not an option. You see, I've already been with your brother."

He froze. Not out of anger—at this point he didn't give a damn about Amber's bedmates—but in shock. Malik?

"It was after he lost his wife," she said. She put her hands on her slender waist, then ran them down her hips. "He was so very sad, and he'd been drinking. I was alone, and one night I thought we could make each other feel better. He was very impressive." Her gaze dropped to his crotch. "I'm hoping it's a family attribute. Shall we see if we are as well-matched?"

Disgust with her curled in his stomach.

She moved closer. "Why wait? We will be married soon enough. In time I'll have sons, Khalil. Your sons. And then you can deny me nothing."

Coldness swept through him. It chilled him to his bones, then froze his soul. Resolve steeled his spine. He would not marry this woman. Somehow he would find a way to keep Aleser in office and avoid bedding this witch of a woman.

"Get out," he told her. "I have no use for a whore this night."

Her expression of good humor slipped a little. "Be careful," she warned. "I'm a formidable enemy."

"As am I, Amber. You believe you can say or do as you wish because I am trapped, but you are wrong. Know this." He took a step toward her. "I will face down the devil himself before I marry you."

"Yes, but will you destroy El Bahar?" she asked as she moved to the chair by the front door and retrieved her wrap. "You see, Khalil, the devil isn't the problem. You are your own worst enemy in this. You're a dutiful prince. You adore your people and your country. You would die for them." She laughed. "You would even marry me for them. So you see, I have nothing to fear."

She gave him a mocking bow, then left. Even as she closed the door, he could hear the light sound of her laughter.

He swore long and loud into the silence. Anger, no rage, raced through him, propelling him back to the window. He curled his hands into useless fists and wished to be anywhere but here.

He would not marry her. He swore by his honor as his father's son he would find a way out of this dilemma. But how? Did Amber have him so neatly trapped that there was no escape?

He paced to the door, then returned to the window. Frustration built inside of him. Could he tell his father privately? Would the king believe him without proof? Khalil shook his head. If he had proof of Amber's true nature, the king would feel obligated to go to his good friend, Aleser, and tell him about his daughter. As far as Khalil could see, all roads led to disaster.

He had paced for nearly an hour when the phone rang. The sharp sound startled him. He crossed to the instrument on the desk in the corner and picked up the receiver. As he did so, he heard Dora's voice.

"Hello?"

Khalil was about to hang up when a man said, "Dora, it's Gerald. Where the hell have you been?"

## Chapter Four

Khalil heard Dora's sharp gasp over the phone. He had the brief thought that he shouldn't listen, then dismissed the idea of hanging up. He was curious about Gerald. The man had behaved inappropriately and was a fool. Dora wasn't especially beautiful, but she was a good worker and he, Khalil, liked her.

"How did you find me?" she asked.

"When you canceled the caterer, you left them a phone number. Now tell me what the hell you think you're doing? You've completely canceled the wedding. How dare you do that without speaking with me first?"

"How dare *I* cancel the wedding? You're the one who had his hand up a married woman's skirt, and you want to know how I dare anything? You're an insensitive cad, Gerald. Do you even know what time it is here?"

"It's a little after ten. What of it?"

"It's after one in the morning. I'm in New York. But

as you never dial your own phone, you probably wouldn't recognize the area code." She sighed. "Not that any of this matters."

"You're damn right it doesn't matter," Gerald growled. "I don't care if you're in New York or Zimbabwe. You get your fat ass back here by the end of the week. Do you hear me?"

Khalil tightened his grip on the phone. Dora's cry of pain was barely audible, but *he* heard it.

"No," she managed, although her voice was a little shaky. "The engagement is over. I can't believe I was so stupid about you. You're nothing but a faithless jerk, and I was a moron to think you were more. I'm glad you're out of my life."

"You don't know how I wish I could stay out of it, Dora, but I can't. Mr. Greene wants to know where you are. However much either of us would like to end it right now, we can't."

She sniffed. "That's where you're wrong. I have ended it."

"The hell you have. What am I supposed to tell Greene?"

"How about the truth? How about telling him the only reason you said we were getting married was that you'd gotten caught? Why don't you tell him that in addition to trying to sleep with me, you've also been doing it with Glenda and Lord only knows who else?"

"I will not lose my job because some dried-up old virgin gets cold feet."

Khalil found himself wondering how Gerald would look after several encounters with a horsewhip.

"You always were an expert at sweet talk," she said sarcastically. "Go to hell, Gerald. I don't want anything to do with you."

''I've been to hell,'' he countered. ''I went there every time I thought about having to make love with you. Did you ever wonder why I never tried? I was actually grateful old man Greene caught us that first night because there was no way I was going to do anything with you. You're already an old woman, and you're barely thirty. You were born a virgin, and you're going to die one. No man in his right mind is ever going to want you. I'd like to—''

Khalil heard a click and knew that Dora had hung up the phone. He replaced his receiver as well, then stood in the silence of the living room. From there he could hear the faint sounds of Dora's sobs. Her pain was as tangible as the furniture in the room.

He shifted uncomfortably. Until this moment, he'd not thought of his temporary assistant as a real person. She was efficient, intelligent and humorous. He'd enjoyed working with her. He'd known she was alive, but he'd not realized she was someone with hopes and dreams, someone with a spirit, someone now bleeding from the inside.

''We've both had a hell of an evening,'' he muttered. He'd had to deal with Amber's threats while she'd been tormented by Gerald. A grim smile tugged at the corners of his mouth. Perhaps he would fix Gerald up with Amber—the two deserved each other.

He crossed to the bar at the far end of the room. He needed a drink. But instead of pouring cognac into the snifter, he paused. An idea formed. It was ridiculous and insane, as was he for even thinking it, but once the idea formed, it wouldn't go away. He set the bottle back on the bar and moved toward the hallway.

There, the semidarkness swallowed him. As he walked, the sounds of Dora's cries were more audible. Gerald hadn't just rejected her, he'd stripped her of the last of her woman's pride. Perhaps he'd tapped into some secret fear she had of not being pretty, or desirable, or whatever it was that worried thirty-year-old virgins.

He paused outside her door. The idea circled in his brain. He had to find a way to break off his engagement with Amber and do so without endangering her father's position in his country's government. He, Khalil, insisted on marrying a virgin. His bride-to-be would be a princess, which was more than license to be ornamental. She had to be intelligent and committed to the betterment of El Bahar. He wanted someone sensible, deferential and even-tempered, yet he wanted to enjoy her company. While marrying for passion would be nice, finding a woman who would be a good mother was more important.

He pictured Dora—her soft brown eyes and easy smile. Her body was harder to imagine, mostly because he'd not paid much attention to it. She had broad hips—childbearing hips. Unlike Amber's slender frame, Dora had been built to give a man strong sons.

She was not deferential, nor was she likely to allow her will to bend to his, but she had nearly all the other qualities he sought in a wife, and she was a virgin.

He hesitated in the hallway, sorting through the information. His father would be furious. It would be some time before Khalil would be forgiven for such an impulsive act. Turning his back on his engagement with Amber would bring momentary dishonor to his family, and the king would not forget. Khalil drew in a deep breath. Perhaps in time he could explain why, but in the short-term, he would have to accept his father's displeasure.

He turned the handle, and the door opened silently. Dora lay curled up on the bed like a child. She'd pulled her knees to her chest, and her hands covered her face. Her sobs had quieted, but her shoulders shook. Once again he could feel her pain and knew that she'd been stabbed down to her very soul. Perhaps she was not whom he would have chosen, but she was better than many others. A man could do much worse.

That decided, he crossed to her bed and sat on the mattress. She jumped and half sat up, then cried out and jerked the covers to her shoulders.

"Khalil, I don't understand. What are you doing here?"

Tears covered her face. Her eyes and mouth were swollen. She was not at her most attractive, yet Khalil found himself strangely drawn to her. He reached out and cupped her cheek, then used his thumb to wipe away her tears. Her skin was soft and damp, and oddly appealing.

"I couldn't stand it," he said. "To hear your pain. Sweet, sweet Dora."

He wrapped his arms around her and pulled her close. Her shock was a tangible presence in the room. He suspected that if he hadn't caught her so off guard, she would never have allowed herself to be drawn against him.

She held herself stiffly. Instead of hugging him back, her arms hung limply at her sides. Yet the feel of her this close was not unpleasant. Until now he'd never noticed the feminine scent of her body. Instinctively he knew the smell didn't come from any expensive store, but was instead her own private perfume. The heady fragrance made him think of warm sunlight and laughter. An odd combination considering it was the dead of night and she was in tears.

"I don't... You can't..." She sniffed. "Khalil?"

"I understand," he told her, again cupping her face, but this time with the intent of kissing her. With the light spilling in from the hall, he could see the outline of her breasts under the cotton gown she wore. How innocent was she? Had any man seen those curves, touched them, tasted them?

He found himself aroused, not just at the thought of her innocence, but by the feel of her womanly body against his. He could already feel the heat of his own growing desire. Making love with Dora was going to be surprisingly easy. In one single act of possession, he was going to solve both their problems.

Dora fought against the emotional fog that clouded her brain. She couldn't think clearly. Obviously she was caught up in some dream—or was it a nightmare—brought on by her own exhaustion and Gerald's phone call. Because there was no other explanation. No way was Khalil actually in her bedroom, sitting next to her and holding her close.

Except her dream was far too real. She could feel the hard planes of his chest, the strength of his arms, and the fiery heat of his body. Long, male fingers stroked her face, brushing away tears she hadn't realized still spilled from the corners of her eyes.

"Khalil?"

"Hush, my love. Hush."

She couldn't be quiet. There were too many questions. "What are you doing here?" she asked again, trying to ignore the fact that he'd called her "love." She looked at him. "Are you drunk?"

For a second, something hot and wild tightened his expression. She had the oddest sensation that he wasn't going to say a word, but instead pull her close and kiss her. Rather than being horrified, she found herself leaning toward him, wanting his kiss, regardless of whether or not this was a dream.

"Of course not," he told her. He rose to his feet and

crossed to her door. A protest formed in the back of her throat. Was he going to leave her? But he didn't. He pulled the door shut, then flipped on the light switch. Instantly the lamp on her nightstand came on and flooded the room with light.

Dora briefly closed her eyes in horror at the thought of what she must look like. No doubt her skin was red and blotchy from her crying, while her hair was a mess, and she was curled up in bed like an invalid. What must Khalil think of her?

Before she could come up with an answer, or even speak the question aloud, her brain reasserted itself, and she realized she still didn't know what he was doing in her room in the middle of the night.

''Khalil?''

She'd thought he might turn on his heel and leave. She'd thought he might start speaking. She even imagined him beginning a detailed conversation on crop management. But she never expected him to cross to the bed, sink back onto the mattress, take her hands in his and begin kissing her fingers.

She blinked several times, wondering if the blood flow to her brain had been interrupted by her crying jag. Or maybe she'd had a small stroke or seizure. There was no way she was really staring at Prince Khalil Khan of El Bahar sitting on her bed, holding her hands and deliberately, passionately kissing her skin.

But even as she doubted her eyes, she couldn't doubt her senses. Shivers rippled up her arms as heat flooded her. He pressed his mouth to each sensitive fingertip, then nibbled on the pad of her thumbs. Sounds collected in the back of her throat, but she could not speak. Air filled her lungs, but she could not exhale. Her legs stirred restlessly as her brain jumped from sensation to sensation, not sure which to settle upon. Between her thighs she felt an unfamiliar pressure, a heaviness and warmth. Her breasts seemed to swell, her nipples ached. Was this really happening to her?

"I will destroy him," he murmured against her skin. "I will have him shot."

"What?" she breathed. "Shot? Who?"

"That son of a jackal. That eater of camel dung. Gerald." He practically spat out the name.

She jumped. "Gerald?"

He raised his head and looked at her. His thick dark hair was no longer perfect and several strands fell over his forehead. His eyes burned with anger and possession. She blinked. Possession? Of her? Impossible.

"I heard you on the phone with him. He is a disgusting excuse for a man. How dare he treat you so badly? He is stupid and worthless. You, sweet Dora, you are a prize. Lovely and intelligent, you are all that a man could want in a woman. I swear I will have him shot, or if you won't agree to that, I'll at least have him horsewhipped."

They'd fallen into an alternate universe. It was the only possible explanation for what was happening. Because this sure wasn't her life. Men did not profess her to be a prize, and if one were to do that, he wouldn't be someone like Khalil.

"I d-don't understand," she managed to say, her voice trembling.

"You're better off without him," he said. "Gerald doesn't deserve you. Be happy that you're free of him." He gripped her hands more tightly. "I want you," he told her hoarsely. "I've wanted you since the first moment I saw you at the airport. It's been as torturous as the fires of hell working with you these past two weeks, playing the employer when the role I truly sought was that of your lover.''

His hot, dark gaze held her captive. She wanted to look away, but she could not. She also wanted to believe him, but she couldn't do that, either. Maybe he'd overheard part of her conversation with Gerald and felt sorry for her. While the sentiment was admirable, she wasn't interested in anyone's pity.

''I don't understand what you think you're doing,'' she began. ''It's very nice of you to be concerned, but I'm fine.'' She thought about her tears, then shrugged. ''Okay, saying I'm fine is pushing it, but I *will* be fine, eventually. You don't have to pretend that you—''

''No!''

His sharp word cut her off in midsentence. She gawked at him.

''Don't patronize me,'' he ordered harshly. ''Don't for a moment believe you understand what I'm thinking or what I want. And don't you dare assume that this is out of pity. I'm not pretending anything.''

He stood up in one quick, fluid movement, then reached for the buttons on his shirt. ''You believe him, this son of a jackal. You listen to his lies and make them your truth. Why? Why do you allow him to hurt you? He knows nothing of you.'' Khalil jerked the last few buttons free then yanked off his shirt and tossed it on the ground. ''He had his chance, and he destroyed it. Now it is my turn. I will not make his mistake.''

Dora half rose into a sitting position and scooted against the headboard. She wasn't afraid, exactly, but it was clear Khalil was going to take off his clothes. Part of her thought it might be a good idea to make a timely escape but the rest of her figured she might not get another shot at seeing a naked man. Lord knows she'd been dying for the experience for years. Besides, he was so beautiful, she couldn't find the strength to look away.

Light from the lamp illuminated his skin, adding shadows and hollows to the movement of muscles and bone. Dark hair began at the top of his broad chest, then narrowed down to his waist. As his fingers worked his belt, then unfastened his trousers, she found herself holding her breath in anticipation.

But he didn't push them down or otherwise expose himself. Instead he drew off his shoes and his socks, then placed his hands on his hips as he stared down at her.

"I want you," he told her. "Only you. I want you in my bed, in my arms. I want to touch all of you, caress you, with both my hands and my tongue. You are my heart's desire. It is not pity, it is not to thank you or heal you. I'm not that selfless. I am here because of the ache in my body." His gaze narrowed. "There are things a man can't pretend. The desire must be real. You understand?"

She nodded slowly. She understood all too well. Gerald had cut her to the core when he'd told her that he'd thought it would be difficult for him to become aroused around her. She knew that she wasn't the prettiest woman in the world, but she'd never thought of herself as so undesirable that no man could want her. Then Khalil tucked his thumbs inside the waistband of his slacks and pushed down.

The fine wool fabric bunched low on his belly. It was only then that she realized the unusual shape she'd barely noticed was the hard proof of what he said. He reached inside and drew out his erection. The trousers slipped unhindered to the floor.

"I want you," he said softly.

"Yes, I can see that." She pressed her hand over her

mouth. "Sorry," she mumbled, "I didn't mean to say that aloud."

But he didn't get angry. Instead he grinned at her. "You're impressed."

"Yes, well…" She waved in the general direction of his…his *member*. "It's quite lovely."

He took a step toward her. "Do you doubt me now?"

He'd given her fairly substantial proof. She wanted to believe him, but she couldn't quite. There were the things Gerald had said, plus why on earth would Khalil be interested in her?

He growled low in his throat. "Stop," he commanded, moving closer, then kneeling on the bed. "Stop the voices in your head and listen only to me. You will be my woman. Mine and only mine. Do you understand?"

She stared into his eyes. He was fierce and possessive, and as she looked at him she could see the wild desert behind the man. A shiver rippled through her. Anticipation? Perhaps. Fear? Certainly. But fear of the unknown, not fear of him.

"Be mine," he whispered, moving closer. "Be mine, Dora. Let me love you."

She was sure there was a perfectly witty response to all that he was saying, but she found herself at a loss for words. She could only wait until he drew his arms around her and pulled her down onto the mattress. Whatever protest she might have wanted to utter was lost at the first touch of his mouth on hers.

She'd been kissed before…at least a couple of times in high school, once at a frat party in her first year of college, and of course by Gerald. Gerald's kiss had been practiced, almost clinical. She'd never been kissed by a wild, sensual man, and certainly not one as seductive as Khalil.

She expected an assault, perhaps with him pushing her,

invading her, *taking* her, but it was nothing like that. His mouth was soft, yet firm, yielding against her own, but leaving her in no doubt of his mastery of the task. He learned the contours of her lips slowly, thoroughly. Every point of contact was fire and heat. He lay next to her, on top of the sheet and blanket, but she could feel the weight of him, and it was delicious.

One of his hands cupped her face as if he feared she might try to escape. Had she the strength or the will to speak, she would have told him that was not possible. She was trapped beneath him—more because she had nowhere else in her life she would rather be than because of his superior strength. She didn't fear Khalil; she knew in her heart he would never hurt her.

"Dora," he murmured against her mouth. "I want you. I want you, my sweet desert rose. You are so soft, so warm, so my match."

His words were as heady as wine. She'd read about people getting drunk on words, but until this moment she hadn't believed it possible. He made her writhe with undefined desire. She *wanted* without knowing what exactly would fulfill her. She needed desperately, but she could not describe the outcome that would most please her.

"Touch me," he commanded, then stroked her bottom lip with his tongue.

She didn't know which shocked her more—his request or the wet pressure on her lip. Instinctively she parted for him. At the same moment, she brought her free arm around and rested her hand on his shoulder. While his tongue slipped into her mouth, her fingers and palm absorbed the hot strength of him. He was all hard muscle and masculine scent. He was also wet and fiery and tempting as he stroked inside of her mouth. She found herself gasping in pleasure, in shock, in desperation that he never ever stop what he was doing.

He stroked his tongue against hers. The sensation and texture of him sent sparks dancing through her blood. He angled his head slightly and deepened the kiss. Fire boiled low in her belly. She couldn't breathe, yet it didn't matter. She was going to die this very moment, and she welcomed the experience. To have been held and kissed by this man was more than she'd ever expected from her small life.

He explored her mouth, learning details and discovering favorite places. He made her gasp and sigh and press up against him. She clung to his shoulder, urging him closer. She rubbed her tongue against his, circled him, then joined him in an erotic dance that left her legs trembling.

Between her thighs a rhythmic pulsing began. She felt blood pooling and a waiting dampness that signaled her readiness. Part of her was ashamed of her body's reaction to this man, but most of her reveled in her awakening. She hadn't known that such pleasures existed.

Khalil broke the kiss by moving his mouth to her neck. There he nibbled and licked the sensitive skin beneath her ear, then moved lower, to her collarbone. He rolled to the edge of the bed and pulled away the covers, tossing them to the foot of the mattress.

Instinctively Dora reached for the hem of her night-gown. It had crawled up until it was well above midthigh. But before she could push the fabric down, she felt a single male finger stroking her bare leg. Up and down, up and down, that lone point of contact moved from the inside of her knee to the top of her left thigh. She shivered. She bit her lower lip. She fought against the need to cry out his name.

The finger lifted, and the absence of his touch caused physical pain. Then he touched her again. One, brief, perfect caress on her erect nipple. As he stroked the tight bud, he stared deeply into her eyes. She found herself lost in his gaze, drowning in a pool so wet and welcoming that she could not imagine ever wanting to be free.

"Say my name," he commanded, then touched her nipple again.

Electricity, pleasure, desire, heat seared through her. "Khalil!" she gasped.

He smiled. "What a passionate creature you are, my efficient Dora. I'm a most fortunate man."

He pulled her up into a sitting position. Before she could gather her wits about her, he'd pulled off her nightgown, and her breasts were bare to his gaze.

She wanted to protest, or at the very least cover herself, but before she could think of the right words needed, he'd lowered her to her back and pressed his lips to her right breast. His hand closed over her other breast. Suddenly being topless didn't seem like such a bad thing.

She closed her eyes and absorbed the wonder of his ministrations. His tongue and lips were soft and wet against her sensitized skin. His fingers matched their movements. He circled her, brushed over her, then suckled her. All the while her body turned to liquid.

Was this what happened between a man and a woman? she thought incoherently. Was this the wonder of which she'd read? So many things became clear to her. That lovers would move mountains to be together. That they would risk death. She would have done anything to prolong the magic.

He moved against her, now licking, nibbling and loving her other breast with his mouth and teasing the first with his fingers. She watched him, then found her eyes would not stay open. She brought her hands to his head and allowed herself to touch his silky, dark hair. It was all too perfect, too incredible.

Then she felt the pressure against the side of her leg. His arousal surged against her in a rhythm so primitive, even she recognized his desire. He wanted her. For reasons that made no sense to her, this handsome, rich, kind man had decided to make love with her. She wasn't sure she believed that he really cared about her, but the proof of his desire was inescapable. That rubbing against her leg was the most precious gift anyone had given her.

Tears formed in her eyes, but not tears of pain or regret. They were of both pleasure and gratitude. How could she ever thank him?

Khalil shifted, moving lower. His fingers pulled at her panties until they lay in a tangle of silk on the floor. He knelt between her thighs and looked at her face.

"You please me," he told her. "Now I will please you."

But he didn't enter her, which is what she'd expected. Instead he bent low and kissed her most feminine place. Shock stole the breath from her lungs. Shock and the silent scream that he couldn't possibly be kissing her *there*. But he was. He gently drew apart the protective folds and touched his tongue to a tiny point of pleasure.

Dora came up off the bed. Her entire body stiffened. She didn't want to tell him to stop, but she wasn't sure she could survive the experience. He didn't seem to notice her reaction, or if he did, he didn't stop to talk about it. Instead he moved against that small bump, licking it gently, slowly, making her both tense and relax and finally sink back against her pillows.

This wasn't happening, she thought as her head moved back and forth, and she found herself pulling her knees up and out to give him more room. Men didn't really do this sort of thing, did they? Except she couldn't deny the waves of pleasure that crashed through her.

With each flick of his tongue, he carried her higher and higher, or at least that was how it seemed. In reality she never left her bed, although it felt as if she were flying. She couldn't get close enough. He had to go faster, no slower, no...

She breathed his name, then she couldn't breathe at all. She begged him to never stop, commanded him to stop, no, wait. Her muscles quivered. Heat flared on her face and her chest. Her heels dug into the mattress. She writhed and pushed and held back and waited.

She didn't know how long it went on. She was lost in a universe in which time had no meaning. She felt the flicker of his tongue and his hot breath. When she screamed his name again, she was sure she felt him smile. Her whole body collected itself and surged toward a goal she couldn't understand. Then he gently inserted one finger inside of her. As his tongue continued to move back and forth, he pressed up from the inside and stroked at the same speed, in perfect counterpoint.

The explosion destroyed her. It was too perfect to survive. She hadn't known that her body could respond, could feel, could experience the primal release of the moment. She was cast up to the heavens, then caught in strong and gentle arms. Shudders rippled through her, breaking her, assembling her, leaving her forever changed. She could only gasp and pray for a road back, then a soft voice called her name, and she found herself cradled in Khalil's arms. He held her close and touched her face.

"So the desert rose is a wildcat," he murmured, then kissed her. "You are quite the surprise, sweet Dora."

Her heart still pounded hard and fast in her chest. "Was it supposed to be that good?" she asked.

He laughed. "Only when two people are very lucky." His smile faded. "We are a good match."

Then he moved over her, again kneeling between her thighs, but this time he wasn't going to kiss her there. He was going to possess her, to change her. When he finished, she would no longer be a virgin.

It was all she could do to keep from begging him to hurry. She desperately wanted to feel him inside of her. She wanted to know what generations of women had known before her, and to become one with this incredible man.

"Tell me you want this," he told her.

"Yes, Khalil," she whispered, staring into his dark eyes and losing herself there. "Please. Be in me. Change me."

Something probed between her legs. He reached between them, guiding himself. She parted her thighs and told herself to relax, that tensing would only make it more difficult. Then he was filling her, stretching her until it nearly hurt. He pushed in deeper, then paused.

"There," he said. "The proof."

His expression tightened. He flexed his hips once and pushed. A sharp pain ripped through her, making her gasp, but he didn't stop. He thrust deeply into her, all the while staring into her eyes. Passion combined with possession. Later she would swear that she remembered the faint whisper of a desert wind as he took her into his embrace and called out to the heavens, "You are mine."

## Chapter Five

Khalil lay in the darkness. He was tired, but he couldn't sleep. Not after what had happened.

He turned his head to the left and stared at the woman curled up next to him. He could barely make out the shape of her body, but the scent of her filled his senses and made him want to pull her close so that they could make love again.

Instead he pushed himself into a sitting position and turned until his feet rested on the floor. For the first time in his life, he'd made love with a virgin. He'd heard Gerald's accusations and had assumed the man was telling the truth, but a part of him had wondered. Dora's hesitantly eager responses had also hinted at the truth, but until he'd felt his arousal pierce the veil of her innocence, he hadn't been sure.

The act of deflowering a virgin had been surprisingly satisfying. He enjoyed knowing that no man had spilled his seed inside of her—that she was, in the most primitive way possible, his.

Khalil smiled, but the gesture was more cynical than humorous. He prided himself on being a modern man, forward thinking in his quest to lead his country into the new millennium. Yet here he sat, pleased that he'd finally bedded a virgin. So much for his thin veneer of civility. He was not as far removed from his savage ancestors as he would like to think.

Which didn't answer his question about the woman. He glanced over his shoulder and watched her sleeping. Could he do this? Was it wrong?

He dismissed the queries as soon as they appeared. He was Khalil Khan, prince of El Bahar. He could do anything he liked. In matters of state, the fate of the country came first. He would not marry Amber and subject himself and his nation to her petty nature. Yet he had to marry and produce sons to carry on for him when he was dead. He was a member of the royal family—he had obligations.

Besides, without him, who was Dora Nelson? A secretary? A nobody who had been badly used by her former employer? With him, she could be so much more. She would, in fact, be honored by his proposal. This was best for all concerned.

That decided, he stretched out on the bed. When the first light of morning crept into the room, he would begin making phone calls. By the time Dora awoke, all would be arranged. He closed his eyes to sleep, but instead of relaxing, he found himself reliving the pleasure he'd found in her arms.

She'd been unskilled, but eager. Her pleasure when he'd touched her most feminine place with his tongue had surprised them both. She'd writhed beneath him like a wildcat. The memory made him smile, then grow hard.

He remembered how tight she'd been. How she'd stiffened from the pain when he'd first pushed through her barrier. But she'd relaxed, allowing him to go more deeply. He'd plunged in and out of her, feeling her give herself up to him. How fiercely she'd wrapped her arms around him as she'd urged him to completion. She'd wanted him to take her, to change her, to make her a woman. When he'd climaxed, she'd clung to him, as if she never wanted him to go.

He'd had every intention of returning to his own room, yet somehow he had not. He'd spent the night here, at her side, listening to her soft breathing and waiting for dawn. Even now, when there were only a few hours left until the new day began, he stayed in her bed. Aroused and wanting, he pulled her close and breathed in the scent of her hair. She stirred against him but did not wake. He would sleep another time. For tonight, this was enough.

Dora stirred slightly under the covers, which seemed especially heavy this morning. She turned over and bumped into something...warm.

Her eyes flew open. Khalil lay next to her, his brown eyes alert, his mouth smiling. "Good morning," he said.

She swallowed hard as memories from the night before crashed into her. Her conversation with Gerald, Khalil's declaration that he couldn't keep his hands off her, the way they'd made love. The last thought brought sensual images to mind, of him touching her, kissing her, taking her. She felt a flush of embarrassment crawl up her face, and she had to fight the need to duck under the covers and never come up.

"Ah, so you *do* remember what happened last night," Khalil said, his voice as low and gentle as his caresses had been. "I'd hoped you might." He placed his hand on her bare shoulder, then stroked her arm. "I think we did very well together." He slipped one leg between her thighs. "So well I had trouble sleeping. All I could think about was wanting to make love with you again."

She blinked at him but didn't have a clue as to what to say. What was the correct social response on the morning after? Especially when the night before had not only been unexpected, but had also been her very first time?

"Thank you," he said, and pressed a kiss to her cheek.

She didn't know whether to laugh or to scream. Here she was, naked, in bed with a handsome prince, who by the way had his bare leg between her bare thighs, and he was thanking *her* for their close encounter. Had the world gone completely crazy? Or was he looking for a way to let her down gently? Was that what this was about? Did he want to find an easy way to let her know that she would be a fool to have any expectations?

"I had a nice time, too," she said at last when it became obvious he was waiting for some kind of response. She wished she could put a little space between them, but she didn't know how to do that without being thought of as rude. She would also like to get up, but she was naked and the only bathrobe nearby was clear across the room in the bathroom. She did not relish the thought of walking around naked in front of Khalil. While his bare body had been sheer perfection, she saw no need to flash her flaws in the light of day.

"I was hoping you would think our lovemaking was more than just nice," he chided. "How about spectacular? Extraordinary? Even magical?"

He was teasing. She could tell by the tone of his voice. His playfulness gave her a little courage. While she had no illusions about his expectations for any kind of relationship with her, perhaps this wasn't going to end badly.

"I think I'll stick with nice," she said primly, then braced herself for his retaliation.

He didn't disappoint her. He waited less than two seconds, then lunged toward her, tickling her stomach and her side. She screamed and tried to wiggle away, but he was much stronger. Using only one hand, he pinned her arms above her head, which gave him free access to her naked torso. But instead of continuing to tickle her, he bent down and licked her nipple. She shivered.

He released her and sat up. "We are well-matched," he said, repeating what he'd told her the previous night. "I was not wrong to choose you."

His words didn't make any sense. "What are you talking about?"

He frowned as if he expected her to intuitively understand. "Isn't that obvious? We are to be married this afternoon. The ceremony will be at five. I've already spoken to the manager of the boutique where you got your other clothes. One of their salespeople will be bringing by a selection of dresses at two."

As he spoke, he rose to his feet and reached for a bathrobe she hadn't noticed draped across a chair. Her ears heard what he told her, her brain absorbed the information, but it had no meaning. He might as well have been discussing the lack of oxygen on Jupiter, or the number of single-celled animals who lived at the bottom of the ocean.

"Married?" she asked, sure she'd misunderstood.

"Yes. That is what I said."

She pressed her lips together and stared at him. Married? *Married?* Them? "You want to marry me?"

"Of course. Why are you surprised?"

How much time did he have to listen to that answer? she wondered grimly. This had to be a joke. A cruel bit of humor that had gone awry. Marriage? To her? Sure. Princes fell in love with their secretaries every day. "We're not in some movie from the forties," she said angrily. She sat up and pulled her knees to her chest, making sure she remained covered by the sheet and blanket. "I don't think this is funny."

"Nor do I," he said coolly.

Her eyes burned. She realized she was close to crying—probably because there was a part of her that wanted to believe it was all true. She'd never allowed herself the fantasy of imagining Khalil caring about her. It was too ridiculous to stand. But he wasn't a heartless man; at least she'd never seen proof of that. So why would he act this way now?

"I don't understand," she whispered. "Why are you doing this to me?"

"It's perfectly clear," he insisted. "I've wanted you from the first moment I saw you. You are intelligent, reliable, honorable and healthy. You have all the qualities I require in a wife. Until last night, you were a virgin. I am Prince Khalil Khan and I do not dishonor women."

This was twisted even for him, she thought, trying to come to grips with what was happening to her. "You can't mean that. You don't really want to marry me."

"Why not?"

There were probably forty-seven thousand reasons. Unfortunately she couldn't come up with one right now. She shrugged and made a vague movement with her hand. "Because."

"Ah, that makes it all clear."

He returned to the bed and settled next to her, then he took one of her hands in his. "What are you afraid of?"

She searched his gaze, wondering if she really dared to speak the truth. But as she couldn't think of anything else to say, she didn't have much choice. "That this is all a game to you. If it is, I don't understand the rules, and I know I'm going to get hurt. I don't want that." The truth was she wasn't sure she would survive more heartache right now, thank you very much. She would prefer to be left alone until she recovered her equilibrium.

He reached toward her and tucked a lock of hair behind her ear, then touched her face. "I understand," he told her, even though he couldn't possibly. "You want to believe me, but you're afraid. What happened to my lovely desert wildcat?"

"She had another appointment this morning and couldn't be with us."

He flashed her a smile. He hadn't showered or shaved yet, and stubble darkened his jaw. He looked rugged and dangerous and she shivered at the thought of them being intimate again.

"I adore you," he said and squeezed her fingers. "I know that this has happened very quickly, but that doesn't make the experience any less valid. Trust me. More importantly, trust yourself, sweet Dora." He leaned close. "I want you, in my bed and in my world. Marry me. Come back with me to El Bahar. Help me with my work. Help me change the world that is my country. You see, I must go back, but I'm not sure I can if you refuse to accompany me."

His words fell like rain in the desert. She soaked up every syllable, drank in the sounds, then let them blossom deep inside of her. Oh how she longed to believe him. Could this be happening? Could someone like her really be so very fortunate?

She stared at him as if the truth lay in his handsome features. From the beginning he'd been autocratic and annoying, and he'd worked her hard, but he'd never been cruel. He'd never lied. She'd listened to him while he dealt with both customers and suppliers. He was tough, but honest. He had a moral code. He wasn't Gerald.

That was what it came down to, she thought. Her fear that like Gerald, he was using her to get something he wanted. Except he was a prince and what on earth could he want that she could give him? She was an unemployed, nearly middle-aged spinster with a few office skills. And he...he was Khalil Khan, prince of El Bahar. In her heart she'd always known that Gerald was much less than she wanted him to be. Something about Khalil made her think he was so much more.

Before she realized what he was doing, he'd taken her in his arms, then stretched her out on the mattress. He reached under the covers and began to stroke her belly.

"Marry me," he murmured against her neck. "Be my wife. Come home with me. Have my sons. I will make you a princess. My sweet, lovely Dora."

It was impossible to think while his fingers tickled her ribs, then moved higher to her breasts. He circled the full curves, then teased her nipples. She gasped as pleasure filled her, and her woman's place dampened in anticipation of his possession.

"Khalil," she breathed.

"Yes," he told her. "Want me, need me, as I have wanted and needed you. Believe in me. Life has just offered you a great prize. Don't be afraid. This once, reach out and grab it with both hands. If you don't, you'll regret it for the rest of your days."

Of all the things he'd said to her, the last statement was the one that got through. She knew all about regrets. She'd lived with them all her life. She regretted her unhappy childhood, her initial college experience, her lack of relationships through her twenties, her relationship—if she could call it that—with Gerald. So many regrets. And not one of them was about something she'd done. She didn't regret her actions, just her *inactions*.

Were her dreams at last coming true?

"Marry me," he urged, still kissing her neck and her throat. "Say yes."

She took a deep breath. Did she want to keep living with regret or did she want to take a chance? She bit her lower lip, then closed her eyes and exhaled a single word.

"Yes."

Khalil sat up. "I knew I could make you see sense. Good."

He bounded to his feet, then reached down and pulled her to hers. Before she had a chance to register her nakedness or be embarrassed, he stepped behind her and gave her a gentle push toward the bathroom.

"Go ahead and shower. There's much to be done before the wedding. I'll meet you in the dining room in twenty minutes."

With that, he was gone. Dora stared after him. Somehow that was not the response she'd expected when she'd agreed to marry Khalil. Married? She shook her head. None of this was really happening. Obviously she was caught up in a weird dream or something. Or maybe she'd hit her head in the night. Either way, she might as well shower, if only to get on with the dream and see what would happen next.

The wedding party consisted of Khalil, Dora, a justice of the peace and the two bodyguards who served as witnesses. Dora glanced around the large parlor in the beautiful hotel suite and told herself that the management had worked a miracle in a very short period of time.

White roses and baby's breath had been woven through

a narrow wooden arch. Large, pale pink urns filled with white roses, lilies and orchids sat on squat tables, which formed a makeshift center aisle in the room. She and Khalil stood on a long, white cloth that had been tacked down from the entrance of the room to the edge of the archway, and soft music played over the suite's sound system.

Dora clutched her bouquet of exotic flowers more firmly in her hands and told herself that considering there had been less than twelve hours to pull it all together, things had gone surprisingly well. Promptly at two the boutique had delivered a half-dozen dresses for her to look at. She'd chosen a simple ivory lace gown that looked like something from the 1920s. She'd managed to pull her shoulder-length hair up into a French twist so that the delicate pearl earrings Khalil had given her at lunch were visible.

She knew she looked pretty good. Khalil was handsome and confident in his dark suit. Under the circumstances, they were doing well. And that was the problem. She wasn't comfortable with the circumstances, nor could she stop shaking. Even now, with the judge talking about sickness and health, she felt as if she were still in her dream. Or maybe she'd gotten trapped in a made-for-television movie. Or maybe it was mental illness. Or maybe it was really happening.

Dora didn't know which would be more frightening. Was she really marrying Khalil Khan, prince of El Bahar? She shook her head slightly, trying to clear her thoughts. Maybe it was the wedding that was messing up her brain, she thought frantically, desperate for an excuse. Nothing was the way she thought it would be. With Gerald, their wedding plans had been a little rushed, but they'd had more than two months in which to come up with a plan.

There had been guests and a church and a reception at a hall, and she'd had a real wedding dress.

She glanced at Khalil who listened attentively to the judge. What was he thinking? She wanted to stop the ceremony and talk to him but she didn't know what words to use. Perhaps he didn't think this was out of the ordinary. After all, when she'd emerged from her room after her shower, she'd found him already working in his office. He'd given her little more than an absentminded greeting, then he'd thrust a stack of folders at her and had turned his attention back to his computer. She'd spent the morning before her wedding dealing with last-minute business problems. As if nothing between them had changed.

"Dora?"

She looked up and realized both Khalil and the judge were staring at her. "What?"

Khalil smiled. "I believe the response he's looking for is more along the lines of 'I do.'"

I do what? she wondered, then it sank in. "Oh. Sure. I mean, I do." She gave a little cough that did nothing to ease the tightness in her throat.

"The ring please," the judge said, taking Dora's flowers from her and setting them on a nearby table.

Khalil reached into his pocket and pulled out a diamond ring. Dora stared, first at the glittering piece of jewelry, then at him. Was that for her?

"Fit for a princess," he murmured and slid it on the ring finger of her left hand.

She opened her mouth to protest. It was too extraordinary, too lovely, too expensive. Then she remembered she was not only marrying royalty, but into one of the richest families in the world. To Khalil this was probably as significant a purchase as her buying a nice pair of panty hose.

The judge started talking again, but she wasn't listening. Instead she found herself captivated by the stunning ring that glittered on her hand. The band was wide, nearly reaching to her knuckle, and the entire ring was a circle of diamonds. Square-cut stones nestled together, each diamond as long as the band was wide. She didn't know how many diamonds it took to make up the ring, but each had to be at least two carats. It wasn't a piece of jewelry she would have picked for herself, but it was lovely and felt as if it had been made for her hand.

"You may kiss the bride."

She looked up in time to watch Khalil bend down and press his lips to hers. The kiss was sweet and far too short. Then he squeezed her hand.

"Do you feel any different?" he asked.

"Being married?"

"That, of course, but I was wondering how it felt to be a princess."

Princess Dora Khan of El Bahar, she thought to herself and had to fight back a burst of hysterical laughter. "I don't think it's sunk in yet," she told him, wondering if it would ever sink in.

"Congratulations, Your Highness," one of the bodyguards said, as he shook her hand.

Dora smiled automatically, but otherwise her body had gone numb. A princess? Yeah, right, that was her. Who was she trying to kid? Reality was she was a secretary from Los Angeles who had stumbled into a crazy situation. She had to get out before she said or did something stupid. Like throw up...or worse...believe all this was really happening.

Except she didn't get to make her escape. Before she'd realized what was going on, the judge was gone and the bodyguards had retreated to their rooms. She was alone with her new husband, watching him pour them each a glass of champagne.

Who was this stranger? she thought warily as she moved to the sofa and settled in the corner. What had she done? Her nervousness increased, as did her shaking, and when he handed her the glass of champagne, it was all she could do to keep from spilling the bubbling liquid all over her lace dress. In an effort to keep that from happening, she swallowed a mouthful of champagne, decided the taste was exceptionally nice, then finished her glass. Khalil refilled it without saying a word.

He put the ice bucket on the table in front of her and settled next to her on the sofa. "Are you all right?" he asked.

He sounded kind and sincere, she thought frantically. So normal, as if he did this kind of thing all the time. Except he couldn't, right? "Isn't this making you crazy?" she blurted.

He took a sip of his drink. "What? The wedding? I thought things went smoothly."

"Oh, yeah, sure. Clockwork in motion, or whatever." She paused. The saying was "poetry in motion," so where did the clocks come from? She rubbed her temple. Her stomach tingled and she thought it might have something to do with the champagne. Just to be sure, she drank a little more. She hadn't eaten that day, and she was also thirsty. The fizziness tickled her throat. Was it her imagination or did her head suddenly feel heavy?

"I think I should probably eat something," she mumbled.

"Of course," Khalil told her. "Dinner is waiting whenever you're ready."

"Great." Except the thought of standing up was suddenly too complex. "Maybe in a minute."

She looked at him, at his handsome face. The lines of his profile were sharp, like a statue of granite. He was dark and dangerous, like the desert at night. Not that she had any personal experience with the desert at night *or* during the day.

"I know this is unfamiliar," he said, lightly touching the back of her hand. "We need to spend a little time getting to know each other. Why don't we talk about our past? After that, we'll eat dinner, and then we'll make love until dawn."

Making love, she thought hazily. Now that would be very nice. Maybe they could skip the other parts and get right to doing it. She hiccuped softly, then took another drink. She wanted to do it again and again until she learned everything about it. She wanted to touch Khalil and have him touch her back. She wanted to see him naked, in fact she thought this little chat about their past might be more enjoyable if he took his clothes off right now. She would very much like to see the "it" that made doing it so very enjoyable.

"Do you have any brothers or sisters?"

His question cut through her fantasies and left her confused. Then she remembered that they were getting to know each other. A sensible plan. Khalil was right—once they knew more details about each other's lives this wouldn't be such a strange situation.

She finished her glass of champagne and started to set it on the coffee table, but Khalil filled it instead. She thought about refusing, after all, her head was already spinning, but wouldn't that be rude? It was his wedding, too, and... What had been his question?

"No, I'm an only child." She leaned back against the sofa. "My mom never said anything, but I think I was a mistake. She and my dad got married about two months before I was born. After that, he was never around much. They divorced when I was seven.''

''I see. I'm the youngest,'' he said. ''I can't imagine what it would have been like to be an only child.''

''It's lonely,'' she said bluntly. ''Probably not for some kids, but it was for me. My mom worked a lot to support us, and my dad wasn't one for regular visitation. Plus, I wasn't really popular at school.'' She shrugged, then rolled her head so that she could look at him. ''Too smart. I wasn't pretty enough to get in with the right girls, and I think I scared all the boys away. Plus I was shy, and I never knew what to say to anyone. It was easier to hide out in the library and read.''

She took another sip of champagne. It tasted tartly sweet and slipped down easily. The tingling in her belly had spread to her whole body, and her brain definitely felt thick, but in a nice way. Like she was protected from anything too scary.

''When did you stop being lonely?'' he asked.

She angled toward him and pulled her knees up onto the sofa. ''Yesterday, I think. I can't really remember.''

Khalil's features started to blur together. Had she had too much to drink? Or was it just the soft lighting in the suite? Her eyes fluttered closed, and she felt warm fingers brush against her cheek.

''College wasn't too bad at first,'' she said dreamily, getting lost in the past. ''I had a scholarship that paid for most things. I liked being in a place where it was considered a good thing to be smart and to work hard. But living on campus cost more than I thought, and I had to get a job to supplement my expenses.''

She opened her eyes and looked at him. ''My mom didn't have any extra money to spare. I don't suppose that's ever been a problem for you.''

"No, it hasn't."

"Must be nice."

"Sometimes, but we've had other problems."

"I guess everyone does. Anyway, I started tutoring. I worked with athletes a lot. Mostly because they paid the most. But they weren't interested in anything but getting by. They didn't want to learn. Isn't that horrible?" She blinked and found that her eyelids were extraordinarily heavy. She swallowed a little more champagne to help her stay awake.

"One day I found my study notes missing. I confronted a couple of the guys, and they wouldn't admit they'd taken them." She sighed remembering the hurtful things those boys had said. "I refused to tutor them anymore. About three weeks after that, a bunch of the guys were caught cheating. They were going to be expelled, but they weren't content to go quietly. They said that they were using a cheating system I'd come up with and had charged them for."

Her words caught in her throat. That had been so long ago, she would have thought it didn't have the power to hurt her anymore, but it did. She remembered her time in the dean's office, when it had been her word against theirs.

"Six of them told the same story. Six," she repeated quietly. "No one believed me, not about the notes or that I refused to work with them, or that I hadn't had any part of the cheating. So I was expelled along with them. I went home, got a job and saved my money. A year later I started at my local community college, then I received my associate's degree."

She pressed her lips together. "This probably isn't what you wanted to know, is it?"

"I want to know whatever you want to tell me."

She tried to smile, but her face felt numb. "I don't think so. I doubt any part of my life is very interesting."

"That's not true." He stroked her cheek again, and the contact felt lovely. "Why didn't you go back to college and get your four-year degree?"

She shrugged. At least it felt like she was shrugging on the inside, even if she didn't feel any movement on the outside. "I was afraid of what might happen. I didn't want to go through that again. Except for when Gerald left me in that airport in Kansas, it was the most alone I've ever felt."

Khalil leaned close and took her glass from her, which was a good thing. When had her fingers gotten so stiff? She could barely bend them.

"You, my desert rose, tell a very sad story," he murmured. "But all that is about to change."

She desperately wanted to believe him. "Do you promise?"

"Yes." He moved next to her and took her in his arms. "Nothing is going to hurt you ever again."

"Not even you?"

"Least of all me."

Then he kissed her. Those wonderful warm, firm lips settled on hers. Her eyes drifted slowly closed as a lethargy filled her body. She was drifting, drifting, drifting... And then there was only darkness.

## Chapter Six

The redheaded model strolled down the center of the showroom, her lithe, insanely slender body barely making any movement under the burnt umber silk of her column dress. Dora stared at the garment and tried to ignore the skinny eighteen-year-old beneath. While she adored the color, the style would never work on her. She shifted uncomfortably on the gilded chair in the exclusive salon Khalil had brought her to this morning. He'd wanted to buy her a new wardrobe before they left for El Bahar later that afternoon.

She told herself to be happy with his generosity. She told herself that he was being kind and attentive, and she very nearly bought into her own story. The only thing holding her back was the fact that she'd awakened alone in her bed that morning, and there hadn't been any evidence that Khalil had ever joined her. But she wasn't sure she had the right to be upset, either, because most of the previous evening was a blur.

She remembered bits of the wedding, and she remembered afterward, when she and Khalil had sat together talking. She certainly remembered the champagne. She pressed two fingers to her temple. Even now her head pounded in a not-so-gentle reminder that too much liquor on an empty stomach did not leave her feeling her best.

At some point she must have fallen asleep—she didn't dare even think the phrase "passed out"—and Khalil had put her to bed. It's not as if she wanted her husband to make love with her while she wasn't conscious, so she shouldn't be upset that she woke up alone. Technically nothing was wrong. Even so she couldn't shake the feeling that something wasn't exactly right, either. After all, she'd spent her wedding night alone.

Babette, the owner of the fashion salon, fingered the delicate silk of the column dress. "The fabric is quite extraordinary," she said. "And the color would be fabulous on madam."

Oh, right, Dora thought glumly. And wouldn't madam look amazing with her hips pulling at the seams and completely destroying the line of the dress. But she didn't say that. She didn't say anything. The exclusive establishment left her feeling out of place and more than a little inadequate. All the saleswomen looked like former models. Babette was petite and incredibly well-dressed. Despite wearing her new favorite blue dress, Dora felt frumpy and fat by comparison.

Babette regarded her thoughtfully. "However, I'm not sure the style is going to flatter madam."

What insight, Dora thought sarcastically. Give that lady a prize. Then she sighed and reminded herself that her defensive attitude came more from fear than because she felt slighted. She didn't belong here. She didn't belong back in Los Angeles, either. She was homeless and confused and to make matters even more stressful, she'd just married a prince.

Khalil had stationed himself at the rear of the viewing room, close to the entrance of the salon. As soon as Dora had been settled, he'd started making calls on his cellular phone. Now he dropped his phone into his jacket pocket and crossed to stand beside her. His gaze raked over the model who had paused to turn in front of him. Her pouty mouth curved up in what was an invitation to look...and maybe more. Dora wanted to slap the teenager and tell her to go back to high school. Instead she told herself that the shopping trip wasn't going to last forever.

Khalil turned to Babette. "The girl looks as if she hasn't eaten in a month. Don't you pay your models?"

Babette's perfectly made-up face blanched. "Your Highness, I assure you—"

He cut her off with a glance. "My wife has a wonderful womanly shape. I not only desire her, I am fortunate to have her as the future mother of my sons. She is a princess, madam. You would do well to remember that."

Babette managed to look both composed and stunned at the same time, while Dora was sure she only looked shocked. Khalil then bent down and pressed his mouth to her cheek. "I still have calls to make. Are you all right?" he asked quietly, his breath tickling her ear.

"I'm fine," she managed to answer.

"Good. Let me know if they give you any trouble."

With that he returned to the counter by the door and reached for his phone. Babette gave her an appraising glance. "He must love you very much, Your Highness. You are a fortunate woman."

Dora didn't have a response, so she just smiled. She

was willing to admit to fortunate, but she was also confused. Did Khalil, as Babette suggested, love her? Dora wanted to believe that was so, but she wasn't sure. Everything had happened so quickly.

She glanced up in time to see the redheaded model disappearing around a screen. Three more models appeared, each in a different type of clothing. One wore a short nightgown that barely skimmed her knees. The light green silk reflected the light, while side slits emphasized thighs, not hips. The second model sashayed along in a hunter-green velvet evening gown that was so beautiful, it made Dora's mouth water. The shoulders were wide and padded, the neckline plunging, while the lightweight velvet skimmed over the lower half of the body. Dora thought she just might have a shot at wearing that dress and looking decent.

The final model had been attired for business, in a navy pin-striped coatdress with a wide collar. Behind the models, three more women appeared, each carrying several outfits.

"We will start with the basics," Babette said, turning to her. "These are all in your size. Why don't you see what you like, and then we can start with the fittings. Marie—" She pointed to a tall, young blonde. "We'll need shoes." Babette looked at Dora. "Your Highness, what size shoes? Oh, and may I offer you some coffee, or perhaps a light snack?"

Three hours later all Dora wanted to do was curl up in a ball and sleep for a week. She hadn't realized that trying on clothes could be so exhausting. She stood in the center of a large dressing room with two fitters working on the dress she wore.

She'd lost track of how many outfits she'd already chosen. Babette had a master list, but for Dora it was all too confusing. There were the clothes themselves and the shoes. Babette had chosen hats for some of the dresses, as well as pins and scarves. There were wraps for evening gowns and a casual coat for her slacks. One clerk had brought out a tray of costume jewelry, but Babette had cast a meaningful glance at Dora's impressive wedding band all the while murmuring that "Her Highness will not bother with artificial stones," and the tray had been whisked away.

The two fitters finished their work. Dora took the moment of freedom to step out of the changing room and go find Khalil. What had he been doing all this time?

She made her way into the front of the showroom and saw him speaking with a young woman. At first Dora thought she was one of the salespeople—she was too short to be a model. Then Dora realized their conversation wasn't the least bit casual.

As she watched, her controlled, elegant husband put his hand on the woman's shoulder and pushed her away from him. The woman, her long, dark hair swaying down to the middle of her back, glared at him and spoke. Dora was too far away to hear their words, but she read the anger in the woman's body language. Rage surrounded her like a venomous cloud.

Khalil gestured. The woman shook her head, then, as if she'd just caught the scent of something unpleasant, she froze and turned.

Instinctively Dora took a step back. But it wasn't enough. The young woman stared at her. She was so beautiful that Dora's breath caught in her throat. Her perfect features were marred only by the look of pure hatred in her large, expressive eyes. For a moment, Dora thought her life was in danger. Then Khalil took the woman's arm and led her out of the boutique. Dora moved toward them, wanting to ask him who the woman was, but before she got close enough, Babette had cornered her.

"Your Highness, you must try on the rest of the shoes."

Dora nodded, but promised herself she wouldn't forget to speak with Khalil later.

"Khalil, who was that woman in the store?" Dora asked as the limo drove them from the hotel to the airport where Khalil's private jet waited. "The pretty one you were speaking with so intently."

Khalil thought about pretending he didn't know what she meant, but he knew her well enough to know that she wouldn't be easily distracted.

The pretty one, he thought with faint humor. Amber would be most insulted by the inadequate description. She wasn't merely pretty—she was a goddess…and a snake.

"She is of no importance," he told her with a smile. "A friend of the family. Her father works in government. I told her about our marriage."

"She didn't seem very happy about it."

Khalil thought of Amber's shriek of rage and her threats to both him and Dora. "She was surprised, nothing more."

He spoke easily because the lies were all Dora needed to know. The fact that Amber had gone for his eyes, then had called him names even he hadn't realized she'd known wasn't anything his wife needed to hear.

His wife. He looked over at the quiet stranger he'd married. She might not be as lovely as Amber, but in every other way she was Amber's superior. If he'd had any doubts, the chance—or perhaps not-so-chance—encounter with his ex-fiancée in the salon had taken care of them. Dora would learn the duties of her new position quickly. She would be loyal, loving, and would never cause a scandal. If he were lucky, she might even grow to be more pliable with time.

He reached over and took her hand. "I'm happy to have married you," he told her.

She gave him a slightly shaky smile. "I'm glad."

He squeezed her fingers, then released her. Yes, he'd been fortunate to find a way out of his dilemma, and he'd found an adequate substitute as well. It had been a very successful trip.

Dora stared out the window of Khalil's jet, but the terrain below was as unfamiliar as a moonscape. She didn't know enough about the region to be able to tell where one country ended and another began, and unlike her school atlas, the different areas weren't neatly color-coded. She could only stare and wonder if they'd crossed into El Bahar yet.

The trip was too long, she thought, trying to hold panic at bay. She'd had too much time to think, especially when Khalil had dimmed the cabin lights, stretched out in his comfortable seat and fallen asleep. Now they were within a few minutes of landing, and she desperately wanted to tell him that she'd changed her mind.

She glanced to her left and saw Khalil lost in a report on waste management. He'd slept for most of the eleven-hour flight, then had awakened in time to eat breakfast, shave and change into a clean shirt. She looked at her own wrinkled dress and wished she'd thought to bring something to put on before they landed, but she hadn't and all her luggage was stowed in the belly of the jet.

*I'm fine,* she told herself, even though she didn't believe the words or the sentiment behind them. She wasn't fine, she was terrified. What on earth was she doing here?

In a panic, she reached for the air phone tucked neatly into her armrest. Then she paused. Who was she going to call? She hadn't seen her father in twenty years, and her mother had passed away the year Dora had turned twenty-five. There weren't any other relatives. As for friends, most of them were more acquaintances than people she would feel comfortable confiding in. Besides, what was she going to say? That in day two of her marriage, she was having serious second thoughts? That she was terrified about leaving her country behind and moving to El Bahar?

She dropped her hand back to her lap and sighed. She was going to have to get through the next few days without doing anything rash. In time, the situation would settle down, and she wouldn't feel so lost in unfamiliar territory.

She looked at Khalil again and saw that he was still reading the same page of his report. Was he distracted as well? Was he having doubts? She desperately wanted to ask him, but then she decided she was afraid of the answer. What would she do if he said yes, that he wasn't sure, either?

If only they'd had one more night in New York before leaving for El Bahar. If only she hadn't gotten so drunk the night of their marriage so they could have talked more and made love. If he could have held her one more time and told her that he cared about her, she would have felt better about everything. But they hadn't. Instead they'd boarded his private jet, repaired at last. There were not only the pilots, but two stewards who had seen to their every need and not given them a moment's privacy.

Pressure built at her ears, and she instinctively swallowed. They were descending. Dora looked out the window and saw that they'd left the vast desert behind. Below them was a sprawling city with wide streets and hundreds of buildings, including modern glass towers. She caught a glimpse of glittering blue.

The Arabian sea, she wondered in astonishment. Had she really come halfway around the world?

"There's the palace," Khalil said, pointing out the window. "On the coast. You can also see the old city walls."

She saw a huge creamy-white structure poised on the edge of the water. Beyond it extensive grounds formed a patchwork of colors. The wall he'd spoken of made a rough square around much of the city, although it didn't include the high-rises she'd noticed earlier.

Excitement began to replace the panic inside of her. From the safety of the jet, El Bahar looked exotic but still welcoming. Perhaps things weren't going to be so frightening after all.

The jet made a smooth landing, then taxied to a small single-story building at the far end of the runway. As Dora stepped out of the jet, she noticed a much larger terminal across the tarmac.

"That's for the commercial aircraft," Khalil said, noticing the direction of her gaze. "Immigration and customs are there, as well. On the far side we have a substantial area for freight companies. They even have their own runways. As you can see, El Bahar is ready for the new century."

"Very impressive," she told him.

She walked down the narrow flight of stairs and drew in her first deep breath of El Baharian air. It was slightly cool, but pleasant. She caught the elusive fragrance of a flower of some kind, but couldn't see anything planted nearby. The sky overhead was an amazing shade of blue, and seemed more vast than any sky she'd seen before. She told herself that she was being fanciful—that this was the same sky she always looked up at. Yet it felt and looked different.

Khalil led the way to the waiting limo. It was white and had two small flags on the hood. The bright gold royal emblem fluttered in the light breeze. As she approached, she noticed the uniformed chauffeur holding open the rear door, but before she could slide onto the back seat, Khalil stopped her with a light touch on her arm.

"Dora, this is Roger, our favorite driver. He's been with my family for as long as I can remember."

The chauffeur, an attractive light-skinned man in his fifties, touched the brim of his cap. "Thank you, Prince Khalil, but I must take offense at the phrase 'for as long as I can remember.' The young lady is going to think I'm as old as dirt." The Englishman smiled as he spoke.

"Maybe not as old as dirt," Khalil admitted. "How about as old as time?"

Roger grinned. "All right, Your Highness. Be that way if you must." He winked at Dora.

She found herself smiling back at the older man. At least the first person she'd met in El Bahar hadn't terrified her.

Khalil gripped Roger's shoulder briefly. "I'm glad you're the one who came to the airport today," he said. "Now Dora won't be so worried about staying in El Bahar."

She glanced at him in some surprise. "How did you know what I was thinking?"

"I'm your husband. Why wouldn't I know?"

She didn't know how to respond to the question. Yes, he was her husband, but he didn't know her very well. At least she didn't think he did. Or had she misjudged him? Perhaps he'd been telling the truth when he said he'd noticed her from the first moment they'd met. The idea left a warm glow in her stomach.

"Your wife?" Roger said, his voice laced with disbelief. "Sir, I had no idea." He pulled off his cap and gave Dora a low bow.

She was so startled by the act of deference that she could do little more than stare at Roger's close-cut sandy-red hair before glancing helplessly at her husband. But Khalil didn't look the least bit upset by the other man's actions. Of course, he was a prince by birth and quite used to this sort of treatment.

"Your Highness," Roger began. "I meant no disrespect. If I'd known—"

Dora might not know much about being a princess, but she knew plenty about getting along with people. "I hope you would have been as friendly to me," she said gently, as she cut him off in midsentence. "The prince is correct. This is my first time in El Bahar, and I'm a little nervous. You've given me a gracious welcome."

"Thank you." Roger nodded his head, then motioned to the open door. "If Your Highness pleases."

Dora slid onto the rear seat. Khalil followed, but not before Roger said, "Well done, sir. She's quite the lady."

Khalil didn't respond. Dora knew that she wasn't supposed to have heard the comment, but it allowed her to relax a little. Perhaps she had a chance of getting it right after all. If only the royal family was as friendly as Roger, she would be just fine.

When the luggage had been loaded into the trunk, Roger got behind the wheel and started the limo. In a matter of minutes they'd left the airport behind and were headed for the city. Dora let her gaze move from window to window as she took in the sights of her new homeland.

They headed south to the coastal highway, then east,

toward the city. The roads were wide and well-maintained, and the cars she saw were a mixture of old and new. The blue sky drew her attention again and again, and she found herself wanting to lower the window so that she could inhale the scents of the air.

"Would you mind?" she asked, lightly touching the control lever.

"Please." Khalil leaned back in the seat. "This is to be your home. I want you to feel comfortable."

She thought about telling him that she'd feel much more comfortable if he would touch her arm or take her hand, but she didn't have the courage. They might technically be married, but she didn't feel she had the right to any of a wife's privileges.

She pressed the lever, and the window on her side lowered soundlessly. Instantly a cool breeze whispered against her face. She could feel the warmth of the sun, inhale the faint salt of the sea, along with that strange, slightly sweet aroma.

They were in the far left lane of the highway, moving along at a fast rate of speed. Dora saw rows of palms along the side of the road. "Date palms?" she asked.

"Yes. Not that long ago they were a staple food supply through the long summer. Now they have become more of an export crop, although they are still a part of the El Baharian diet. Look." He pointed to her left.

She turned and saw a man in nomadic dress leading two camels laden with burlap bags.

"He's heading for the *souk*—the marketplace," he added. "One of the largest and oldest in the city is by the palace. I'll take you there sometime."

Despite her nerves, Dora felt a flicker of excitement at the thought of all the exotic adventures awaiting her.

They continued toward the city. As they passed through

the financial district, she strained her neck to try to see the tops of the glass high-rises. Several of the names on the signs out front were from companies she recognized.

"Jamal, my middle brother, handles the country's finances, as well as the family money." Khalil jerked his head toward the cluster of Western-style buildings. "While my father had the idea of making El Bahar the financial center of the Arab world, Jamal is the one who made it happen. He designed the packages that brought the big banking and financial companies here. Of course our billions are substantially less than the Bahanians' wealth."

"Who?" she asked.

"Bahania—it's our neighbor to the northeast. Between us and Yemen. My father always says that his troubles are nothing when compared with the king of Bahania. Where I am one of three sons, the king of Bahania has four sons and a daughter." He shook his head. "The two fathers are good friends, and for a while my brothers and I thought there would be an arranged match between the two countries, but my grandmother is Bahanian, and there was concern about mixing the blood lines."

Dora stared at him, her interest in the city temporarily forgotten. "Your father has arranged marriages for his sons?"

"Of course. We're a royal family."

As if that explained it all. Except it explained nothing. "But you don't have an arranged marriage." Horror gripped her. "You have. You have other wives." Her stomach tightened as a cold fever swept through her. Wasn't El Bahar a Muslim country? Weren't men allowed four wives? Dear God, she'd made a hideously, awful mistake and she had to—

Khalil laughed. "I'm not sure what you're thinking

right now, but you look as frightened as a mouse about to be eaten by a hawk. I have no wife other than you, Dora. El Bahar allows its people to celebrate many religions, but a man may take only one wife. My father claims for some men that's one wife too many.''

She licked her suddenly dry lips. ''Are you sure?''

His expression turned indulgent. ''Quite sure. I've lived here all my life, and I'm familiar with the customs. Now stop asking questions and look. We're coming up to the palace.''

Only then did she notice that they'd turned off the main road and were on a side street. Although the street was smoothly paved, the alleys leading off between buildings were cobblestoned. She could see storefronts and small houses right next to an apartment building with brightly colored laundry lining the balconies. In a large side yard, a half-dozen children played soccer. One of the boys—a child of maybe eight or nine—saw the car and called out to his friends. Immediately all the children ran toward the limo. They waved and called out greetings. Khalil put down the window on his side and waved back.

''Prince Khalil! Prince Khalil! Welcome home.''

One of the little girls bent down, picked a flower and tossed it toward the slow-moving car.

Dora felt as if she'd found her way into central casting for some movie from the fifties. ''They speak English,'' she said.

''Most people here do,'' he told her. ''It's required in all the schools, and we encourage it in business transactions. El Bahar is preparing itself to be a major player in this century.''

''I see.''

Dora continued to watch as the car turned down a long, tree-lined street. So far all that she'd seen had made her feel better about her situation. No doubt the worst was behind her.

"There," Khalil said, pointing straight ahead. "The entrance to the palace."

They drove through huge gates that were open. Nearly a dozen guards stood on duty. Once inside the walled complex, the driveway circled lazily through lush gardens. Through the thick foliage she caught sight of buildings, ponds, tennis courts and an army of gardeners.

"The palace grounds are open to the public twice a week," he said. "There is a small zoo, as well as gardens and walking paths. Different entertainments are provided during holidays and festival times. Residents are never charged, for the palace is as much theirs as ours, while visitors to our country pay a small fee."

The sweet smell grew stronger. Dora inhaled it, then felt her breath catch in her throat when they rounded the last bend in the road and pulled up in front of a huge, cream-colored building.

The structure extended for what seemed like miles in both directions. It was at least three stories tall with a beautiful tile roof that shimmered in the midday sun. Balconies clustered together, their black wrought-iron railings contrasting with the clean lines of the palace.

A huge archway led inside. As Roger opened the rear door and held out his hand to assist her, she saw that the circular area in front was paved in tiny cobalt-blue tiles. They formed a pattern that looked like the ocean, with fish and boats existing in harmony. It was exquisite and made her feel instantly at home.

"Welcome, Princess Dora," Roger said, then gave her a wink. "Ready to meet everyone?"

"I hope so." She glanced at Khalil who stood beside her. Roger had been surprised to learn that the youngest prince had married. What about Khalil's family—specifically his father? "Do they know about me?"

"My father does. He was delighted when I told him."

It was a small lie, Khalil thought, but one that Dora needed to hear. He didn't have to know her well to sense her nervousness, although he couldn't blame her. It wasn't every day that one met one's in-laws. The situation would be worse for a woman marrying into a royal family. Especially as she wasn't anyone the family would have picked.

He thought about his conversation with his father the previous day. King Givon Khan had roared out his displeasure, refusing to listen to anything his son had to say. Khalil doubted the old man had settled down since then.

They walked across the courtyard with its dozen or so fountains and the guards posted every few feet. El Bahar was a peaceful country, and the men were mostly there for show. The automatic weapons and ammunition draped across their chest were most impressive. Dora pressed close to his side.

Up ahead he saw that the entire family had turned out to greet him. His two brothers lounged against the large pillars in front of the open double doors leading into the palace itself. Malik, Jamal and himself all shared the Khan family characteristics of dark hair and eyes. The three men were more than six feet tall, with Malik topping the other two by about a half inch. They were handsome, although Khalil privately considered himself the best looking in the group.

His grandmother waited on the bottom step. Her slender, nearly frail body gave fools the impression she was weak and feeble, but Fatima Khan could still outwit them all. He found himself hoping his grandmother would take to his new wife. Fatima's acceptance would make a great difference to Dora's life in the palace.

Finally Khalil's gaze settled on his father. Givon Khan was nearly sixty, yet he looked as straight and strong as a man twenty years younger. Despite his preference for Western-style dress, he was often an old-fashioned king. He ruled El Bahar with wisdom and patience…a patience he rarely showed to his sons. Khalil saw the disappointment and anger in his father's eyes and knew there was going to be trouble.

Khalil and Dora paused in front of the group. No one spoke. His grandmother glared at her son, the king, which meant they'd already had words about Khalil's marriage, but the old woman didn't move toward him. Khalil placed his hands on Dora's shoulders and felt her tremble. He squeezed slightly to give her courage.

"Father, I would like to introduce Princess Dora Khan. Dora, this is my father, King Givon of El Bahar."

Dora surprised him by stepping forward and giving his father a very smooth curtsy. "Your Majesty, thank you for welcoming me to your most wonderful country."

Givon glared at her, nodded briefly, then turned his attention on his son. "Khalil, I have been angry with you in the past, I have been frustrated, but this is the first time I have wished you were not my son."

Dora turned and gave him a stunned, hurt look. Khalil wanted to reassure her, but this wasn't the time. He thought about trying to explain the situation, but again, he had to wait. Eventually he would tell his father the truth about Amber and their engagement, but not right now. First he had to establish his place—and Dora's—in the palace.

He drew his wife into the protective embrace of his arm, then faced the king. "You may say what you wish to me, Father, but you will treat my wife with the respect she deserves. I would ask that you welcome her as your new daughter.''

Young eyes glared into old. Tension cracked in the air. It was a battle of wills, something that Khalil had never won before. But then nothing had ever been this important. He waited. Dora trembled again.

The king took three steps forward until he stood in front of Khalil's wife, then he put his hands on her shoulders, leaned forward and kissed both her cheeks. ''Welcome daughter, to the house of your new family. May you be blessed with long life, many sons and peace in your old age.''

Dora smiled at the king. ''Nothing about love?''

The king looked as startled as Khalil felt. He hadn't expected her to *speak*. This wasn't some New York City restaurant with his father acting as the lunchtime manager.

''I fear your new husband will not be with you long enough for love to endure.''

''If you're so angry that you're going to kill him, then I don't suppose I can hold out much hope for those sons you promised me.''

Khalil was shocked when his father's stern mouth curved up at the corners. ''Perhaps I'll just have him flogged.''

She leaned toward the king and lowered her voice to a confidential whisper. ''I know exactly how you feel.''

Givon, king of El Bahar, laughed out loud, then drew Dora into a warm embrace. ''I have the first hint as to why my son turned his back on tradition and married you. All right, I'll put my anger aside for now. Come, Princess Dora. Come and see your new home.''

## Chapter Seven

The rest of the introductions passed in a blur. Before Dora could put names to faces, she found herself being led down a long, wide hallway by a dark-haired servant, then shown into a stunning three-room suite. The young woman was talking, but Dora couldn't hear anything. She could only stare in disbelief.

The main parlor was at least thirty by forty feet with twenty-foot ceilings. Cool marble covered the floor, but the walls were creamy white—nearly the same color as the palace itself. A large mural of a mother camel and her baby at an oasis decorated the wall to her left, while tapestries hung on the right.

Western-style furniture made an attempt to fill the vast space, but there was enough open area to hold an aerobics class. Still, the most spectacular feature of the room was the wall of windows leading out to a balcony overlooking the Arabian sea.

Dora walked to the French doors and let herself out. Instantly soft sea air surrounded her. The faintly sweet scent teased her, making her relax. There were small tables and chairs along the balcony and she realized it was common to all the rooms on this floor. The individual balconies with their wrought-iron railings were one floor above.

As she had been when she'd first stepped off the airplane, Dora was swamped with a sense of entering a very foreign world. While she seemed to have made a good impression on the king, it hadn't lasted very long. He'd been anxious to get rid of her—probably so he could speak with his wayward son. If the family wasn't happy with her marriage to Khalil that must mean that they'd had other plans for him. Which made sense. He was a prince, after all. It wasn't as if they were going to let him pick his future wife.

"Oh, Khalil, what have you done?" she asked softly and covered her face with her hands. Why hadn't she thought this through? He wasn't a regular man who got to choose his future bride. He was royalty. Marriages like his required state approval, didn't they? Or was that just in England? She glanced down at the heavy diamond ring she wore. Perhaps they weren't even married.

"Your Highness?"

Dora straightened, then turned to see the servant standing just inside the living room. "Yes?"

The woman was in her early twenties, very pretty, with large dark eyes and beautiful hair pulled back into a bun. She wore a short-sleeved gray dress with sensible flat shoes.

"Your suitcases have arrived. I would like your permission to begin unpacking your things."

Dora felt as if she were suddenly in a movie where she

was to play the innocent American tourist thrust into a difficult situation. But she had a bad feeling her problems weren't going to be neatly solved in less than two hours.

"What's your name?"

"Rihana, Your Highness." The young woman gave a slight curtsy. "It is my honor to serve you."

Dora wished she could say that it was her honor to be served, but she knew it would take her a long time to get used to that. "Are you allowed to call me anything but 'Your Highness'?"

Rihana smiled. "Of course. Princess Dora is an acceptable title."

"Then let's use that, instead. If I hear my name, I have a better chance of realizing you want a response." Dora glanced to her left and saw oversize double doors. "Is the bedroom in there?"

"Yes."

"Then why don't I unpack my clothes myself? That way I'll know where they are."

Rihana frowned. "Princess Dora, my job is to take care of you."

"And before I arrived, what was your job then?"

"I am part of the household staff."

"I see." Dora smiled. "But as I've just arrived, I'm going to guess that your assignment to help me is recent. Therefore you probably still have some household tasks to complete."

Rihana looked confused. "Of course, but they will not interfere with my service of you, Princess. I am a hard worker."

"I have no doubt." She drew in a deep breath. "I'm not used to the ways of this country, or of the palace and it's going to take me a little while to fit in. For now, let me unpack myself. I promise tomorrow you may serve as you see fit.''

Rihana hesitated. Dora smiled, then pointed to the door. ''It's all right, Rihana.''

The young woman made her way toward the exit. ''If you change your mind, simply pick up the telephone and ask for me.''

''I will. Thank you.''

When she was alone, Dora stepped into the bedroom. This room was slightly smaller than the living room, but no less impressive. A four-poster bed stood on a raised platform in the center of the room. The opposite wall was glass, with French doors leading out to the common balcony. Blue, green and gold tiles formed a mosaic on the walls, the colors circling each other in exotic disarray.

The furniture was slightly more Oriental, with black-lacquered sides and gold Chinese characters for drawer pulls. Dora crossed the marble floor and pulled open the wooden closet doors, then blinked in stunned surprise at the empty space before her.

This wasn't Khalil's suite of rooms; she hadn't been put in with her husband. Instead she'd been shown to guest quarters, who knows how far from the family's section of the palace.

Fear and worry knotted in her stomach. What did this mean? Was it a mistake? Would Khalil come looking for her when he realized she wasn't to share his room? Or was this the way of royal life in El Bahar? Why on earth hadn't she done some research before they'd left New York?

Fear turned to panic when she realized that except for Khalil and his family, no one in the world knew where she was. Everything had happened so quickly, she hadn't had time to call any of her acquaintances. Her mother was gone, she hadn't seen her father in years. She could simply disappear, and no one would ever miss her.

She walked into the living room and paused by the entrance. Was she a prisoner here? Scenes from old movies filled her brain. Pictures of women trapped, stolen, killed. Her mouth went dry as she wondered if she would ever see the land of her birth again. Sadness filled her as she realized she had only herself to blame for this situation. She'd been so excited to have a man interested in her that she hadn't thought about the consequences of her decision. A prince had appeared in her sad little world, and she'd jumped at his offer of marriage.

She had to get out of here. Now!

Dora pulled open the door to her suite and stepped into the hallway. Her first shock was that the door opened easily, the second was that there wasn't a guard posted in the hallway. She still remembered those fierce, armed men by the entrance to the palace.

She looked one way, then the other, trying to remember the direction to the front of the palace. If her suite faced the water then that was south and the palace faced...

"Princess Dora, may I help you with something?"

"What?"

She looked up and saw an elderly man standing in front of her. He carried several thick towels in his thin, brown arms. His dress wasn't familiar to her—an open robe over light-colored loose trousers and an equally loose shirt—but his expression was friendly and welcoming.

"Are you hungry, Your Highness? May I bring you a tray of food? Or would you like me to call Rihana?"

She opened her mouth then closed it. Obviously if she wanted to escape, she needed a plan. "I'm fine," she said. "Thank you."

She retreated to her room. First things first, she thought,

as she shut her door. Item one—calm her heart rate. Item two—figure out a plan.

She collected a pad of fine linen paper from the desk in the corner, then settled on the sofa. After drawing a rough outline of the palace as she remembered seeing it when they'd flown over on their way to the airport, she began filling in the rooms she knew. Which meant she could write in the entrance, a hallway and her suite. Nothing else. Maybe she could ask Rihana to take her on a tour.

Dora leaned back into the comfortable cushions. Perhaps she was making this too difficult, she thought. Maybe she should simply pick up the phone and ask to be connected with Khalil. After all, he was her husband. If they could speak, if she could at least *see* him, things would be better. That decided, she closed her eyes for just a minute. She hadn't slept the night before on the plane. She'd been too tense, with too much on her mind. Just for a second, she thought drowsily. One little second...

"I'm sorry, child, but you don't have much time," a voice said.

Dora stirred, then blinked and realized she was in a most awkward position, sprawled in a corner of the sofa. She looked up and saw a tall, slender woman with streaks of gray in her thick, dark hair. A beautifully tailored sapphire-colored suit made her look regal, while matching stones glittered at her ears. But it was her face that captured Dora's attention. Despite her obvious age and the tiny wrinkles in her paper-thin skin, she was an amazing beauty.

"Fatima," Dora breathed as she first sat up, then rose to her feet. She realized she was speaking with a woman who was both the mother of the king and a queen in her own right. "I mean, Your Highness." She gave a shaky curtsy.

Fatima patted her smooth chignon and gave a quick wave. "Oh, please, we're family, my dear. If Grandmother is too familiar, then call me Fatima. Or 'Exalted One.' I've always enjoyed that particular title. Of course it was first spoken to me by a visiting head of state some forty years ago. The man in question had his hand sliding up my inner thigh as he said it. I informed him that I was more than willing to be his lover but when my husband, the king, found out about our affair, and I was very bad at keeping secrets, he would make sure that particular dignitary lost his ability to ever be with a woman again. If you get my meaning."

Fatima winked, then her expression turned slightly sad. "I miss him. My husband, not the other man. Despite my teasing, I was a good and faithful wife for nearly forty years. We had a wonderful marriage." She touched the neckline of her suit. "It's Chanel. Don't you simply adore the Chanel line? I knew Coco, but then at my age, it's easy to have known everyone. So you're Khalil's new wife. I would guess that you're quite confused by all this." She motioned to the room.

"More now than before," Dora replied without thinking, then pressed her fingers to her mouth. "I'm sorry. I didn't mean to say that."

Fatima surprised her by laughing. "Yes, but the point is you were thinking it." The older woman took a seat on the far end of the sofa, then patted the cushion next to her, indicating Dora should sit as well. Dora sank down gratefully.

"I'm a bit eccentric," Fatima continued. "Some of it is age, but a lot of it is just me. I've had more than seventy years to perfect my oddness and I take great pleasure in doing or being the unexpected." She leaned forward and lowered her voice. "We're surrounded by men, my dear. If you haven't noticed, you will. Givon's sweet wife died some years ago and I can't get him to remarry. He had three sons. Bahania, our neighbor to the east and the land of my birth, has a royal family with four sons and only one daughter. We women have to stick together."

Dora didn't know what to say to Fatima, so she kept quiet. She still had the oddest sensation of being caught up in a dream. Of course, she'd been living with that feeling since Khalil had first walked into her bedroom and told her that he wanted her.

"The palace is in an uproar," Fatima said. "Part of the problem is that the youngest son of the king married in a foreign country in a civil ceremony to a complete stranger." Fatima leaned forward again and patted the back of Dora's hand. "No offense, dear, but we don't know you, do we?"

Dora could only manage a weak, "I suppose not," in response.

"Then there's the whole issue of Khalil not being like this at all. I won't say he's the most arrogant of his brothers because they can all be difficult, but he's not impulsive. Now if Malik had suddenly shown up with a bride in tow, that would have been more understandable. But not Khalil." Fatima frowned thoughtfully. "How well do you know my grandson?"

Dora swallowed. "I, um, worked for him while he was in the United States. I was his secretary."

Finely plucked eyebrows rose at her statement. No doubt Fatima knew that Khalil had been away for all of three weeks.

"An impulse," the dowager queen said more to herself than Dora. "Has he told you about his scar?"

The unexpected question left Dora blinking in confusion. "The one on his face?"

"It's the only one I know about, although if he has a more interesting scar you must tell me the story."

Dora felt as if she'd taken a wrong turn and ended up in an alternative universe. "I don't know how he received the scar on his face and that is the only scar I know about."

"Too bad." Fatima laced her hands together on her lap. "You must ask him about it, then. From that scar Khalil learned many things, including not to speak without thinking first. I simply do not understand. I'm sure you're a lovely girl, but you're nothing like Amber. Is that why he married you?"

Coldness returned to Dora, and with it the sense of stepping off into darkness. "Who is Amber?"

Fatima studied her for a long time. Dora didn't know what the other woman was thinking, and she didn't want to know. She had a feeling that things had just gone from bad to worse.

"Until your marriage, Khalil was engaged to the youngest daughter of El Bahar's prime minister. I take it he never mentioned this to you?"

Dora could only shake her head. Engaged? He'd been engaged? She swallowed, but the sick feeling in her stomach didn't go away. Then why had he married *her?* That first night he'd talked of being swept away, but that couldn't be it, could it? Had he really fallen for her? She wanted to believe that was the reason he'd acted so hastily, but she'd never had that kind of luck before.

"When were they to have been married?" she asked, her voice low and scratchy.

"Khalil never agreed to a date," Fatima said thoughtfully. "I hadn't realized that before, but it all makes sense now. He was waiting to fall in love. How very romantic."

Dora tried to look suitably impressed herself, but she had a feeling she still looked a little green and unstable. Khalil desperately in love with her? She wanted it to be true. More than anything. Was it possible?

"Here's what we shall do," Fatima told her. "El Bahar moves quickly into the modern world, but we also remain steeped in our traditions. The people will not approve of the youngest son of the king marrying a woman in a foreign country. It smacks of—" Her gaze widened. "Oh, dear, you didn't marry because you were pregnant did you?"

"I've known him less than a month," Dora blurted. Then there was the matter of them only doing it the one time. Pregnancy was hardly an issue.

"Of course. Well then, to dispel that rumor and any others, I suggest you two have a second marriage ceremony. This one a bit more traditional. Say in two weeks? In the meantime we can all start mending fences with the prime minister and his family."

"I don't know what to say," Dora told her honestly. "If you think that will help, then I'm happy to participate."

"Good." Fatima rose to her feet. "Now it's time to dress for dinner. I don't suppose Khalil bought you anything from Chanel, did he? The boys did not inherit my sense of style."

She walked into the bedroom and moved to the open suitcases on the bed. Dora trailed after her. By the time she reached Fatima's side, the older woman had been through most of her things and had created two piles. Dora guessed they were "keep" and "discard."

"The blue will look lovely," Fatima said, holding up

Dora's favorite dress. "It's light enough in color so we won't look as if we're trying to dress alike." She gave an impish smile. "Or would you like to greet your new husband by wearing traditional dress?"

"I don't think either of us are ready for that."

"I would guess you're correct on that account." Fatima handed her the dress, then touched her arm. "Don't be frightened of us, Dora. Or if you are, don't let us see. We respect strength and determination in El Bahar, even in our women. My son is angry and disappointed right now, but it's directed at Khalil, not you. So if he appears curt, don't let him know that he's hurt you. You must be strong. If you let any of the Khan men dominate you, you are setting yourself up for a life of servitude. Do you understand?"

"I think so," Dora said, wondering if she ever would understand.

Fatima gave her a little push toward the bathroom. "Go dress. I'll wait, then I'll take you down to dinner. I received a not-so-subtle message from my son that the meal was to be for the men only, so we'll be catching them off guard. Always a good thing. Now hurry."

Thirty minutes later Dora followed Fatima down endless hallways. She caught glimpses of large rooms, filled with both Eastern- and Western-style furniture. There were fountains tucked into alcoves and beautifully lit gardens. While she was still confused and nervous, she couldn't help being excited at the thought of exploring this beautiful palace and its grounds.

They rounded a corner and found themselves in an intimate dining room. The long table could seat ten or twelve, but there were only four place settings that evening. The king sat at the head of the table, with two of his sons on his right and Khalil on his left. All four men looked up as they entered.

"Are we late?" Fatima asked, ignoring the king's expression of displeasure. "I was just telling Dora that tonight there would be a family dinner where we'll discuss how to handle the crisis. The timing is unfortunate. After all, this *is* her first night in El Bahar. However, I thought that having her here with us all was certainly better than leaving her alone in her room."

Khalil nearly grinned as his grandmother's frosty glare caught the king's gaze and held it. Givon Khan might be one of the five or six most wealthy men in the world, and a beloved and powerful monarch, but he was still a man who had to deal with a formidable mother. Fatima was in her seventies, but she wasn't someone to be taken lightly.

Khalil waited for his father to draw his battle lines. Not unexpectedly, the king decided this wasn't the time or place for a confrontation. He nodded toward one of the servants waiting patiently at the rear of the room. Two more place settings appeared.

"Mother, your willingness to think of others is what has made you the woman you are," Givon said, rising and holding open his arms. "As always, you are wise beyond your years."

Fatima walked toward him and let herself be folded into his embrace. She touched his cheek. "I'm seventy-three, Givon. It's time to stop saying I'm wise beyond my years, don't you think?" She turned her attention toward the table. "Dora, sit next to your husband. Jamal, move over. I'll sit between you and your brother."

In a matter of seconds Fatima had the table arranged to her liking. She settled between her two oldest grandsons, but shot Khalil a look that warned him he would have much to answer for later. Khalil found himself looking forward to the exchange. He'd avoided marrying Amber. Nothing else mattered.

He glanced at his bride. Dora tried to give him a smile, but it quivered at the corners, then failed completely. He knew that his father had settled her in a suite on the far side of the palace. More proof that the monarch did not approve. Khalil braced himself for the next round of tirades against his thoughtless, irresponsible behavior. He told himself it didn't matter what his father said; the marriage was binding.

"I am still not sure what I'm supposed to tell Aleser," Givon said as a servant served a salad of fresh greens and goat cheese. "He has been my most loyal adviser for more than thirty years. We grew up together. We always agreed that his oldest daughter would marry one of the princes from Bahania, cementing the relationship between our two countries."

"Whose fault is that?" Fatima asked blandly. "You're the one who didn't have any daughters. Besides, his oldest daughter *did* marry one of the princes."

Givon ignored his mother and continued to focus his attention on Khalil. "In return, his youngest daughter would marry into our royal family. She was engaged to you, Khalil. We had all agreed."

"Apparently not all of us," Fatima said. She speared a piece of arugula. "I quite like Dora, and I think she'll be a far better match than Amber. The girl's smart, and she's got backbone. My grandsons are too stubborn. They need women with backbone."

Khalil forced himself not to laugh or look at his father, although he could imagine the older man's outrage at his mother's comments. But there was little Givon could do. He couldn't force Khalil to divorce his wife. Fatima's approval was not easily given and not something the king could ignore.

Khalil glanced at his grandmother. Why had the old woman sided with him on this matter? Did she know something of Amber's antics?

He noticed that Dora hadn't touched her food. He wanted to tell her to relax, that everything was going to work out, but he didn't want to speak in front of his family. Instead he slipped his hand under the table and found hers, then squeezed her fingers. She gave him a grateful smile.

"The problem is easily solved," Fatima said. "In two weeks, we'll have a traditional ceremony. That will appease the people."

"What about Aleser?" the king asked. "How are we to appease him?"

"The man has children of his own. I suspect he understands they can be difficult at times." Fatima took another bite of salad. Her sharp, brown eyes glittered with amusement. "In the meantime, Dora can come live with me in the harem. I will teach her all she needs to know to be a good wife to a prince."

Khalil frowned. He'd known that his father had moved Dora into her own suite as an expression of his displeasure, but Khalil had planned to change that arrangement this very evening. She might not be the woman of his dreams, but he'd married her, and he had every intention of bedding her. For one thing, he wanted sons. For another, he'd enjoyed their lovemaking, and he wanted to experience it again. But if she was in the harem, she was out of reach to him.

"That's not possible," Khalil said curtly. "Dora and I are married. We will share quarters."

Fatima raised her eyebrows. "You weren't in a hurry to correct the situation this afternoon."

"I was with my father." Having his hide taken off, he thought grimly.

"No matter. It won't hurt you to wait two weeks to share time with your bride."

"As I said, that's not possible. If nothing else, Dora works for me."

"Not anymore, Khalil," Fatima informed him with a triumphant smile. "She's a princess now, not a secretary. You're just going to have to do without her."

When they'd finished dinner, Khalil walked a quiet Dora to the door of the harem. He'd brought up their living arrangements twice more, but Fatima had been adamant. Dora was to spend the next two weeks with her, learning how to be a proper wife. Khalil wasn't sure what those lessons would entail, but he doubted Dora would take well to them. She was a very Western woman.

"I'm sorry about this," he said when they stopped in front of an ornate gold door. A design of an exquisite garden had been etched into the precious metal. "I thought we'd be together, but it's only for a couple of weeks."

He was speaking as much to himself as to her. For reasons he didn't understand, a need had built inside of him and made him ache. He wanted her more than he'd wanted anyone in a long time.

She turned on him. "Our living arrangements are the least of our problems, Khalil. Why didn't you tell me you were engaged?"

He shifted uncomfortably. "Yes, well, perhaps I should have mentioned that."

"Perhaps? That's the best you can do? How do you

think I felt when I found out that you were supposed to marry someone else?''

''Why does it matter? I married you.''

''Which leads to a couple of dozen other questions.'' She turned away from him and pressed her fingers against the door.

''Is this real gold?''

Her question made no sense to him. ''Of course.''

Her laugh sounded strangled. ''Golden doors and broken engagements. So why did you marry me instead of her? What's her name? Amber?''

He hadn't expected to answer questions about his ex-fiancée, so he wasn't prepared. The truth was unacceptable. Dora would never understand. He wanted to pound his fist against the wall and scream out his frustration. What had seemed like a sensible plan when he'd been in New York had quickly turned into a disaster. Why couldn't everyone leave him alone? He was married—his wife was, if not suitable, then someone who could be made suitable.

''I didn't love her,'' he said at last.

Dora stared at him expectantly, but he didn't have any more to say. He wondered briefly how strange all this must seem to her. A new country, in-laws, a palace.

''You won't have to stay here two weeks,'' he promised. ''I'll speak to my father and have your things moved into my room.'' As he studied her, he remembered how it had been between them. The feel of her soft skin and her body, so hesitant, yet yielding. Hot blood coursed through him, arousing him. He moved closer.

''It was good between us,'' he murmured, leaning close and touching her mouth with his. ''I want you.''

She drew back. ''I wasn't sure what to think. You haven't wanted to, well, be together since that first time.

I thought maybe you'd decided our marriage was a mistake.''

Doubts filled her brown eyes. Doubts and questions. In New York it had been easy to lie to her, but it was more difficult now. Was that because of their location, or did it have something to do with the fact that he knew her better? She was no longer an employee, but a person.

He slipped his hand around the back of her neck and drew her next to him. ''It wasn't a mistake.''

''So you still love me,'' she breathed in relief and closed her eyes.

''There will be none of that!''

A sharp voice cut through the quiet. Khalil jumped back and saw his grandmother standing next to him. Fatima took Dora's arm and led her into the harem. Khalil took a step forward, as if he would go with them, but he had known since he was a young boy that this gold door marked a point of no return for him. He'd never once set foot inside the harem and that wasn't going to change tonight.

Biting back a curse of frustration, he stalked down the hall and out onto the common balcony. He breathed in the familiar scent of the ocean and the fragrance that was unique to El Bahar.

''I wouldn't be happy, either,'' a familiar voice said.

Khalil looked up and saw Malik, his oldest brother, standing by the balcony.

''You've been married, what, three days, and you've already lost your bride.''

''I know. I'll speak to Father.''

''Save your breath,'' Malik told him. ''He's not going against Grandmother. Not in this matter.''

Khalil knew that Malik was right, but he didn't have to like it.

Malik moved close and rested his hand on his brother's shoulder. Dark, wide eyes, similar to his own, stared into his face. ''For what it's worth, I think you've made a good choice. Amber was not suited for the life of a princess.''

And then Malik was gone, leaving Khalil to wonder if his brother recalled more about his night with Amber than she had realized.

## Chapter Eight

Dora studied the chart in front of her. It listed positions in the El Baharian government, but not the names of the officials currently in office. She went across the chart from left to right and supplied the name for each position.

Fatima beamed. "You learn quickly. I had hoped my grandsons would marry intelligent women, but with princes, one never knows."

"Thank you."

Dora looked at Khalil's grandmother. As always, the elderly woman was beautifully coiffured, with perfect hair and makeup. Today she wore a tailored blouse and skirt with pumps that showed off her slender ankles. While there were subtle, telltale signs of her age, for the most part she could pass for a woman in her early fifties.

They sat on one of the low sofas in the palace harem. Dora had been living behind the sheltered walls for eleven days. Just three more days until her wedding. Everything around her was new and strange, yet in some ways it was as if she'd always lived here. She had the oddest sensation of having been thrust back in time.

"Now I want to talk about history," Fatima told her. "Do you remember—" She broke off as Rihana, the young servant, came in carrying a large tray with tea and tiny sandwiches.

"Is it four already?" Fatima asked, glancing at her elegant gold watch. "The afternoon has flown."

Rihana paused. "Would you like me to come back later, Your Highness?"

"No. Of course not." Fatima sniffed. "Ah, there's cinnamon sticks for the tea. My favorite." Her beautiful face softened into a smile. "You do spoil me, child."

Rihana set the tray down and began to place the contents on the table in front of the sofa. Dora had already seen the ritual acted out every afternoon. She rose to her feet and crossed to the balcony on the far side of the room.

Unlike the regular living quarters and main offices of the palace, the harem didn't face the sea. Instead the rooms had a view of the gardens. On her first evening, Fatima had taken her on a tour of the complex suite, which had been designed to please women, as well as hold them captive. There were dozens of sleeping chambers, some large, some small. The size of the room was a statement of the occupant's status with the king. The communal baths were works of art, with mosaics depicting erotic couplings between mermaids and sailors. Water poured from gold faucets, and the jewels studding the back of the hand mirrors were large and genuine.

The common rooms had arched doorways, but few doors, giving the area an open feel. Fatima had taken her up the hidden staircase to the small, closed room where the chief eunuch had once watched over the women in his care and the king had viewed his beauties before deciding his choice for the night.

The harem had its own private gardens, lush with tropical plants and a small formal English garden. A few elderly parrots survived in the trees inside the lattice-covered grounds. Fatima had told her at one time dozens of parrots had been kept by the harem to cover the sounds of the women's voices so that no man would be tempted to enter. She'd also whispered that the parrots had served to cover the women's screams when they were beaten for a transgression.

Now, Dora stood in that same garden, a woman of the twenty-first century. So different from those long-ago women whose only purpose in life had been to bring pleasure to a king…and yet very much the same. While she was in El Bahar, most of her world revolved around the whim of the prince. The man she'd married impulsively and had not seen except at dinner for the past eleven days. The evening meal, taken in the company of the family, was her only contact with Khalil, and they had never once been left alone.

She shivered as she remembered his heated gaze the night before. How he'd looked at her with such desire that she'd lost her ability to eat or drink. She could only stare back at him, captured by his dark eyes, wondering how she could ever have doubted his desire.

Every look, every word, every touch told her he wanted her desperately. Whether or not he loved her remained in question, but for now, the wanting would have to be enough. Only three more days until they were married in a traditional ceremony. A ceremony with rituals and meanings as old as time.

She heard the soft *click* of the harem's outer door closing and returned to the central chamber. Fatima had already poured tea for them both and divided the plate of sandwiches.

"You were never occupied by the British," Dora said as she resumed her seat on the sofa. "So why English tea?"

Fatima smiled as she handed her a delicate bone china cup. "It's very civilized. We were never occupied by the Americans, yet we use electricity—which I believe your Thomas Edison first invented."

"Point well taken," Dora said, stirring in a drop of milk, then sipping the strong, hot brew.

Fatima patted her neatly coiled chignon. "You have learned much of our history in these past few days."

"The books you loaned me were very interesting. I want to learn as much as I can about my new country."

Shrewd dark eyes regarded her thoughtfully. "I have traveled all over the world, Dora. Some of that time was spent in your native country. I know a bit about American culture. You are bright, well-spoken, organized and a natural leader," Fatima said. "There are many business opportunities available to women. So why were you working as Khalil's secretary?"

Dora set her cup on the table and smoothed her hands over her skirt. "Why wasn't I an executive in some company?" she asked.

"Exactly."

"I don't have a four-year degree. I had a scholarship, but things didn't work out, so I earned a two-year degree, instead." She paused, not sure she wanted to go into the mucky details of her past. Fatima was warm and friendly, but she was a woman of class and breeding. Dora doubted she would understand how Dora could have gotten herself in such a mess.

"You never went back to complete your education?"

Dora pressed her lips together. She'd meant to. Once the pain and the humiliation had faded, she'd thought she might apply to one of the many colleges in the Los Angeles area. If enough time had passed, perhaps no one would care about the scandal.

"Time slipped away from me," was all she said.

Fatima continued to study her. Dora felt as if the older woman could read her thoughts. She wasn't the least bit surprised when Fatima guessed the source of her problems.

"Men are odd creatures," Khalil's grandmother said at last. "The weak ones run away from their problems and blame the world. The strong ones accept responsibility, but they have other flaws. They resist admitting they need someone to be complete. They want what they can't have. Sometimes they need to almost lose something to appreciate it."

Dora smiled. "Is that why you have me living in the harem?"

"Perhaps. Does Khalil need to be tricked into seeing that he has married a jewel?"

She was charmed by the compliment and uncomfortable with the question in equal measures. "I hope not."

Fatima nibbled on a watercress sandwich. When she'd finished she wiped her fingers on a linen napkin. "I have enjoyed having you with me in the harem."

Dora glanced around at the luxurious quarters. "It's even more lovely than I'd imagined." She grinned. "And my education is quite different from what I'd thought it would be."

Fatima made a dismissive gesture. "You were thinking we would discuss sexual arts. There is plenty of time for that. The first year or so of your marriage will be a time of great passion. It is all about quantity and emotional bonding. After the first child is born, we'll talk of men and women, of lovemaking. Then you'll be ready to learn the ancient secrets.''

Dora felt herself flushing at the other woman's candor. Were there really secrets she could use to keep Khalil in her bed? She thought about their single night of lovemaking. It had been wild and amazing, and she couldn't imagine anything better than when he'd held her in his arms. She'd spent many hours reliving their intimacy, remembering the touch of his fingers, his tongue as he'd—

''Why did you marry Khalil?'' Fatima asked sharply, the question jerking Dora out of her reverie.

Dora stiffened and stared at her. Fatima's expression was unreadable.

''He swept me off my feet,'' she blurted without thinking. ''I was deeply impressed by him, but I didn't think he would ever notice me. I thought he assumed I was simply a very efficient robot. But that wasn't true. When he told me he cared about me and wanted me, I couldn't resist him.''

''I see.'' Fatima's eyes gave nothing away. ''He is not an easy man. Of course, look at his brothers, or his father for that matter. They don't understand the heart of a woman. You will have to be the slender reed, bending in the storm.'' She sighed. ''How I loathe to speak in clichés, but it's true in this case. The men of the Khan family are great leaders, honorable and just, but they are also arrogant and unyielding. So stubborn I wanted to hit my husband with a frying pan more than once.''

Dora didn't know how to respond to Fatima's confession. She pictured the slender, well-dressed queen of El Bahar toting an oversize frying pan from room to room in search of her annoying husband.

''Khalil is a man worth having, but only if the woman

is worthy and strong,'' Fatima continued. ''You must be those things, my dear. Even if you don't yet feel them.''

Dora swallowed, but didn't respond. Nor did she ask how this wise old woman had figured out the truth...that Dora didn't feel the least bit worthy of Khalil or her new title. Nor did she know if she would be able to bend like a reed. While it wasn't in her nature to fight for something, she wasn't sure she could simply acquiesce, either.

Fatima changed the subject, mentioning a charity fashion show that they would attend together at the end of the month. Dora listened, grateful that Khalil's grandmother hadn't asked anything difficult...like why Khalil had wanted to marry *her*. Dora knew it had happened; she had the wedding license and the ring to prove it. She saw the passion in his eyes, a fire so bright she could almost believe it. But none of that answered the real question of why he'd chosen her.

Dora stared at the henna staining her hands. The intricate pattern worked its way across her palm, then circled each finger, like dark lace.

Fatima brushed the back of her hand. ''Tradition has it that a bride does not do work in the household until the last of the henna has faded. It marks the end of the honeymoon. You can imagine how for centuries young brides avoided water, or anything else that might hasten the fading process.'' Fatima smiled fondly. ''That is not for you to worry about, however. You're a princess in this great house, and we're unlikely to set you to work in the kitchen.''

''I don't know,'' Dora teased. ''I peel a pretty mean potato.''

Fatima didn't return her smile. ''I would imagine you can do anything you set your mind to. Don't forget that, child. Don't give up too easily.'' She rose to her feet. ''Listen to me, prattling on like the old woman I am. Stand up, and let me look at you.''

Dora did as she requested. Like Fatima, she dressed traditionally for the ceremony. A simple silk chemise served as her only undergarment. Over that she wore a long-sleeved lace dress, fitted to the waist, then falling loose to the floor. Heavily embroidered robes went over the dress and covered her completely. Rihana had worked wonders with her hair, pulling it up and securing it with a diamond headdress. Except for the gold thread from the embroidery, she was dressed entirely in white.

Fatima, whose slender body was draped in exquisite robes of blue and green, circled her. ''Just lovely. This wedding robe is more than a hundred years old. I was married in it myself.''

Dora glanced over her shoulder so that she could see the expanse of fabric in the mirror. El Baharian tradition prescribed that each bride add something to the marriage robe, a small picture of something symbolic to her alone. In the royal family, the picture was chosen by the groom and sewn by a female relative in his household. Fatima had stayed up late several nights completing her contribution to the robe.

The older woman touched a small design of a tree with many branches, just over Dora's right hip. ''That is the symbol of my homeland of Bahania. There was much discussion about what symbol would be added for you.'' Fatima laughed. ''Jamal suggested a portrait of Elvis, while Malik favored the American flag.''

She couldn't imagine the king agreeing to either. ''What did Khalil pick?''

''This.'' Fatima touched a small flower near the hem. ''Khalil said he wanted a symbol of the desert rose.'' She smiled. "But he specified that one of the leaves was to be made to look like the paw print of the desert cat. As we have no such creature in our country, I thought it was a most unusual request."

Dora could feel herself blushing. She remembered their night of lovemaking, when he'd first compared her to a desert rose, then afterward had called her his desert wildcat.

"Very interesting," she said without meeting Fatima's gaze.

The older woman moved in front of her and kissed her cheek. "Don't be afraid. I have cast your fortune upon the water, and the future has been revealed to me. You will need to be strong, but if you trust your heart and stay on the true course, you will achieve your soul's desire."

Then she secured the sheer white veil across the lower half of Dora's face and left the room.

Dora stood alone within the protective walls of the harem. She couldn't believe all that had happened to her in the past month. Her life had changed so dramatically, she couldn't seem to catch her breath. Ironically her wedding ceremony today, to Khalil, would occur the day after she'd been scheduled to marry Gerald.

She turned slowly so that she could see herself in the large mirror across the room. Instead of a thirty-year-old woman in a traditional wedding gown, she stared into the dark eyes of a stranger. Heavy garments covered her from her shoulders to her toes, and the sheer veil concealed the details of her features. She looked exotic and other-worldly, not at all the timid woman she'd been a month before.

Fatima had promised that she could achieve her soul's desire, if she was strong and trusted her heart. Dora squeezed her hennaed fingers so tightly together that her

nails dug into her skin. Her soul's desire was to find her
one true love. To be cared for, and to care in return; to
have children, to raise those children, and then to grow
old next to a wonderful man. Not riches, not titles, not
power—just the joy of being part of a warm, loving marriage.

As heart's desires went, it was fairly standard. Surely
she wasn't asking for too much.

"Are you nervous?"

Dora glanced up and saw a beautiful young woman
standing behind her. She hadn't heard her enter the harem.

She turned and looked at the petite, dark-haired goddess
dressed in a shimmering gold-and-white dress that emphasized the incredible shape of her body. Her face was
exquisite with perfect features that looked amazingly familiar. Dora stared and tried to remember—then it came
back to her. This was the woman Khalil had argued with
in the clothing store in New York.

"We haven't met," the young woman said, moving
toward Dora, but not holding out her hand in greeting.
"My name is Amber. I'm Khalil's fiancée." She paused,
then touched perfectly manicured, long red fingernails to
her pouty mouth. "Oh, dear. That was a slip of the tongue.
I should say Khalil's *former* fiancée."

The heavy silk robes might conceal Dora's body from
view, but she knew that her own pear shape was no competition for the young beauty in front of her. Amber was
everything she'd ever wanted to be—everything she'd
ever admired. How could Khalil have turned his back on
this vision to marry *her?*

"Cat got your tongue?" Amber asked in a low, husky
voice.

"No, of course not. I'm just surprised to see you."

"I can only imagine." Amber gave her an imperfect

smile, then began to walk in a slow circle around her. "My, my, my. You're not at all what I pictured. I had hoped he might have at least chosen someone more..." She made a fluttering gesture with her right hand.

Amber's thick, long hair had been piled on top of her head, giving her a few added inches of height. Large diamonds twinkled in the upswept curls. As Dora stared at them, she reached up and touched her own headdress. It was only then that she realized the other woman's dress resembled a robe, although the fabric of Amber's gown was thin enough to mold to her body. In fact, everything about Amber's appearance was either a mockery or an imitation of Dora's wedding garb. Her heart sank.

"What are you doing here?"

"At the wedding?" Amber asked, deliberately misunderstanding. "I'm the daughter of the prime minister and a close friend of the family. That makes me a very important guest. Of course I'd expected to attend this wedding in a slightly different capacity." Something flickered in her brown eyes as she continued to circle Dora.

"This is a disaster for all of us," Amber continued. "I blame myself, of course. If I hadn't fought with Khalil while he was in New York, none of this would have happened." She paused and lowered her gaze. "It was a lover's spat. We were both so silly. Khalil insists on dictating my life, and I couldn't stand it anymore. I told him it was over."

She stared directly at Dora. "He was so furious. So I left. But instead of coming after me, he came to you. Into your virgin bed."

Dora stiffened. How had Amber known that Dora hadn't...

"He told me," Amber said, answering the silent question. "He tells me everything. You can imagine how distraught he was to find out that you were innocent. He is, after all, a most honorable man. How could he turn his back on what he'd done? So he proposed. Of course neither of us thought you would accept.''

Dora's stomach turned over, and her throat tightened. This fabulous creature in front of her was lying. She had to be lying. It hadn't happened like that.

''He insisted,'' she murmured, forcing the words past suddenly dry lips.

''Did he?'' Amber asked languidly. She paused in front of the mirror and patted her perfectly coiffed hair. ''He can be most convincing. But how awkward for all of us that you believed him. My father is distraught, as is most of the country. I am a favored daughter while you are…not.''

Dora took a step back. She didn't know what to think or feel. She could only retreat.

Amber smiled sadly. ''Then there is the matter of us still loving each other. I don't know what to do about that.'' Their gazes met in the mirror.

''He doesn't love you,'' Dora said shakily, unable to believe what was happening. This wasn't real. It couldn't be real. She was dreaming except that her body was too cold, too bruised for her to be anything but very awake. Dreams never hurt this much.

Amber turned to face her. Compassion added incredible beauty to already perfect features. ''Dora, has Khalil made love with you once since that first night?''

Dora opened her mouth, but she couldn't seem to form words. Mutely she shook her head.

''And since you've been in *my* country, has he ever been with you?''

''I've been in the harem,'' she managed to whisper.

Amber shrugged. ''Khalil has managed to find his way

inside my father's house, which is halfway across the city and as well-guarded as the palace. If he'd wanted to, don't you think he could have made his way down the hall?''

Dora could feel her face flushing, then growing cold. Her eyes burned, but she could not give in to the tears. Was Amber speaking the truth? Dora didn't want to believe her, but the young woman knew too many details. Had Khalil discussed this with her? The humiliation made her stomach twist and rise. She had to swallow the taste of bile.

"He's been with me every night," Amber said quietly. "We've been wild for each other. I suppose some of it is the lure of the forbidden." She sighed. "He's so filled with passion that it lingers in his eyes even after we've sated ourselves."

A sob formed in Dora's throat. She didn't want to believe anything Amber said, but it was too hard to dispute so many facts. If Khalil hadn't been making his way to Amber's bed every night, how would she know that he wasn't with her, Dora? What about the fact that they hadn't made love since that first night? Dora had been so sure she'd seen passion in his eyes, but had it just been for Amber?

If things had happened differently between herself and Khalil, if they'd been spending time together, she might be able to make sense of this, but they hadn't. Except for dinner with his family, she never saw Khalil. It had been two weeks since she'd been alone with him. These were hardly the actions of a man deeply in love with his new wife.

Worse, a part of her had never believed what he told her. She'd always wondered how he could have been so swept away by her. She wasn't the type to inspire that kind of passion. She was just an ordinary woman… nothing like Amber.

Dora motioned to her wedding garb. "Then why is he doing this? Marrying me, I mean."

"Does he have a choice?" Amber asked, bitterness sharpening her words. "Did you give him the out he needed? Did you ever once think of anyone but yourself? Of course not. He was married before he had time to consider the alternatives, and you took advantage of him. You're greedy and selfish."

Dora took another step back. "It wasn't like that," she said softy. "I never—"

Amber dismissed her with a wave of her hand. "You think we don't know the truth? The very day after your wedding, you went shopping and spent thousands of dollars on clothes. What about that wedding ring and the jewels?"

"There aren't any jewels," she protested weakly. "The hair ornament is Fatima's. And I didn't ask for any clothes."

"No, but you took them, didn't you. You refused nothing."

Amber made her sound so horrible. Dora held on to the last thread of her dignity and refused to cry. Khalil had insisted on the clothes. She hadn't wanted to go shopping at all. Amber could say what she liked about that, but Dora knew what had happened.

"You're wrong," she said.

Amber glared at her. "Am I? We'll just see. You've trapped Khalil into marriage, but that's just for now. In time his passion for me will overcome his duty, and he'll leave you. El Bahar has made much progress in the past fifty years, and it's surprisingly easy for a man to divorce his wife...even a prince. I wouldn't get too used to living in the palace if I were you.''

''He wouldn't,'' Dora whispered, even as she knew he very well could.

''Don't count on it. I know Khalil. I know him down to his soul. I know that I am in possession of his heart. Can you say the same?''

With that she turned and left as quietly as she'd come. Dora stared after her. Pain swept through her, agonizing waves that left her broken and disillusioned. All she'd wanted, all she'd hoped for, it had all been a lie. Khalil didn't want her—he'd never wanted her. She'd been an impulse and then a mistake. He hadn't wanted to marry her. Why hadn't she seen that?

''Princess Dora?''

Dora looked up and saw Rihana standing in the doorway to the harem.

The pretty, young servant smiled at her. ''Come, it is time for you to be married.''

## Chapter Nine

The old man in front of them spoke ancient words. Around them, dozens of people sat on fat pillows, while candles lit the vastness of the room. But for Dora, the world had been reduced to a sharp pain, a futile quest for forgetfulness, and the death of a dream.

Even as Khalil took one of her hands in his and spoke, she couldn't think about anything but what that woman had said. The lies, dear God, they had to be lies. She couldn't have been speaking the truth. That wasn't possible. Khalil *had* said he wasn't sure he could leave New York without her, hadn't he? She pressed her fingertips to her temple and tried to remember what, exactly, had happened the night they'd made love...and the next morning. Had she misunderstood? Was that possible? Had his proposal been a courtesy, nothing more?

No, she thought frantically. He'd insisted. She'd thought it was all a joke, but he'd pursued her, hadn't he?

Just as he'd really convinced her that he wanted her. She remembered him taking off his clothes so that he could show her the proof of his desire. She hadn't imagined that—after all, she'd never seen a naked man before. So that part had really happened. Surely he couldn't have been able to pretend to want her if he hadn't felt that way. Except she didn't know enough about men to figure out any of this. Could he have been aroused for other reasons? Had he been thinking about Amber instead? But if he'd been thinking about his fiancée, why had he come to Dora's bed?

The holy man spoke more words. Incense filled the large hall. The room seemed to tilt and spin, and then Khalil removed her veil and pressed his mouth to hers.

The intimate contact caught her off guard. She flinched in surprise, then tried not to feel the familiar heat of his mouth. Despite her pain and confusion, just the lightest brush of his lips against hers sent liquid heat pouring through her body. If he had continued kissing her, or if he'd touched her anywhere else, she would have found herself unable to resist him.

The reality of her need for this man terrified her. They'd only been together once. How could she have changed so much in such a short period of time, and how could she go back to what she'd been before? She didn't want to be vulnerable to him; she needed to be strong.

When Khalil raised his head, the crowd around them cheered. He grinned as he tucked the veil back in place. "Now you are officially my wife, little desert rose. What do you say to that?"

She searched his face, desperate to find a clue, a hint that he was happy and that this was what he wanted. But she didn't know him well enough to read his expression.

She could only guess, and the new questions in her mind made her question everything she found.

"Khalil?"

But he was torn from her before he could say anything. A group of men spirited him away, while dozens of women led her in the opposite direction. In a matter of minutes she and Khalil had been led across the hall into an even larger room set with dozens of huge tables. They were seated next to each other at the center of the largest banquet table. A feast lay before them, but the thought of eating churned Dora's stomach.

She tried to concentrate on her surroundings. The beauty of the room, ancient tapestries hanging from an arched ceiling nearly three dozen feet overhead, the open windows and doorways leading to balconies overlooking the sea, the lush displays of tropical flowers filling corners and overflowing the tables, caught her eye if not her attention.

Conversation and laughter filled the room, but she couldn't participate. The wild desert music made her head pound. She ignored the food Khalil set on her plate and barely sipped her wine.

"You are quiet," Khalil said, leaning close to be heard over the crowd. "Did the ceremony disappoint you?"

"Not at all." She cleared her throat. This wasn't the time to have a talk about what Amber had said. "I have a slight headache."

His dark eyes flashed. "I hope it gets better soon. I have missed my desert cat and had hoped I would get to visit her again this night." He put a hand on her thigh, then slipped it between her legs for a brief, erotic caress. "It's been too long."

She stared at him, not sure what to believe. Unfortunately it was impossible to think with his fingers rubbing against that magical center of her being. Shivers rippled through her, and her breasts swelled. She wanted to let her legs fall open so that he could touch her again and again until she found her release. Even as she acknowledged that he could have been lying about everything, she sensed that he would always have sexual power over her. The situation was intolerable...worse, it was inescapable.

She suffered through the rest of the meal, trying to smile and pretend that all was well. When the dessert trays were brought out, Khalil leaned close again.

"Everyone will understand if we make our escape now. Rihana has packed your bag for the night."

She blinked. "What bag? For what night?"

He gave her a slow, lazy smile. "You've spent two weeks in the harem. Didn't my grandmother tell you about the traditional wedding night?"

Mutely Dora shook her head.

"Ah, then I suspect you will enjoy the surprise," he told her. "I know I will enjoy sharing it with you."

As he rose, the pace of the music changed. The beat increased, as did the volume. Instantly they became the center of attention.

"You sneak away so soon?" Malik called from his place at the far end of the table. "But then my little brother was always impatient."

Khalil waved him off. "We have far to go. It's late."

"You need to go far so she won't be able to run away in horror," Jamal, Khalil's middle brother joked. At least Dora assumed it was a joke. Everyone laughed out loud.

Khalil ignored that comment and the others that followed. He took Dora's hand and started for the door. But dozens of people stopped them, the men offering congratulations, the women smiling at her with friendliness, or envy. Dora's numbness crept down to her bones, and she found herself barely able to register what was going on.

Then, just as they were to make their escape, Amber appeared in front of them. If Dora had any doubts, they were dispelled when she felt her husband stiffen as if he'd slammed into a wall. He obviously felt some strong emotion for this woman.

Amber, as beautiful as the most perfect statue ever created by man, stared up mutely. Tears clung to her lower lashes, but did not fall. Her lips trembled. She was a vision of pain.

"Khalil," she breathed softly. "I love you."

For Dora, the confession was a knife to the heart. She had to force herself to stay silent, to not cry out. Why had this happened? Why had she been a fool for the second time in her life?

Khalil pushed past Amber without saying a word. In a matter of minutes, Dora found herself in the passenger seat of a four-wheel-drive vehicle, heading away from the palace.

"Khalil?"

He drove with easy confidence. "Relax. We aren't going that far. Tradition states that we ride to our destination, but I didn't think you'd be up to that."

"Ride?"

He shot her a grin. "Horses."

Her brain refused to function. She turned the thought over in her mind a few times until she realized he meant that the usual tradition was for the bride and groom to ride away on horseback. "Where are we going?"

"You'll see. It's just over the rise."

Buildings quickly fell away. To the left and right, the city rose around them, but in front was only wilderness.

"This is all royal land," Khalil told her. He pulled off

his traditional headdress and tossed it into the back seat. He still wore robes that were only a few shades darker than her own. They emphasized his height and strength, leaving her feeling slightly vulnerable, as well as confused and foolish.

"Much of the city sits on land that is owned by the royal family, although it is granted to the government in hundred-year blocks, and we don't require any rent. But this section is kept private and undeveloped."

Dora glanced around and tried to take an interest in her surroundings. There was a wild sort of beauty to the untamed vastness that was the desert. In less than ten minutes they'd left the city and palace behind, and now it seemed they were the only two people around for miles.

They reached the peak of the hill. Below lay a shallow valley with an oasis in the center. Dora had never seen such a thing before, except perhaps in books or movies, but she recognized the startlingly green island of life in the middle of brown emptiness. Slender palms formed a half circle around a deep blue pool. Lush plants and bushes grew everywhere. On the far side of the pool, animal tracks littered the muddy banks, and to the left stood a large beige tent.

"Your palace for the night, milady," Khalil said, his voice teasing.

Dora could only stare. One of the flaps had been tied open, inviting them inside. As Khalil drew closer, she could see several Jeeps already parked behind the tent, and armed men patrolling the area.

"Who are they?" she asked stiffly.

"They are the unfortunate reminder of reality. Tradition dictates that we spend our first night as man and wife out in the desert. It's something my family has been doing for generations. However, times have changed, and it's no longer a simple matter for a prince to take his bride away for the night. So we have a few guards with us." He gave her a reassuring pat on the hand. "Don't worry. They'll stay well back—we'll have our privacy."

A tent, the desert, guards? Where would this madness end? What had she been thinking when she'd accepted his proposal? Or perhaps she hadn't been thinking. Maybe that was her problem. She'd wanted to believe so very much that she'd ignored the obvious...that a man like him could never want a woman like her.

Khalil parked next to the tent, then walked around and opened her door. She stepped out because she couldn't think of anything to say, and for now it was easier to go with him.

One of the guards moved close as they approached and held open the loose tent flap. His expression was closed and forbidding, and when they entered, he secured the flap behind them.

"Don't they make you nervous?" Dora asked.

"On the contrary. They make me feel very safe."

She supposed that he was right—better to be protected than not. Then she turned and faced the interior of the tent and thankfully, she didn't have to think about anything at all for a few minutes. It was far better to lose herself in the magic that had been created at the edge of a small oasis.

A smaller inner tent filled the larger one. Dora stepped into a cream-and-gold wonderland of thick rugs and wall hangings, dozens and dozens of deep red pillows. A bed stood in the corner on a dais, the covers pulled back, the soft white linens offering welcome.

To the right sat a table laden with covered dishes. Champagne—for the Khan family was not Muslim—chilled in an ice bucket. The rugs deceived her feet and the tapestries deceived her eyes. Had she not seen the tent for herself, she would have thought she were in some luxurious home in an exotic town.

"It's lovely," she told Khalil.

"We know how to travel in style," he said lightly. "Something we learned more than a thousand years ago."

He came up behind her and placed his hands on her shoulders. She told herself not to react, or at the very least, not to overreact. But it was impossible. Before she could stop herself, she flinched violently, then tore herself away and spun to face him.

"Don't!" she ordered. "Don't touch me."

Khalil stepped back in surprise. "What's wrong?" He stared at her, his dark eyes searching her face. "This is more than wedding nerves, isn't it? Something has happened."

"How perceptive," she said sarcastically. "What was your first clue?"

He frowned. "What is it, Dora? Why are you acting like this? It's not in your nature to be a petty female. You are usually so reasonable. Tell me?"

She stared at him, at this man to whom she had been bound in separate ceremonies nearly half a world apart. "You don't know me at all," she said softly. "But that's only fair, because I don't know you, either."

He gestured impatiently. In his traditional robes, he looked very much the part of the prince of a desert kingdom. A prince who would never have willingly chosen her for his wife.

"You haven't answered the question," he said. "What's wrong?"

"Amber came to see me," she told him. "Today, just before the ceremony."

His expression didn't change at all. She might as well

have told him about the weather for all he seemed to care. "She is not to be trusted," he said. "Ignore everything she said."

"It's not that easy. Don't you want to know what she said to me?"

"Not really."

She wanted to laugh, but it hurt too much. Pressure tightened in her throat. "I wish I could forget, but I can't. The words are burned into my brain."

She drew in a deep breath. "Khalil, she said that you had a fight with her while you were in New York. She said that was the reason you came to—" She paused. "The reason you were intimate with me was to get back at her. That it was never about me at all."

As she spoke she stared at him, desperately hoping for a sign that it was all false. She wanted him to get angry and frustrated, to pull her close and say that Amber had the heart of a worm and that of course he loved her, Dora. She wanted reassurance and kind words and patience, and then she wanted him to make gentle love to her.

Instead Khalil stalked to the doorway and clutched the thick fabric. "I see."

It was not what she wanted to hear. The pressure in her chest increased, and she was suddenly cold. If she'd eaten anything that day she would have thrown up, but mercifully her stomach was empty.

The silence grew around them. She found herself filling the space with ugly words.

"She said that you were shocked to find out I was a virgin. Shocked and h-horrified." She could feel the tears burning in her eyes, and she blinked them back. "She said you proposed out of a sense of duty and that neither of you expected me to say yes." Her voice dropped to a whisper. "She said you would divorce me so you could marry her."

"Enough!" he growled. "She tells you lies. All lies. We will not speak of this again."

She didn't remember ever being this cold. The tears fell, and there was nothing she could do to stop them.

"That's not good enough," she told him. "I want to know the truth."

"Why?" he asked as he turned to look at her. Anger sharpened his features. "What will it change? You are my wife, and you will stay my wife."

She gave a strangled sound and sank onto one of the thick cushions. Amber had been right about everything. What had she done? "She said you were with her. All these past nights when I was in the harem, she said you stole into her father's house and took her. That was why you didn't come to me."

Khalil stalked toward her, then stopped and loomed above her. "I didn't come to you because I respect my father and grandmother's wishes. The sanctuary of the harem is absolute. No man may enter. I have lived in the palace all my life, and I have not once stepped foot behind that golden door."

He placed his hands on his hips and glared. "I thought you were different. I thought you could be logical about all of this, but I see that's impossible."

Dora barely heard his words. Too many lies woven through too little truth. She pressed her hands to her face and tried to stop the flow of tears. She had to go. She had to get back to…to…to where? To what? She had no life anymore. Everything she'd known was gone.

"I just want to know," she whispered.

Khalil sighed. "All right. I'll tell you the truth." He bent down and cupped her chin, forcing her to look at him. "All of it. Then we'll have it out in the open and be able to put it behind us. We'll start our marriage with a clean slate and go on from there."

He released her face and began to pace in the tent. His long strides ate up the distance quickly, and he was forced to turn after a mere five steps.

Dora brushed away her tears and ignored the steady dampness that replaced them. She told herself this was a good thing—that once she knew how bad it was, they could talk about fixing the problems. But the coldness only increased, and her heart braced itself for even more pain.

"Amber and I had been engaged from the time we were children. It was the wish of both our fathers." He paused as if searching for the right words. "We did fight in New York, but only because I told her I didn't want to marry her."

She raised her head. "What?"

"I didn't want to marry her. Amber is not..." He hesitated. "She would not be a good wife or mother. I didn't know how to break the engagement in such a way as to avoid scandal. Then I heard you on the phone with Gerald, and I thought you might be a good solution to my dilemma. You are intelligent and even-tempered. I thought you could learn the duties and be a good mother. You were also a virgin." He paused. "I needed a wife, and you were a likely candidate."

She'd heard too much, she thought, wishing she could transport herself to another place, or even another time. How could she continue to breathe through the gaping hole in her chest? How could her heart continue to beat, her blood flow? Why hadn't the pain killed her yet?

And then she knew the awful truth—that no matter how much it hurt, she would never die from the agony. She was destined to survive, even though she didn't want to. She was going to keep on living and suffering and going through the motions because there was no mercy, no escape, no hope.

"So it was all lies," she said dully. "All of it. When you told me that you wanted me, that you'd wanted me from the beginning." It was hard for her to talk, nearly impossible for her to go on, but she forced herself to continue. She had to speak the truth. Once she faced it, she could begin the incredibly slow process of putting the pieces back together again...if that were even possible.

"You lied about the passion, you lied when you told me it would be impossible to leave me behind in New York. You made me feel special and important, and it was all a lie."

Life had become a cruel joke—nearly as cruel as her new husband.

Khalil stopped in front of her. "The past is finished, and there's no reason to dwell on it. Yes, I stretched the truth to make you feel better. Until the night I heard you on the phone with Gerald, I never thought of you as anything but efficient. I didn't have any particular regard for you at the time, but you're my wife, now. I believe we have a chance to make this union successful."

"Successful? Are you insane?" she asked, pushing herself to her feet.

"Not at all. I made vows to you, and I fully intend to honor them."

"But nothing is real," she protested. "You lied about everything."

"You're making too much of this."

"And you're making too little. You toyed with me. You made me believe in you."

His mouth twisted. "You wanted to believe me. You

were desperate to believe that a prince from a fairy tale had arrived to take you away from your sad, little life. You lied to yourself as much as I lied to you.''

She glared at him. "But *I* never lied to you. You can't excuse your own behavior by pointing the finger at me.''

"What about when you told me you loved me? You don't even know me.''

"I never told you I loved you.''

He met her gaze, then shifted uncomfortably. Silence grew, then pressed down upon them. She *hadn't* said she loved him. She was too afraid of the words to ever speak them casually. He was right that she'd wanted to believe in the possibilities, but was that so great a sin?

"What do you want from me?" he asked. "Fine, I lied. I convinced you to marry me, using false pretenses. We're married now. So we'll make the best of it. We'll start over.'' He reached for her. "Dora, some of what I told you was true. I think you will make a fine wife. You will be a good mother my sons, and you have the perfect body to allow my sons to grow healthy inside of you.''

She sucked in her breath. It wasn't enough that he ripped out her heart—now he wanted to talk about her hips, too? "No. I don't want to be married to you. I want to go home.''

"Where is home? With Gerald?''

She flinched, but didn't back down. "Anywhere but here. I won't stay.''

"You don't have a choice.'' He moved closer and reached out to touch her.

Despite her desire to stand up for herself, she backed away quickly, knowing that if he stroked any part of her body she would be lost.

"Don't,'' she told him, folding her arms over her chest. She needed time to think.

Except he wasn't going to give her time. Even as she struggled to collect her thoughts, he advanced.

She took another step back, then another. The pain was still there. She didn't know what to believe. He hadn't wanted her. He hadn't longed for her. He'd picked her because she was a convenient virgin. That was hardly the basis of a successful marriage.

But that wasn't what hurt the most. What ripped her open and left her bleeding was that she'd done it to herself. She'd been a fool...again. First with Gerald and now with Khalil. With Gerald, she'd been so lonely that she'd allowed herself to believe that he had qualities that didn't exist in him at all. The small conciliation was that with Khalil, he'd fed her deception with pretty words.

"Dora."

His warm hand settled on her shoulder. She gave a sharp cry and ran toward the entrance. Once outside, she realized she was in the middle of the desert with no idea which direction was home. Probably because she wasn't sure where home was. El Bahar? Of course not. Los Angeles? Not anymore. Where did she want to go?

Khalil grabbed her arm and pulled her back inside. "Do not run away from me again," he growled.

"Or what? You'll have me locked up or maybe beaten. You seem a very practiced bully."

Dark eyes flashed with fire. "I have never bullied you."

She hated that he spoke the truth. "You used me."

"You let yourself be used. You welcomed me into your bed."

Color flooded her face. She swallowed her shame. "Don't make the mistake of thinking that's ever going to happen again. I want a divorce. I want to leave you and this country."

He leaned close until his face nearly touched hers. "Never."

"I won't let you destroy me."

He laughed cruelly. "Destroy what?" he asked mockingly. "You were wandering around at an airport when I found you. You had nothing. Your fiancé had left you, you had no job, no money. I saved you. I married you and brought you to my country where you have a chance at a life beyond anything you have ever imagined. Here you will have wealth and power and a title. You are an honored member of the house of Khan. Do not forget that. You will be my wife, and you will bear me many sons."

"I would rather be married to a dirt farmer than you, prince or not, and I will never have your children because I will never let you touch me. I want a divorce."

"Never. You are mine."

"I am not a possession."

"You are my wife and my woman. Do not make the mistake of challenging me because I will always win."

"Not this time—not with me."

"Wife of mine, *you are wrong*."

She sensed his intention before he moved, but she was too slow. Even as she tried to step away, he grabbed her arm and pulled her up against him.

Anger, pain, sadness, loneliness, betrayal all blended inside of her, draining her strength and her will to fight.

"I want you," he said, his mouth inches from hers. "I will have you."

"You're going to have to force me, because I'm not going to do this willingly."

His dark eyes gleamed. "Didn't I just warn you about challenging me?"

Then he kissed her. Not the soft, tempting kiss he'd used the first time they'd made love, but a powerful, claiming kiss that forced a response, even as it promised the sweetest of rewards for giving in.

"No!" She pressed against his shoulders, trying to push him away.

He laughed, his lips still against hers. "Fight me, my desert cat. Fight me, then claim me as your rightful mate."

"Never!"

But even as she breathed the promise, she felt the first tendrils of desire coiling through her. Heat hot enough to melt resolve, even hot enough to warm the very ice from her bones, crept through her like dawn would creep across the thick, plush carpets. It moved slowly, filling her from the inside out, sucking away her will.

His tongue swept across her lower lip, back and forth, back and forth, whispering for admittance. She wanted to resist. She told herself to be strong—that she hated him, that he was horrible, that he'd used her and hurt her and…and…

He untied the tiny bows that held her robe together, then slipped his hand through the gap in the heavy silk. Even as she swore to herself that she would stand firm against him, his fingers brushed against the tight bud of her nipple. At the same moment his tongue slipped between her suddenly parted lips.

She pushed against him one last time, then sobbed out her defeat. Hating him, hating herself more, she wrapped her arms around his neck and pulled him close.

Dora shut her eyes, not wanting to see the look of triumph on his face, but instead of gloating, Khalil broke the kiss long enough to gently whisper, "You are my wife, little desert cat. I will always keep you safe."

Perhaps he thought he could, for he would never see that the greatest threat to her safety was no one else but him.

## *Chapter Ten*

"Don't resist," Khalil said, still whispering against her mouth. "Want me back. Need me. Make love with me."

Dora shivered in his embrace, trying to disconnect herself from what was happening, even as her body responded to his nearness. She kept her arms around his neck and her eyes firmly closed as he unfastened all the tiny ties down the front of her robe. When he drew her arms down so he could push the robe off her shoulders, she steadfastly refused to look at him.

The heavy silk slid down to pool around her feet. Underneath, she wore a lace dress, and under that was a silk chemise. The traditional garb did not allow for panties or a bra, and she felt oddly vulnerable as she stood before him.

"Dora," he said, stroking her cheek. "Give in with grace. Why would you want to win this battle? How would that be a victory?"

''I would have my dignity,'' she said into the darkness.

''And a cold bed. Is that what you want?''

What she wanted was a real marriage with a man who cared about her. At this point she would accept respect and liking, with the hope that love would grow. What she had instead was lies.

''I don't want you.''

One fingertip brushed against her hard nipple. ''Your body says otherwise.''

She shivered involuntarily, and her eyes snapped open. ''I can't help my response to you, but it doesn't mean anything. It's the same as when the doctor taps on your knee, and your leg jerks. In this case the nerves are not connected to my brain. My weak outer self might react to the sexual act, but my heart and soul are completely detached.''

Dark eyes regarded her thoughtfully. ''A very pretty speech. Shall we test your theory?''

''What do you mean?''

''You're saying that we can make love and that you can respond to me sexually, but that the act won't touch you on the inside.''

''Exactly.'' She believed completely in what she told him—she just hoped she wasn't fooling herself.

He took her hand in his and pushed up the loose, long sleeve to the elbow, exposing the underside of her forearm. ''You're saying that when I touch you like this—'' He lightly traced a line from the inside of her wrist to her elbow. ''That any reaction you have is the same as automatically pulling back when you touch a hot stove?''

''Yes.'' She ignored the trembling that began inside of her and the goose bumps that erupted on her skin. Just standing this close to Khalil made it difficult to think, let alone banter with him.

He turned her hand over and stared at the back, then traced the lacy lines of the henna. "Do you know that somewhere in this decorative pattern I will find my name?"

She blinked. She knew he was talking...she could hear the words...but it was so hard to concentrate when he touched her. There was a traffic jam in her nervous system and only the emergency vehicles, in this case the sensation of his fingers on her skin, were getting through. Everything else, like conversation, had to wait.

"Your name?" she repeated dully as he circled round and round on the back of her hand, then traced the length of each of her fingers.

"Yes. Tradition dictates that the husband's name be woven into the henna pattern." He looked at her, his dark eyes smoldering with hot, heavy, *ready* desire. "Where is my name, Dora?"

"I don't know," she said, her voice trembling. "I didn't watch Rihana when she painted me."

"So I'll have to go searching. How sad that they only paint your hands and feet."

It was sad, she thought vaguely. If only they'd painted her all over. There would be more places for Khalil to search.

The thought of his fingers and perhaps even his tongue on her body made her thighs quiver. She remembered what it had been like before...when he'd touched her and then kissed her between her legs. She remembered the feel of him against her and the passion of her release. She remembered all of it and even though she knew it was wrong and made her weak, she wanted to experience it again.

He led her to the bed. There they paused while he pulled off the lace dress, leaving her in a calf-length chemise and nothing else. Dora shivered again, but it wasn't from the cold. In his robes, with his eyes blazing passion, Khalil was a dark, mysterious stranger. She was far from anything she'd ever known. She'd married this man standing in front of her. For all she knew he had the power of life and death over her. She wasn't sure how she felt about him, nor did she know why he'd married her. She was committed to resisting him in all ways, including physically. And she'd never in her life known such incredible physical longing.

She hadn't known it was possible to stand and breathe and *want* with such powerful need. She ached, she shook, she melted, she cried out deep inside for him to take her. Even as she knew she should resist. Even as she knew she would hate herself for her weakness...she wanted him.

He urged her to sit on the edge of the bed. The dais was covered with carpets, and her toes curled into the thick weave. Khalil settled next to her and took possession of her left hand. He held it palm up in his, studying the pattern made by the henna. The stain was a dark orange-brown on her skin. Fatima had told her it would turn a little red as it faded over time. The design was exotic on her pale skin, bringing to mind how out of place she was in this foreign land.

He lightly scraped the tip of his fingers over her palm. "I don't see my name here, do you?"

She thought about telling him that she couldn't really see her hand, that he held it too far and angled away from her, but the tingles shooting up her arm made it difficult to talk. He turned her hand over and stroked it.

"Nor here," he murmured before pressing her fingertips to his mouth and rubbing the sensitive pads with his tongue.

Had she not been sitting, she would have fallen in a heap on the floor. Muscles quivered, joints gave way. She wanted to sag against him, to sigh, to moan. Instead she bit her lower lip and endured the exquisite torture.

He licked and nibbled his way across her palm, then up the inside of her wrist and arm, all the while speaking of his name and hers, of the weaving of time and futures and how she belonged to him. She didn't really listen. They didn't have a future, she didn't belong to him, and right now she didn't care about anything but the way he touched her.

His mouth pressed against the inside of her elbow. Strong hands splayed across her back as he urged her to recline against the mound of pillows on the bed. She thought about protesting, but it was too late for pride. She was here because she couldn't imagine surviving without knowing what it was like to make love with him again. She might play the fool, but she wouldn't play the hypocrite.

When she'd stretched out on the bed, he leaned over her. "Dora," he whispered, speaking her name with a husky passion that made her ache inside. She was already wet between her thighs, wet and swollen and so very ready for him. She wanted to know his body again, his weight on hers, his maleness pressing inside of her.

She waited for his kiss, but he didn't touch her lips. Instead he nibbled on her shoulder, then moved lower, taking her nipple in his mouth.

She still wore her silk chemise. As he suckled her, the thin, gossamer fabric dampened. When he raised his head she saw that the material was now transparent. She could see the peachy-pink bud puckering against the undergarment. He saw it, too. Holding her gaze, he deliberately touched the tip of his tongue to the sensitized peak. To see as well as feel his seduction was more than she could stand. She half raised herself, grasping his head, pulling him down so she could kiss him.

Their mouths met in frenzied passion. She needed all of him. Next to her, in her, on top of her. More and more of him. She pushed at his clothes, fumbling for the ties of his robe. He shrugged out of them quickly, then pulled off his loose shirt. He had to leave the bed to remove his trousers, and she was shocked to hear herself whimper when he stood up to shed the garments.

But then he stood before her, naked and so incredibly beautiful. She studied the hard planes of his chest, the thick coils of his muscles, the dark hair crowning his arousal.

"Tell me," he commanded, standing by the bed but just out of reach. "Say the words. Tell me that you want me."

She shook her head. "I can't."

"Want me, or say it?"

Both, she thought, but she wouldn't tell him that. He moved closer…close enough that she was able to reach out her hand and stroke the powerful length of him. She encircled him with her fingers and moved back and forth, savoring the feel of him. Baby-soft skin over the unyielding pulse of his desire. She looked up at him and found herself caught in his hooded gaze. Only the tightening muscle at his jaw indicated that he was the least bit affected by her ministrations.

Slowly, gently, she moved lower and slipped her hand to his hard thighs. The hair on his legs tickled her palms. She moved up and down, learning his textures, his body, and in the process, arousing herself even more.

Without warning, he bent over and reached for her right foot. He examined the pattern made by the henna, tracing lines and circles with the tip of his finger. When he tickled her, she squirmed and laughed. She tried to pull away, but he wouldn't release her. She was caught.

''Tell me,'' he commanded, moving onto the bed and settling between her ankles. ''Tell me you want me.''

She mutely shook her head, then closed her eyes when he pushed up her gown and kissed the inside of her thighs. Her legs moved of their own accord, falling open, knees pulling back. There were no panties to impede him, no reticence on her part. She wanted him to touch her and kiss her there. She wanted to experience the passion and then the release.

He moved under her chemise and parted the secret folds of her flesh. She couldn't see what he was doing, but she felt the first warm caress of his lips and tongue on that most sensitive spot. He teased her, touching her lightly, circling, moving away and then returning.

It was more intense than it had been before, probably because she knew what to expect. She knew the glory at the end of the road and she tensed, rushing toward her paradise.

Involuntarily her hips moved in time with his tiny strokes. Her breathing increased, and her body heated. The coldness was long gone, as was her anger and her pain. All that remained was the wanting, the needing, the man. Khalil. Her husband.

He moved faster, bringing her closer to her release, then slowing, driving her mad. He pressed a finger into her, pushing up and teasing her from the inside. Then he slid that single finger in and out, imitating the love act to follow.

Pressure increased. Need increased. She wanted, desperately, to find her peace. Her heels dug into the mattress, her hips raised. She moaned his name. He moved faster and faster, lighter, better, closer and closer and closer.

In one quick movement, he sat back on his heels and pulled her into a sitting position. She stared at him unable to believe that he'd stopped what he was doing. Didn't he realize that she was going to die?

The wanting continued to grow inside of her. It became a hungry beast that consumed her. Desperately she reached for him, wanting more. Wanting it all.

But he ignored her questing hands that would have urged him back into place. Instead he tugged until her chemise was free of her hips, then he drew it over her head and tossed it away. His gaze fell to her breasts, and pleasure lit his eyes.

"So lovely," he told her as he leaned forward and took a nipple in his mouth.

It was as if there were a direct line from her breast to the very center of her being. With each tug of his lips, she felt an answering response between her legs. Even as his hands roamed up and down her back, even as he suckled her, she found herself spiraling closer and closer. She needed him, desperately.

"Khalil, please."

He raised his head. Dark hair tumbled onto his forehead. Untamed desire tightened the lines of his face, leaving her no doubt that his ancestors were wild savages who had ruled fearlessly. Did she really think she could stand up to him and win?

One of his hands slipped between their bodies. He rubbed her swollen point of pleasure until she whimpered, but stopped before she could climax.

"Tell me."

He was the devil, and the price was her soul. Why hadn't she seen what he wanted? "I can't."

''But you do want me.''

Their gazes locked. She could feel both their hearts beating. His arousal pressed against her belly. He pressed her onto her back and cupped her breasts. Finger and thumb teased her nipples. His hardness rode against her hot center, tormenting her by bringing her higher, but not allowing her to release.

She raised her hands and brought his head down to hers, then she kissed him. With her lips and her tongue she told him that she wanted him, but she refused to give in verbally. Between her legs, he rubbed hard, faster, making her ache and want, but she would not speak.

''Your will is not stronger than mine,'' he growled against her mouth.

''Yes, it is.''

''No!''

He raised up and guided himself inside. As he filled her, stretching her, making her cry out with pleasure, he reached down and touched that one, tiny spot.

The combination was too much. She felt herself collecting, rising, building, the tension growing until it exploded into light and glory.

Khalil felt the first rippling response of her body. Her muscles convulsed, contracting and releasing in a perfect rhythm. He cursed, he resisted, and it was all a waste of time. He'd played the game too well. In his effort to force her to submit, he'd allowed himself to get too aroused. Now, in the vortex of her release, he felt himself being caught and flung into the same tornado. Even as he tried to withdraw and gain control, it was already too late. Clutching her, he passed the point of no return and cried out her name.

The pleasure grew. He pumped harder, going deeper. Incredibly her contractions began again. She wrapped her

arms around him, clinging, urging him on. Again and
again she convulsed, until he had no choice but to explode
his seed inside of her. They shuddered together, two people lost in a storm.

When at last his breathing returned to normal, he raised
himself up on his arms and stared at her. She lay with her
eyes closed, her lips tightly pressed together. Tears flowed
down her temples and into her hair.

"Dora?"

"Go away. You won."

"We both won," he said, although technically she had
been the real victor. He hadn't been able to make her say
that she wanted him.

She pushed at his shoulder. He shifted off her, suddenly
feeling as awkward as a teenager. What was wrong?

When Dora was free of him, she sat up. "Is there a
bathroom?"

He pointed to several hanging rugs on the far side of
the tent. "In there. We have running water, but not very
much, so be cautious."

She nodded, but didn't speak. As she climbed out of
bed, she reached for her gown and covered herself. Khalil
watched her slow progress across the floor. She moved as
if she were in pain. Had he hurt her? He shook his head.
That wasn't possible. At the end, she'd been clinging to
him, wanting him as much as he wanted her. Women.
They were all temperamental creatures.

By the time she returned to the bed, he'd slipped under
the covers and had arranged the pillows. He saw that she'd
washed away all traces of her tears. She got in next to
him, but instead of cuddling close, she curled up with her
back to him.

"You're being a child," he told her.

"Leave me alone. You got what you wanted. The rest of it shouldn't matter."

He stared at her for another minute, then flopped down on his back. Fine. If she wanted to be that way, he didn't care. She was right. He'd gotten what he wanted. He'd made love with her. The rest of it was nonsense.

Except he found himself aching to hold her. As the night wore on, his side of the bed seemed to grow until he felt he was in a separate country. Once, when he knew she was truly sleeping, he'd moved close and put his arm around her. But even in sleep she shrugged him off, so he retreated to his own side.

Something cold and dark took residence in his chest. He hated the feeling that he'd acted rashly and had made a mistake that couldn't be corrected. Involuntarily he raised a hand to his face and touched the thin scar on his cheek. History was not repeating itself, he thought grimly. He would make sure things were different. Of course they were different. The situations had nothing in common.

And yet, far into the night, he wondered.

Dora awoke in Khalil's arms. As she stirred, she felt heat beneath her cheek and something heavy across her waist. She opened her eyes and saw that sometime in the night she'd rolled over and curled into his arms.

She stiffened and started to pull away, but the hand on her waist tightened. She looked up and saw that he was awake.

"Good morning," he said, his voice low and husky.

She hated that just the sound sent a shiver through her body and made her want to melt against him. Wasn't it enough that he'd humiliated her the previous night, tempting her until she'd thrown her convictions aside and had surrendered? Was this going to be an ongoing battle between them?

A slow smile curved at the corners of his mouth. "You resist and you want in equal measures, my desert cat. Which part of you is going to win?"

He shifted as he spoke, turning on his side until he faced her, slipping one knee between her legs and pressing it against her swollen woman's place. It took every ounce of strength not to arch against him. The need was as instant as it was powerful. How could her body betray her this way?

"I'll never surrender willingly," she told him, staring into his eyes. Her words were a vow. "You might be able to make my body react, but you'll never touch my heart."

"Is that a challenge? Didn't I warn you about making challenges? You are destined to be defeated." He pressed a kiss to her forehead. "In the most delicious way possible, of course. Besides, the chase is part of the appeal."

She wanted to scream out her frustration. How could this be happening to her? How could she have allowed herself to get into this position—both figuratively and literally? Even as she lay next to him, she felt his growing arousal pressing into her hip. Her woman's place dampened in response, readying for him. It didn't matter that he'd hurt her and lied to her and used her—every cell of her body still ached for his possession.

"You will be mine," he said confidently.

"Never. I'll keep turning away from you."

"And night after night, I will seduce you." He laughed. "If you're looking to punish me, Dora, you're going to have to find something better than that." His humor faded. "Then, in time, you'll grow to love me as a dutiful wife should."

She didn't know if he was still teasing or not, but it

didn't matter. Inside she'd grown empty and cold again, as she had the night before. She knew that he would be true to his word. He *would* seduce her as often as it amused him, and regardless of how much she resisted, she would eventually submit. In time his relentless assault would leave her spirit crushed and broken.

"I will never love you," she promised.

"You say that now, but I wonder if you've already fallen a bit in love with me. Am I your fantasy, my desert cat? Am I who you dreamed about in your lonely virgin bed?"

She wrenched herself free of him and stumbled out of bed. As she glared at him, he merely smiled and tossed away the covers so that she could see that he was hard and ready.

She turned her back on him and made a feeble effort to gather some kind of control. She had to learn how to protect herself from him. She had to be strong. If she didn't figure it out, his words would become a prophecy. He was an arrogant, selfish bastard...and he was right. He *was* the kind of man she'd dreamed about through her loneliness. Not the self-centered prince who forced his will on his reluctant wife, but the charming lover who had seduced her that first night.

She dreamed about the kind man who had rescued her in Kansas and the intelligent businessman she'd worked for in New York. Those were the men who had captured her attention and perhaps even a bit of her heart. But she did not love the Prince of El Bahar.

She found her lace dress and drew it over her head, then pulled on the heavy silk robes. Only when she was completely covered did she turn back to face him.

"I cannot speak for loving," she said quietly, "but I

will never like or respect you. If you insist on keeping me here, you will have to be content with duty.''

He raised dark eyebrows. ''A dutiful wife during the day and a wildcat in my bed at night. You, my dear, are my fantasy.''

She felt the tears begin to burn, but she blinked them away. ''How fortunate for you, Khalil. To me you are nothing more than a nightmare from which I can only pray to awake.''

She continued to stare at him, but not even by the flicker of a lash did he betray his thoughts. Then she turned away because she could feel her pain growing stronger, and she was determined to never let him see her cry again.

## Chapter Eleven

They drove back to the palace in silence. Khalil waited for Dora to comment on the beauty of the morning, or their four-car escort of guards, but instead she sat quietly in her seat, staring straight ahead, saying nothing. Fine, he thought angrily. If she wanted to play that game, he could do it as well...or better.

What had started out as a simple, even logical arrangement had turned into something more—something difficult. Why did she have to be so emotional? Perhaps he had misled her about his feelings at the beginning, but why did that matter now? He'd married her. He intended to treat her with the respect and consideration his wife deserved. They would live at the palace, have many sons. By virtue of their marriage, she had entered a life of wealth and privilege. What was she so upset about?

He gripped the steering wheel more tightly and told himself he would never understand women. They were difficult, emotional creatures, best left to their own devices. In time, Dora would see that this was all for the better. She would come around.

Or would she, a voice in his head whispered. Dora was not like other women he'd known. She was by far the most intelligent and certainly more independent of all his female companions. He quickly glanced at her, then returned his attention to the rutted track that became paved road as they neared the palace. She would not allow herself to be manipulated, and while he respected her for that, he also resented the extra work it was going to mean for him.

He would ignore her for a while, he thought. That would teach her. Except…visions of their lovemaking the previous night filled his mind. Memories of how it had been to touch her, to be touched. She'd been stubborn and unyielding to the end, refusing to tell him that she wanted him. But even without words, she'd let him know how much she desired him. Her body had spoken eloquently and without sound when she'd clung to him, begging him to go deeper, faster, harder.

He shook off the erotic images filling his brain and had to consciously slow his breathing. Perhaps he was hasty in his decision to ignore Dora. Perhaps there was a better way to reach her. Perhaps he wasn't giving her the benefit of the doubt—if she was so smart, she would figure out that he'd made the best decision for both of them. She would see that their marriage was the right thing for her, and she would be grateful to him for all that he'd done on her behalf.

As they neared the palace, he glanced at her again. She wore a long-sleeved dress that Rihana had packed for her. Both of their wedding robes were in the back seat. She'd brushed her short, dark hair away from her face, exposing her profile to him.

She wasn't beautiful like Amber or many of the other women who had been a part of his life, but she was quite lovely in her own right. He liked the way her eyes flashed when she grew angry with him and the way her mouth betrayed her when she was trying not to smile. He looked forward to speaking with her, hearing both her words and the sound of her voice. He welcomed the feel of her soft skin pressing against his, and the hot dampness that greeted his entry. She might not have been his first choice, but she was all things a man could want in a wife. He'd been fortunate to find her.

When they drove into the courtyard and he turned off the engine, he tried to think about what he should say to start their lives together on better footing. Some words of, if not atonement, then reconciliation. He could say that while he didn't understand or agree with her position he believed she thought it was important, so he would respect that. Maybe if he mentioned—

She opened the passenger door and stepped out. Instantly one of the servants was there to help her. She thanked the man and started walking toward the entrance to the palace.

Khalil stared after her. She hadn't waited for him. How dare she go striding off, as if he wasn't anyone more important than the chauffeur.

"Dora," he called as he scrambled to open his door and step outside. He brushed off the servant's greeting and hurried after her. "Dora, where do you think you're going?"

She paused to glance over her shoulder. "I would have thought that was obvious. I'm going to my rooms."

He caught up with her in the grand foyer. The sound

of running water from the main stone fountain provided idyllic background music. He touched her cheek. "You don't live in the harem anymore, my little wildcat. You live with me."

Her brown eyes widened at the news. She glared. He could almost see her temper rising inside her, and he held back his grin. They would fight, then they would make up. He looked forward to both events with equal anticipation. He hadn't thought that being married would require so much energy, but then he also hadn't realized the rewards.

Rihana appeared from the shadows and bowed low. "Welcome back." She gave Dora a shy smile. "I have moved your belongings into your husband's rooms. May I please show you the way?"

"No," Dora said sharply, not taking her gaze from Khalil's face. "Please take my things to the guest suite I was shown to when I first came to the palace. I'll be staying there."

Khalil frowned. "Dora, this is ridiculous. What do you hope to accomplish by this game? You're my wife."

Her gaze turned icy. "I am, aren't I. That makes me a princess. As such, I assume I'm allowed to give the servants instructions, and I can expect those instructions to be followed. Is that correct?"

She'd boxed him neatly into a corner. If she was his wife and therefore a princess in the palace, the servants would be expected to obey her. As her husband, he could not take away her power on her very first day. If he did, that decision would affect her position in the palace for the rest of her life.

He gritted his teeth and glared at her. They would have to take this up another time.

"Rihana, you will do as my wife requests," he said stiffly.

Rihana looked troubled, then nodded slowly. "This way, Princess," she said and turned away from the corridor leading to his rooms. Dora gave him a smug smile before she left to follow the girl. Khalil stood there alone, wondering how the hell everything had gone so wrong and what he was supposed to do about it now.

Dora stood alone on the balcony, staring out at the sea. She'd spent the past six hours alone in her suite of rooms, trying to savor her victory. But it didn't taste as sweet as she'd thought it would. She was away from Khalil, which is what she wanted, but she was also by herself. The rest of the day stretched long and lonely in front of her, as did all the days in her future. What was she going to do with herself?

She turned her back on the glorious view, and paced toward the French doors leading into her living quarters. How long would Khalil keep her in El Bahar before realizing their marriage was a mistake? She believed it was just a matter of time until he came to his senses and divorced her. Then she would be free. Until then, she would make the best of a bad situation by enduring her solitude. There had to be something she could do with her time. Maybe—

A light knock on the door interrupted her thoughts. She hurried across the large living room and opened her door. But instead of Rihana, or even Khalil, she saw that Fatima was her visitor.

She smiled at the older woman. "What a nice surprise. Please, come in."

Fatima did as she requested. She glanced around at the suite, as if she'd never seen the rooms before, then settled on one of the sofas facing the view. "I heard that you had chosen to live here instead of with Khalil. I didn't realize that privacy was so very important to you. I must apologize for making you uncomfortable by asking you to live with me in the harem."

Color and heat flared on Dora's cheeks as she sat opposite her guest. She placed her hands in her lap. "You disapprove of what I've done."

Fatima's thick hair lay coiled at the base of her neck. Her deep purple suit, all elegant lines with a neatly tailored jacket, emphasized her trim figure. She looked like a successful businesswoman about to attend an important meeting.

"It is not my place to approve or disapprove. Marriage is private between the two parties involved." She pressed her lips together. "I heard about what happened with Rihana, how you forced Khalil to choose between your obedience and your power in the household. While it was a tidy trick, I'm reminded of an old expression. It's originally British, I believe. Perhaps you've heard it—something about winning the battle, but losing the war."

"We're not fighting," Dora said evenly.

"Aren't you? When a husband and wife choose separate living quarters, it is rarely an indication that all is well, but then I'm from a different generation."

Dora lowered her head. She didn't like misleading Fatima. Khalil's grandmother had been very kind and generous to her. "Khalil and I have some things we need to sort out," she said. Actually, she had to do most of the sorting. She was still so confused and hurt by all that had happened.

"If you're waiting for my grandson to bend, you're going to be living here a long time. Khalil doesn't give in."

"Then it might be time for him to learn." Dora raised her head and straightened her spine. "I haven't forgotten your advice about bending, Fatima, but there are times when one has to make a stand. This is one of those times."

The older woman studied her. "Are you going to tell me what my grandson has done?"

"I can't." It was too humiliating to discuss with anyone, even someone as kind as Fatima. Besides, Dora knew that when push came to shove, Fatima would side with her family, not with her grandson's new wife. "I'm making the best of a difficult situation."

Fatima's shrewd, dark eyes seemed to see right through her. "And if he doesn't change? Then what?"

"I don't know."

Then she would leave, she thought. She would find a way to insist that Khalil divorce her, and she would be free. The fact that she had nowhere to go didn't matter. She wouldn't stay where she wasn't wanted and respected.

"I thought you loved him," Fatima said as she rose to her feet. "I'm sorry that I was wrong."

Dora felt as if she were six years old, and she'd just been scolded for being clumsy. "I do care for him," she hedged.

"But you don't love him. Or if you do, it's not strong enough that you'll fight for him." Fatima walked toward the door.

"Goodbye," she said as she stepped into the hall. To Dora, the words sounded very final.

When Fatima had left, Dora stood alone in the center of her silent rooms. She wanted to cry out that it wasn't fair—that Khalil had been the one to lie and deceive her, so why was *she* being punished? She'd married him with the best of intentions. She'd wanted to make her marriage work, she'd wanted to love him and be with him. But he'd hurt her. Worse, he wouldn't even take responsibility for his actions. He expected her to just understand and get over it. How could she have a relationship with a man who didn't see her as someone worth common courtesy?

She paced the length of the room, then returned to the balcony. The blue of the sea soothed her battered spirits but couldn't quiet her mind. Questions continued to fill her. What happened now? Could she stay in this suite indefinitely? Would Khalil want to divorce her? What would happen if he came to her expecting them to make love again? She doubted she had the power to resist him. As much as she didn't want to give in, her body betrayed her.

Dora sank down onto one of the chairs and covered her face with her hands. Had she won the battle but lost the war? Was she wrong to want more of Khalil? He'd hurt her so deeply. With him, she'd allowed herself to believe, only to find out it was all a lie. He'd used her because she was convenient and because he thought she would make a decent wife. Hardly the declarations of love that a woman longed to hear. So what happened now?

She didn't have an answer. So she continued to sit there alone until the sun set. Her only visitor that night was Rihana, bringing her a tray for dinner. Apparently Dora was not to be included in the family meal. She went alone to her bed and stayed alone that night and all through the next day.

Two nights later Khalil appeared in her room. There was no other way to describe it. One minute Dora had been reading and the next her husband loomed in front of her.

"Good evening," he said and settled next to her on the sofa.

Part of Dora wanted to start screaming at him, demanding that he get out, but only after making arrangements for her to return to the United States, but the rest of her was so grateful for someone to talk to that she nearly wept in relief. Since Fatima's visit, the only face she'd seen was Rihana's. And Dora hadn't had the courage to go in search of company on her own.

"Khalil." She nodded.

He wore dark slacks and a white shirt with the sleeves rolled up to his elbows. Something about his mussed hair and a slight air of weariness told her that he'd been working all day. She longed to return to her job as his assistant, or to any job, just so she could get out of her suite and do something with her time.

"I have honored your wishes," he said curtly.

"What wishes are those?"

"That you be left alone. Are you enjoying your solitude?"

She closed her book and set it on the table next to her. "I never requested solitude, I simply asked for separate quarters. However, you chose to take advantage of that and cut me off from the world. Does it make you feel big and strong to treat me this way? Is this a game of power? If so, you're only playing with yourself. I'm not interested in one-upmanship."

He looked at her for several seconds. "It seems whatever I do, you are determined to assume the worst about me. I honestly believed you wanted to be alone. You are my wife, and as such, a member of this family. You are welcome to leave your suite and join us for any meals you wish. This is a palace, Dora, not a prison."

She didn't know what to make of his words. Was he

telling the truth, or was this all another act? She stared into his handsome face and had to curl her fingers into her palm to keep from reaching out to touch the slender scar on his left cheek.

"All right," she said at last. "Thank you."

"You may also return to work," he announced. "I will expect you in my office at eight in the morning."

If he'd asked if she would like to return to work, she would have probably said yes. If he'd even hinted that she had a choice, or that it was her decision, everything would have been fine. But for him to have the nerve to give her *permission* to help him... She sucked in a breath and felt her temper beginning to rise.

"I don't think so," she said coolly, as she rose to her feet. She crossed to the open French doors and stepped out onto the balcony. The sun had long since disappeared behind the horizon, leaving the ocean a dark and mysterious glimmering slate of blackness. She stared out into the night sky and pretended to be fascinated by the stars.

"I am giving you my permission," Khalil said as he followed her onto the marble balcony.

"Yes, I know. I'm telling you that I'm not interested." She smiled sweetly.

"I want you working for me."

She shrugged. "I want you to apologize for what you said to me in New York, for lying and for tricking me into marriage. I want you to admit that you were wrong, and then I want you to tell me that you care about me. I suspect that neither of us is going to get what we want."

She heard him take a step toward her. "You will not toy with me, wife."

Finally she turned to face him. "And here I thought that was what you wanted."

His expression tightened. "I am Khalil Khan, prince—"

She cut him off with a wave. "Prince of El Bahar. Yes, I know. I've heard this speech a hundred times before. What exactly is your point?"

He froze in place, obviously stunned by her impertinence. Dora was a little surprised herself, but in a good way. Maybe she'd needed time alone to give her the courage to stand up to Khalil. Right or wrong, it was the only way she knew to change things. As much as she might tell herself she wanted a divorce and to go back home, the truth was a little less clear. In her heart of hearts she was willing to admit that she would prefer to stay here— but only as Khalil's true wife. He didn't have to love her but he had to care about her and treat her with respect.

"Being the prince doesn't give you the right to use people," she went on, praying her courage lasted five seconds longer than his visit. "You were cruel to me. You lied, and you treated me as if my feelings had no consequence. You took advantage of my innocence."

"I married you."

"Right. As if being married to you is any kind of picnic."

He took one more step closer. Now he was within touching distance…as was she. He took her hand in his and rubbed his thumb across her palm. Instantly shivers rippled through her as heat flamed and her body came to life. She disentangled herself and retreated to the railing.

"Come to work for me," he said.

Ignoring her still tingling palm, she smiled. "I'm the princess of El Bahar. I don't work. Besides—" She held up her hands "My henna hasn't worn off. Tradition states—"

This time he was the one to cut *her* off. "I'm well

aware of the tradition. I was born here.'' He glared. ''If this is what you wish, so be it. You may stay in your rooms but do not attempt to leave them. You will exist within these four walls. For all I care, you can rot here.'' He spun on his heel and headed for the door.

Dora swallowed. She heard Fatima's words again—the ones about winning the battle but losing the war. Was she doing that again? To live by another quote, pride goes before the fall. Did she really want to spend all her time alone in this suite?

''Khalil?'' she called before she could stop herself. ''I'll come work with you, but not as your secretary.''

He paused in midstride. ''I suppose you want to run the country.''

She ignored his sarcasm. ''No,'' she said as she crossed to stand next to him. ''I want to work with the Western companies who have come here to do business. I've been doing a lot of reading in the past couple of days.'' She motioned to the stack of magazines and books by the sofa. ''There isn't a single department to coordinate the efforts of Western companies interested in setting up facilities here in El Bahar. I want to be a facilitator between the government and the private companies in the West. I have plenty of experience working with corporate America, and I'm learning more each day about El Bahar.''

He stared at her but didn't speak.

''It makes sense,'' she went on quickly, trying to hang on to her rapidly fading courage. ''As a member of the royal family, I would be considered more of a figurehead than a policymaker. That will appease men in government. The companies interested in coming here will be impressed that El Bahar would put a woman in such a visible position.''

He opened his mouth, then closed it. "You are my wife."

"I'm aware of that."

He turned away. Dora held her breath, then let it out slowly. The idea had come to her in the night, but she hadn't known who to talk to. She doubted she was much in favor with any member of the family right now. So she'd decided she would just wait for the right opportunity. Was it too soon? Should she have gone to work as Khalil's secretary for a few weeks first, gaining his trust, before she approached him with her idea?

Too late now, she thought, and didn't have a clue as to what she would do if he said no.

"You would have to work under the jurisdiction of my office," he said, not looking at her. He seemed to be studying a portrait of an old man on the far wall.

Her heart began to thunder in her chest. Was he really saying yes? "That isn't a problem."

"You would not be allowed to meet alone with any man, and you must dress conservatively. Otherwise my reputation will be called into question."

"I understand. I have no desire to meet alone with any man, and conservative dress is fine with me."

He looked at her. She tried to read his expression, but couldn't. What was he thinking? Why had he agreed?

"For the sake of appearances, we will need to be the happy couple," he told her. "You will take lunch with me each day."

Her tension eased, and a spark of hope burst to life. She remembered their working lunches in New York. Some of the time had been spent dealing with business, but much of their conversation had been more personal. They'd argued politics, discussed books and music. She remembered the heated debates, the laughter, the teasing.

She'd missed those times so much—had Khalil missed them as well?

"I would like that very much," she said.

"Good. Then we are agreed."

He smiled at her, a slow satisfied smile of a male who had gotten his way. Some of Dora's happiness faded. Please, God, don't let him spoil the moment by trying to make it more. But God was busy, or Khalil had a mind of his own, for her husband cupped her face in his hands and stared down at her.

"I want you," he told her.

His words were like a slap. She was a fool to think that anything had changed between them. She stiffened and willed herself to move away, but it was already too late. Just the feel of hands against her jaw and cheeks was enough to melt both her bones and her resolve. She was trapped in a web of her own making—desiring a man she both wanted and hated.

"Don't," she said, at last jerking free of his gentle touch. "I don't feel well."

Khalil grabbed her by her upper arms and hauled her against him. When she was pressed flush against him, he rotated his hips, grinding his erection into her belly.

"Call me names," he growled. "Fight me, hit me, hate me, refuse me, but do not lie to me."

She felt her eyes burning with tears and loathed herself for the weakness. "Of course. Lying is your job."

Instead of getting angry, he smiled. "I thought I was marrying someone sensible, but a bit boring. Instead I find myself with a feisty, sexual wildcat. Do you bite, little kitten of mine? I know you try to scratch, although your claws aren't sharp enough."

"I hate you," she shouted, struggling to get free. "You are nothing but a manhandling piece of pond scum, and

I never want to see you again.'' His fingers held on tight and he didn't let her go. Finally she stopped the fruitless attempt to break free and glared at him. ''I will never surrender willingly.''

''So many absolutes,'' he murmured, lowering his head and brushing her lips with his. ''So many promises. How much energy you waste. And here I was hoping you'd be more aggressive in bed.''

She tried to raise her hand to slap him, but he held her arms firmly at her side and laughed. ''I assume your temper means that you feel fine?'' he asked.

''I'm not sick, I just don't want to have sex with you.''

He released one arm and slowly pulled up her dress. She knew what he was going to do and told herself to run, for pride's sake, if nothing else. But she couldn't move, couldn't turn away. She could only stare into his eyes as he slipped his hand into her panties, then moved lower until he touched her waiting dampness. She shuddered as he rubbed against her swollen core.

''Who's the liar now?'' he asked, then kissed her.

Dora didn't answer. Not because she was too busy kissing him back, but because she didn't know what to say. She couldn't deny her body's obvious reaction to his nearness. And later, when they were both naked and his tongue caressed every part of her, she couldn't quiet her moans of pleasure.

Once again, her husband had been victorious.

## *Chapter Twelve*

Dora paused outside the entrance to the office wing of the palace and smoothed her sweaty hands on her skirt. She'd thrown down the gauntlet, and Khalil had responded. She now had an office of her own, a title and even an assistant. The question was—did she know how to do the job?

She resisted the urge to run back to her lonely quarters and send Khalil a message telling him she'd just been kidding. Because it *was* a joke. Did she really think she had the training and experience required to act as liaison between the El Baharian government and Fortune 500 companies wanting to set up offices or manufacturing facilities? El Bahar was a peaceful country with a reputation of being the Switzerland of the Middle East so corporations interested in expansion in this part of the world frequently began in El Bahar. She was meddling in a multibillion-dollar arena, and she had absolutely no idea what she'd been thinking.

Except that she'd spent most of her time alone reading business magazines and books, and the common theme she'd come across was the difficulty companies had when expanding internationally. She'd had some experience with that while working for Gerald. He'd been a jerk and more than willing to let her shoulder his responsibilities whenever possible. Was that enough training? She drew in a deep breath and opened the door leading to the suites of offices. She supposed she was about to find out.

The frosted-glass double doors led into a large, plush waiting area decorated with leather sofas and fabulous Impressionist paintings. It took her a second to realize that they were all originals. She found herself wanting to pause in front of the huge canvases, then remembered she was here to work, not admire, and approached the trim middle-aged man sitting behind an oversize desk. He looked up and smiled.

"Good morning, Your Highness. I'm Martin Wingbird. Prince Khalil told me you would be arriving this morning. May I have the honor of showing you to your office?"

The man was perfectly dressed in a tailored suit, and his accent was British. From what Dora had been able to figure out, much of the staff was international. While she was still living in the harem, Fatima had entertained her with stories about wild arguments between the two head chefs, one of whom was French, the other American *and* a woman. Apparently while they avoided blows, they weren't above throwing the crockery at each other.

"Thank you, Mr. Wingbird."

Behind the main reception desk, two corridors jutted out, one going left, the other right. Martin took the left corridor, walking briskly down a long, carpeted hallway.

Dora hurried after him as best she could. She'd dressed in a long, straight skirt that came nearly to her ankles. While it was conservative enough to meet any exacting standards, it also prevented her from taking long strides.

They passed several large offices, complete with computers, faxes and copy machines. The desert might be only a half dozen or so miles away, but here in the palace, the staff had long moved into the modern age.

As they approached the end of the corridor, Dora saw two massive doors standing open. Three assistants, two men and a woman, worked in front of two more doors.

"Prince Khalil's staff is here," Martin Wingbird said. "And that door on the left leads to your office."

He introduced the assistants, and she found that the lone female, a beautiful Asian woman named Eva, worked for her.

Dora had to smile. "I'm curious about the staffing arrangements," she told Martin. "Do I have a woman working for me because no man would dare work for a woman in this country, or is it a matter of propriety? And if it's the latter, what is to prevent the staff from crossing the line?"

Martin's serious expression didn't change, but she saw a flicker of humor in his blue eyes. "I'm sure I don't know, ma'am."

"How clever of you. In your position, I wouldn't know, either." She nodded. "Thank you for you help, Martin."

"My pleasure, Your Highness." He bowed once and left.

Eva had already opened the door to Dora's office, and now the assistant led the way inside. Dora followed her into a plush space filled with French country-style furniture, paintings of flowers and a large spray of roses in a vase on the coffee table in front of a small sitting area. Windows gave her a view of a formal English garden.

She looked around at the bright colors in the Oriental rug and the little touches of lace on the throw pillows tossed casually on the sofa. "The room is so perfect, I want to believe it has been decorated just for me," Dora said more to herself than to Eva. But that wasn't possible. She and Khalil had spoken about her working for him less than forty-eight hours ago. The office couldn't have been put together that quickly, could it?

"Prince Khalil arranged everything himself," Eva said. "He spent all of yesterday overseeing everything." She smiled. "Your husband was most particular about the furniture he chose and had many items sent back into storage before he approved this."

Khalil? Her husband? The man who demanded his way in everything, most especially her submission to him? She couldn't imagine him caring about decor, let alone picking out furniture and throw pillows.

Eva walked over to the desk and touched a few keys on the computer. "I've begun to work on your calendar," she said. "You have two meetings scheduled for this afternoon. They're to introduce you to the local presidents of two of our largest foreign banks."

The woman kept speaking, but Dora could no longer hear the words. She'd gone into panic mode, wondering what on earth she'd thought when she'd told Khalil she'd wanted this particular job. She was going to fall on her butt and it was going to be very public and very—

"Your Highness?" Eva asked. "Is everything all right?"

The young woman was exceptionally pretty, with beautiful, thick hair cut in a fashionable wedge and a long jacket and skirt outlining a slender body.

"I'm fine," Dora assured her. "Would you please upload files on those two presidents and their banks. I'm interested in their last yearly report, figures we have for the most recent two quarters, as well as copies of articles from local papers. I want to see what kind of press they've been getting in El Bahar. Oh, and general information on banking in general. The number of local versus foreign banks, the percent of citizens using local banks rather than foreign banks, any estimations on offshore accounts here."

Eva scribbled notes as Dora talked. "Anything else, Your Highness?"

Dora sighed. "I know it's important to address me respectfully, Eva, but we're going to have to come up with something shorter than 'Your Highness.'"

Eva smiled. "I'll get right on all of this, ma'am."

"You do that. Let me know when you start uploading files to my computer."

Eva nodded and started to leave, but before she could pull the door shut behind her, Khalil appeared and pushed his way inside.

Her office was a big room, but Khalil stood well over six feet, and with him filling the space, the walls seemed to shrink together. Dora looked at her husband, half enjoying, half hating the swell of gladness that rushed through her. Despite the fact that he made her crazy, he was a very handsome man and easy to look at.

Today he wore a tailored suit that emphasized the powerful lines of his body...a body that she'd touched and tasted the previous evening until they were both breathless with desire. She'd kept true to her word and resisted him whenever he tried to make love with her. He'd also told the truth when he'd promised to seduce her night after night. They were playing a silly game, and she wasn't sure when it was going to end, or how they were going to determine a winner. She only knew that she was ridiculously happy to see him and that she was going to do her best to keep him from knowing.

"Do you like it?" he asked, prowling around the room. "My office is right next door. I know you would have preferred something on your own, but there are proprieties. The king wasn't sure about the wife of a prince going to work, even as a liaison."

Dora hadn't thought of that. "I'm sorry, Khalil. Did I make trouble between you and your father?"

He shrugged. "He came around."

He paused in front of her desk and ran his fingers across the smooth surface. The deeply colored wood had been polished until it gleamed and reflected the brass lamp sitting by the desk blotter.

He walked to the armoire by the door and pulled it open. "The printer is in here, along with your own fax machine. It will be quieter in the cabinet. There's a small button on your desk that will tell you when you have a fax coming in."

He moved back to the desk and touched the phone. "My number is preprogrammed. Just push star-one and you'll be connected right to my office. Malik is star-two and Jamal is star-three."

"Why would I need to call your brothers?"

Khalil straightened and looked at her. "You'll be taking over projects from all of us. While I'm responsible for all resource development, except for oil, as well as assisting emerging industries, Jamal handles the country's finances while Malik looks after our oil interests and, as the crown prince and heir, represents El Bahar abroad. All of us have dealings with foreign businesses. Your responsibilities will put you in contact with all three of us on a regular basis.''

Dora swallowed and tried not to let her nervousness show. Once again she realized she'd been arrogant and presumptuous in her request for this job. She hadn't thought through the scope of what she would be doing.

''I've asked Eva to schedule introductory meetings over the next few days,'' he said. ''They should get you up to speed. As you're my wife, you'll be reporting directly to me.''

''Yes, of course,'' she said, still stunned by her blunder. Could she really do this?

''You're not afraid, are you?''

She looked up and squared her shoulders. ''Of course not. I'm more than capable.''

Khalil's gaze was steady, as if he knew she was terrified. But he was obviously willing to let her bluff her way through. She decided that however much work it took, she *would* master this job and make both of them proud of her.

She crossed to her desk and took a seat. ''So, do I get paid?''

She'd meant the comment as a joke, but Khalil didn't smile. ''Why would you need the money?''

To be honest, she hadn't much thought about it. ''I suppose I don't.''

He braced his hands on the desk and leaned forward, crowding her and making her want to roll her chair away. ''Make no mistake about your place in all of this. You are my wife, and you will stay my wife.''

His direct gaze burned down to her very confused heart. Until that moment, Dora had assumed that Khalil was going to find a way to divorce her. She still didn't understand all the circumstances of their marriage. She knew what she'd believed and what Amber had said, but the truth remained a mystery. Did he really plan to keep her in his life?

"I will not let you go," he told her. "El Bahar does not permit a royal wife to divorce her husband without his consent, and I will never agree."

Oddly enough, his words comforted her. Despite their differences, or maybe because of them, she didn't want to go. A part of her was still hoping for the dream of a fantasy prince to love her forever. Which only proved she hadn't learned a damn thing, despite having her heart broken by two men in less than two months.

"You were amazing last night," he said, abruptly changing the subject. He continued to stare at her, and she saw the fire glowing in his eyes. Fire that instantly sparked an answering flame deep in her woman's place.

"Thank you," she murmured. Last night she'd been bold. Once he'd broken through her initial reserve, she'd attacked him, touching him, taking him in her hands and then in her mouth. She still remembered his shocked cries of pleasure.

The memory made her squirm against her seat. Her panties grew damp as her breasts swelled. "Khalil..."

He smiled, the slow, satisfied smile of a male who had won. "I knew you would come around. You want me. Admit it."

Her passion fled as quickly as it had arrived. She straightened and stared at him with cold disinterest. "Just because I'm your wife doesn't mean you have the right to sexually harass me, Khalil. While we're in the office, I want to discuss business and nothing else."

He straightened and glared at her. "How do you do that? How can you want me one minute and then freeze me out the next? Why won't you give in on this? You know I will win in the end.''

"Will you?" She shrugged. "I happen to think I'm going to win. I can be very stubborn.''

"I know. It's not your most attractive feature.''

"Would you like a list of your own faults?''

His look of surprise nearly made her smile. "I have no faults.''

She leaned back in her chair. "Honey, you have a list so long, I'd get a cramp in my hand if I tried to write it.''

"Not true," he said. "I remind you that I am your husband, and I will be treated with respect.''

Well, it was an improvement to the "I'm Prince Khalil Khan, etc." which he'd been throwing in her face since they first met. "Nine to five we work together. No chitchat about sex. I mean it, Khalil.''

"What? Do you think you can take that tone with me and get your way?''

She thought for a moment, then smiled. "Absolutely.''

He glared. "You are an impossible woman.''

"Yes, but I'm your impossible woman. Now get back to work, and leave me alone.''

"We're dining together at twelve-thirty," he said as he headed for the door. "And I'm leaving because I have things to do, not because you told me to.''

"Of course. Just as long as you're leaving.''

He paused to look at her. "Do not think you have more power than you do, my desert wildcat. I will still be the one you submit to this night.''

"I will never submit.''

He shrugged. "You may play your game of resisting at the beginning, but we both know that you will soon be in my arms, begging me to touch you and take you to paradise.''

Then he was gone. And Dora was left with the uncomfortable realization that he spoke the absolute truth.

Fatima accepted the cup of tea Khalil's assistant offered, then waited until the young man had left them alone in his office. Khalil stretched out his legs in front of him and waited. His grandmother had requested this meeting, and she would get to her point in her own time.

She didn't keep him in suspense long. "Your father has begun to speak of Dora in terms of grudging respect, which I assume means that she's doing extremely well in her work."

Khalil couldn't help giving his grandmother a satisfied grin. "Right now she's meeting with a computer manufacturing company and instead of walking in dictating terms, as they'd expected, they're conceding on every point she's brought up."

"So you are pleased with her as well."

Pleased didn't begin to describe his feelings. At first Dora had been cautious and hadn't expressed many opinions. He'd made the mistake of assuming she was going to be timid and not much use...as had the men she'd met with. But by the end of the first week, she'd been asking for more than they wanted to give and standing up to them when they refused. A major European bank had received a thumbs-down from her. Khalil had backed up her decision, even though he'd thought she'd gone too far. Three days later that bank's competitor had come in with a package that would fund El Bahar's budding computer chip manufacturing industry. Two hotels were bidding for property east of the city and there was talk of a cooperative venture between two American universities and the leading El Baharian hospital for several research projects. All this in less than a month.

"She is an asset to us all," he said at last. "Despite her lack of formal training, she is a shrewd negotiator. I've watched her use American casualness to lull her opponents into trusting her, then turn into a royal princess to intimidate at exactly the right moment."

"And the marriage progresses equally well?" Fatima asked, then took a sip of tea.

Her well-groomed hair was swept away from her face. Several rings decorated her long, elegant fingers. She looked like a well-dressed matron making a social call, but Khalil knew better. Unlike Dora's opponents, he'd learned not to underestimate the power of a female in the royal family.

"Dora and I are very happy," he said.

Fatima didn't respond. First she nibbled on a shortbread cookie, then patted her mouth with a small, linen napkin.

Khalil wanted to stand up and start pacing, but he refused to let his grandmother intimidate him in his own office. He stayed silent. As did Fatima. The clock in the corner ticked off the seconds. Tension grew. He swore he wasn't going to give in first.

Finally he couldn't stand it anymore. He bounced to his feet and stalked to the window. "She's stubborn and irritating," he growled, his back to the room. He stared out at a view of the gardens, but didn't see any of the lush plants. Instead he saw Dora turning away from him, as she had the previous night. Telling him silently that she didn't want him, forcing him to reduce her to mindless pleading, until her body spoke a truth her lips refused to utter.

"At least she's intelligent," Fatima said calmly. "That's something."

"Not when the intelligence is used against me." He

turned to face his grandmother. "Her two weeks in the harem taught her nothing of being a good wife."

"Oh, is that what we were supposed to be doing? How foolish of me. I arranged for her to learn El Baharian customs and history. Perhaps you should send her back to me. Then I can teach her all she needs to know about cleaning and cooking and mending. Would the young prince be more happy then?"

He glared at Queen Fatima and was reminded that his grandfather had always respected his wife...and with good reason. "I have no need for another servant. I want a wife."

"Perhaps if you weren't living in separate quarters," she suggested.

Khalil stiffened. He hated that Dora refused to move into his suite. He was a married man, and it was damned humiliating to have to traipse halfway across the palace just to spend the night in his wife's bed.

"She refuses to move in with me."

"Really?" Fatima set down her cup and looked at him. "What did you do wrong?"

His hot temper flared. "Why do you assume that it's my fault? She's the one who won't do as she's told."

"I see."

Those two, short words spoke volumes. He hated the way Fatima could make him feel young and small again and had to resist the urge to remind her that he was Prince Khalil Khan of El Bahar. She'd never been much impressed by that.

"I thought you'd learned, Khalil," Fatima said. She touched her left cheek, making him instantly aware of the faint scar on his own face. "I thought you would remember the lesson that some words come with a high price."

"These situations have nothing in common," he insisted.

"So you have said nothing to Dora that you might regret?"

He didn't answer. Instead he turned back to the window, refusing to remember the words he'd spoken that first night they'd made love in New York. How he'd convinced Dora that he'd desperately wanted her when in fact he'd found her mostly convenient. But his grandmother's arrow had found its mark, and he had the sharp cut to prove it.

Dora had told him she wanted him to apologize for what he'd said and to admit that he cared about her. That was her price for her affection. Until then she promised to turn away from his advances, resisting his lovemaking until he forced her to surrender. Every night she kept her word, as did he, breaking her will until she was weak with longing. In the test of stubbornness, they were at a draw.

"You have nothing to be concerned about," Fatima said calmly. "Your wife is intelligent, healthy and well-mannered. She will not dishonor you or El Bahar. In fact, she is proving to be a great asset. In time she will bear you healthy sons."

Something in her tone made him wonder where she was going with this. He looked at her. "I agree. All *is* well."

Fatima took another sip of her tea. "In time, of course, she will grow to hate you, but this is the way of these kinds of marriages."

"No!" Khalil said before he could stop himself. "I don't want her to hate me."

Fatima raised her eyebrows. "Khalil, you couldn't possibly care about this girl, could you?"

"Of course not."

But the words lacked conviction. He didn't want to ad-

mit it, but he *did* care. He hated that night after night he
had to seduce her into wanting him. More times than not,
when they had finished making love, Dora turned away
from him and cried. She made no sound, but he felt the
sobs silently shaking her body. If he touched her face, his
fingers grew wet with her tears.

"What do I do?" he asked the woman who had been
a second mother to him.

"Oh, Khalil, why do you men make everything so difficult?" She gave him a kind smile. "You woo her. Be
the kind of man she can admire. Be tender and attentive,
and most of all apologize for whatever it is you have done
to hurt her. Make amends. Bend a little. For once in your
life, remember you are first a man, and second a prince."

"Never. What you suggest is unacceptable."

"Then get used to roaming the halls of the palace every
night."

He didn't want that, either. "I will force her to move
into my rooms."

Fatima looked at him as if he were a very simple child.
"Yes, I can tell how well that will work with Dora. Why
did you ask me what to do if you're not going to listen?"

"I have listened. You're not giving me good advice. I
am Prince Khalil Khan of El Bahar, and I do not woo
women."

"You are a stubborn fool who is going to live his life
alone. Is that what you want?"

He didn't answer the question and in time, his grandmother left. He paced his office searching for solutions
that continued to elude him. He was not going to woo his
wife. How degrading. How impossible. She would laugh.
He refused to humiliate himself in such a manner.

And yet…the alternative was the standoff that existed
between them now. Is that what he wanted? That and the
very real possibility that Dora would grow to hate him?

## *Chapter Thirteen*

Dora poured more iced tea into her glass and stared at the handsome man sitting across from her. Khalil was telling her about a meeting he'd had that morning with the American scientists who were working on desert reclamation.

"I should have let you deal with them," he said as he set his fork next to his plate. "They were most difficult."

"Oh, so now you're going to give me your dirty work, is that it?" she asked with a smile.

His gaze settled on her face. She wasn't sure what he was thinking, but his expression was affectionate enough to get her heart fluttering a little faster. It was early April. She'd been in El Bahar nearly three months. Khalil visited her room and her bed nearly every night, and he still had the power to make her weak with longing with just a glance or a light touch of his hand.

"Not my dirty work," he told her. "You're better with

the scientists than I am. I think it has something to do with your being a woman. You lull them with humor or flash your ankles at them.''

She glanced down at the long skirt that fell nearly to the floor. As per El Baharian custom, and her husband's request, she wore conservative clothes that covered her arms to the wrist and her legs almost to the ankle. In the privacy of her quarters she sometimes got wild and slipped on an old pair of blue jeans.

''That's me, the ankle flasher,'' she said with a smile.

She was only teasing, but Khalil frowned. ''I do not want you exposing yourself to other men.''

She stared at the man she'd married and lived near and worked with for the past three months. At times she knew everything he was thinking, but every now and then, when he once again became the prince of El Bahar, she realized she didn't know him at all.

''It was a joke, Khalil,'' she told him.

''It is not humorous to me.''

''I don't understand how you can be so possessive in some ways and so insensitive in others.'' She paused. Their lunches together were one of her favorite times of the day. ''I'm sorry. I shouldn't have said that. I don't want to fight.''

He leaned across the small table set up in a corner of his office. ''This isn't fighting,'' he told her. ''We don't fight, we talk.''

''What's the difference?''

''You never throw anything.'' His mouth twisted down at the corners. ''You're a Western woman, with coldness and propriety flowing through your veins.''

''You want me to start throwing dishes?'' He couldn't be serious.

''It would be preferable to the silences. Don't you feel

any passion?'' He made a dismissive gesture with his hand. ''I'm not talking about in bed, but in life. Do you fight for things?''

''Of course. When they're important.''

She glanced around the well-appointed office. The hand-carved desk dated back to the seventeenth century. They were in the middle of a palace in the capitol of El Bahar. Life was different here, as were the people. Sometimes she forgot that.

''We have different styles,'' she told him. ''But that doesn't mean that my way is wrong.''

''Perhaps. But what have you fought for in your life? Not this marriage.''

She straightened and raised her chin. ''What do you mean by that?''

''It's been many weeks but still you live on the other side of the palace. You haven't once come to my room or touched me first. Every night I am forced to make the journey to your room, to hold you and kiss you until you finally surrender to me.''

''That was your decision,'' she told him stiffly. ''I swore I wouldn't give in to you until you apologized for what you did and admitted that you cared about me. You said that you didn't mind having to seduce me every time. That it was a challenge.''

He stared at her. Despite the tailored suit and tie, he was not like the other men she'd worked with. He was part successful businessman, part prince. For the first few weeks, she'd enjoyed the businessman and had tolerated the prince, but that was slowly changing. The more she learned about Khalil, the more she could care about all of him. But he was a difficult man and refused to ever admit that he was wrong. As much as she longed to give in to him, she knew it would be a mistake. She had to make him see that she was a person with feelings—someone worthy of his affection and consideration.

"You are most stubborn," he complained.

She shrugged. "As are you. That's probably why the trait is so irritating in me." She drew in a deep breath. "Is it so very hard to apologize?" she asked. "All I want is for you to admit that you shouldn't have lied to me that first night. If you'd come to me and explained the situation, I might have cooperated."

"You would have thought I was crazy," he said, dismissing her. "Or you would have put conditions on the marriage. No, my way was better."

"What about my feelings? What about the fact that you lied to me and made me believe in you? What about being honest? I still don't know why you wanted to marry me rather than Amber. All you've said is that she wouldn't have been a good wife and mother. What does that mean? Why do you have to keep so many secrets?"

He glared at her. "I am most concerned about your feelings. Didn't I give you this job? Don't I allow you to work?"

"Allow? Allow? You're kidding, right?" She rose to her feet and stared down at him. "I swear, Khalil, if you're looking for me to start throwing things, you're getting awfully close." She placed her hands on her hips. "You might think you *allow* me to have this job, but you and your country are getting a hell of a lot of benefit, and you know it. If you gave me the chance, then I've more than earned my right to stay here. I've made a difference. I've gotten dozens of improvements on our contracts with foreign companies. Don't for a moment think that you can dismiss my contribution."

"I'm not saying you haven't helped," he hedged. "But

I don't understand why you have to be so difficult. You're ruining things between us.''

She couldn't believe the audacity of the man. "Me? No, Khalil, you don't get to pass this one off on me. You want to ignore the ugly reality that is the foundation of our marriage. Until that is fixed, until the past is atoned for, nothing lasting can be built here. We can try, but whatever we build is destined to crumble.''

She dropped her hands to her sides. "I'm willing to meet you more than halfway, but I can't do it all. You have to be willing to take responsibility for your mistakes. Is it so horrible to admit that you were wrong?''

He rose to his feet and glanced at his watch. "I have a meeting.''

Defeated, Dora nodded. Obviously there was no getting through to him. She walked out of the room and headed for her own office.

Once there she stood at the window and stared out at the garden. What was she doing wrong? Was she wishing for the moon? A part of her simply wanted to surrender. After all, Khalil wasn't like other men. He was strong, stubborn, opinionated, difficult, a prince. Did the ordinary rules apply to him?

Dora rested her forehead against the cool glass. Outside the temperature had climbed into the nineties. Summer approached with a relentlessness that made her hope the air-conditioning never failed.

Was she wrong? Should she forget what had happened between them and start over? A part of her wanted to say yes. That soft woman's place deep inside longed to have a real marriage with Khalil. She wanted to move into his suite and sleep with him every night. She wanted to live with him, laugh with him, see him first thing in the morning, feel his body close to hers, not just when they were making love, but at other times. She wanted to be free to touch him and tell him that she wanted him. She wanted a real marriage.

But if she gave in… Dora didn't have a simple answer for that concern. If she gave in, how could she ever respect herself? She knew that it wasn't enough that he was nice to her now; he had to understand that she was a person with feelings he had to respect. His casual disregard for her had hurt terribly. Even now the wounds remained raw.

If she gave in he would never treat her any differently. She would only reinforce the idea that if he was stubborn enough, he would get his way. She wanted a shared partnership, or as much of one as was possible with a living, breathing prince for a husband. For that to happen, she would have to be strong.

And if it didn't, a voice in her head whispered. Another question that didn't have an answer. If it didn't, she would have to speak to the king about leaving El Bahar. If Khalil didn't come around, she would have to get a divorce.

The night was cool after the heat of the day, and Khalil appreciated the sea breeze as he paced on the balcony facing the ocean. He walked back and forth, his hands shoved into his pockets, his mind swirling and racing as he grappled with the reality that was his life.

Damn her to hell, he thought grimly. Then he stopped and smiled. Yes, he wanted to curse his wife and somehow force her to obey him, but he also respected her in ways he never thought he *could* respect a woman. She was a hard worker—intelligent, resourceful, dedicated. As she'd pointed out at lunch that morning, she'd done great things for El Bahar. She made him proud. So why wouldn't she surrender to him? Did she really think she could bend him to her will? She couldn't and yet...

What he hated most was that her siege had started to get to him. Here he was, Prince of El Bahar, actually thinking about listening to his grandmother's advice. He'd spoken to Fatima several weeks ago, but her words had not faded from his mind. Woo her. Woo Dora. Be all those things a woman wanted a man to be. Adore her, respect her, admire her.

Khalil glared into the darkness. Why should he have to woo his wife? He felt all those things for her already. He had great respect and admiration for her. He did adore her, and if she couldn't see that, she wasn't worth the trouble.

The words sounded perfect...in theory. But the truth was, he'd grown tired of their game. He wanted her to want him. He wanted her in his life and his bed, and not because he'd forced her. He wanted her willing and loving.

He froze in midstride. Loving? Did he want Dora to love him?

He physically took a step back. No, not love. He didn't need a mere woman to love him. He was Prince Khalil Khan of—

"Khalil?"

He turned at the sound of his name and saw his brother, Malik, and his father standing on the balcony. He walked over to them.

Givon grasped his upper arm and squeezed. "My son, I was wrong to be so harsh with you."

Khalil stared from one to the other. "What are you talking about?"

Malik leaned against the railing. "I went to our father and told him what happened with Amber. I don't remember very much about the night. It was a long time ago, and I was quite drunk. At first I thought it was a dream. The betrothed of my brother wouldn't have come to my bed and been with me. I told myself to forget it, but her scent lingered on the pillow.'' He shrugged. ''I didn't know what to do, so I waited.''

Khalil knew that Amber's behavior wasn't his responsibility, but he still felt a sense of shame.

''I wanted to tell you before,'' Malik admitted, ''but I didn't know what to say. I had no real proof, and it might have been someone else.'' He looked up into the night. ''How was I supposed to apologize to you for what had happened?''

Givon patted Khalil's back. ''He came to me earlier today and told me the truth.''

Khalil looked at his brother. ''Why now?''

''Because I'm finally sure. Amber visited me while I was in Paris. I offered to take her to dinner. Before we'd left the hotel for the restaurant, she offered to 'renew our acquaintance.' I knew then that I hadn't been wrong about that night.''

The king nodded. ''So much makes sense to me. Khalil, you were trying to protect both the country and Aleser. You believed, and rightly so, that if he knew the truth about his daughter he would have to resign.'' The older man shook his head. ''I should have realized there was something amiss when you married impulsively.''

''Now what?'' Malik asked. ''I don't think Aleser needs to know Amber's real nature. He adores her—it would break his heart.''

''It breaks mine,'' the king admitted. ''She was like a daughter to me, as well. That's why I was so pleased with the betrothal.'' He sighed. ''But you are right. We will keep this to ourselves. Fatima will speak with Amber and let her know that she is not welcome in El Bahar except for family visits. She has always traveled so it is unlikely Aleser will comment on any extended absence.''

Malik glanced at his father, then nodded. Khalil had the sense that there was more to discuss, but if so, Malik wasn't a party to the conversation.

''I'm sorry, Khalil,'' Malik said and offered his hand. They shook.

''I appreciate the thought,'' Khalil told him, ''but you were as much the injured party as myself. Perhaps in time Amber will change, but for now we are best to be rid of her before she can do more damage.''

Malik disappeared back into the palace.

Khalil stood in the darkness and waited for his father to speak. At times like this, the king could not be rushed.

''You were quite ingenious,'' Givon said a few minutes later. ''You found a way to avoid marriage with Amber and yet not disgrace Aleser and his family. The only price was my displeasure.''

''I knew you'd come around,'' Khalil said, leaning against the railing and staring out into the darkness. Although the apology was late in coming, he was pleased to hear the words.

His father joined him. ''Dora has surprised us all. She is very good at her job. I'll admit I was skeptical at first. A woman as liaison with Western companies? A royal princess employed?''

''You should have heard us arguing over her salary,'' Khalil said proudly. ''Not that she keeps it—the entire amount is donated to the children's hospital, but she wasn't going to let me off easily just because we're married.''

''I will understand if you wish to have the marriage annulled,'' the king said quietly. ''Dora could have the choice of staying in El Bahar in her present job or returning to the United States. She would want for nothing. Then you would be free to find someone else to marry. I promise this time not to arrange a match."

Khalil stared at him. An annulment? Dora leaving El Bahar? He remembered her words from earlier that day. She'd told him that until the foundation of their marriage was repaired, they could not build anything lasting.

"No," he said sharply. "Dora and I are married, and we will stay married. She is my wife, regardless of what anyone thinks, including her!"

Early the next morning Khalil stormed into Dora's room. He turned on a light and tossed a bundle of clothing onto her bed.

"What on earth?" she asked, then glanced at the clock. "It's five in the morning. Is everything all right?"

He pointed at the clothes. "They're for riding. You will get up and put them on."

It was only then that she noticed what he was wearing. Khalil had dressed in light-colored slacks and a loose shirt. Riding boots gleamed to his knees. He looked like the sheik prince prepared to ride out and survey his kingdom. Despite her best efforts to keep herself under control, she couldn't stop the thrill of pleasure that raced through her.

"Why?" she asked.

He stared down at her. "We are going riding," he told her. "I am wooing you. You will find the ride very romantic and notice that I am an amusing companion. Then, when we return, you'll be overcome, and we'll make love."

He looked completely serious as he spoke. Wooing her?

Whose idea was this? Khalil was not the type to voluntarily woo a mere woman.

"You can't simply announce all of this and expect me to fall in with your plans," she said.

"Of course I can. I'm Prince—"

She waved him off with her hand. "Yes, yes, I know that part by heart. You might be Prince Khalil Khan but pigs will fly before I give in to you. Besides, I don't know how to ride."

"Not a problem. I'll teach you." His gaze sharpened. "And you *will* give in because I have warned you about challenging me. You are my wife. You will be most impressed, and you will find yourself falling hopelessly in love with me."

He turned on his heel and headed for the door. "Meet me by the horse stables in thirty minutes."

"Get out," she yelled, tossing a pillow at him.

He laughed as he shut the door behind him.

Dora pulled her knees up to her chest and wrapped her arms around her legs. Had her husband really said that he was wooing her? Was it possible that he was actually starting to care about their marriage? She desperately wanted to believe it was true, but she wasn't sure. She'd been disappointed many times before.

The riding clothes lay next to her on the bed. She looked at them, then at the clock. How would a man like him make a woman fall hopelessly in love with him? She had a feeling that his idea of wooing and hers would be quite different.

Dora rose to her feet and picked up the clothes. She would very much like to go riding with her husband. In fact she would be happy to do anything with him. For the past couple of months she'd been afraid he would force her hand by refusing to change at all. Given the choice, she would much rather stay and fight for her marriage than run away and get a divorce.

She pulled off her nightgown and started toward the bathroom. As for his plans to make her fall desperately in love with him…thank goodness he didn't know how close she already was.

## Chapter Fourteen

The warm desert air blew softly across Dora's face. Her mount, a gentle gelding with the patience of Job, cantered along next to Khalil's powerful stallion. It was early, barely fifteen minutes after sunrise, but they'd already left the palace far in the distance.

Dora found herself laughing aloud with sheer joy as she savored the wonder of the morning. In the past few weeks she'd grown passionate about her rides with Khalil. Thanks to his surprising patience, she'd quickly learned to ride. He'd spent several mornings with her in a training ring before bringing her out into the desert. But after her first ride into the vastness of the quiet dawn, she'd been determined to make the rides a part of her daily schedule.

Up ahead she spotted the small oasis where they frequently stopped. The staff would have put a thermos of rich El Baharian coffee and some fresh pastries into their saddlebags. More often than not, she and Khalil shared breakfast as well as each other's company on the rides.

When he'd first told her that he was setting out to woo her, she hadn't much thought what that would be like. She'd expected a few curt compliments, perhaps flowers sent to her office, and of course the occasional ride in the desert. But he had proved more clever than that. He'd tried to scale the walls of her stubbornness with long conversations about the state of the nation and how they could together create change. He'd taken her on a tour of the poor parts of the city and had seriously listened to her suggestions. When parliament met at the beginning of the new term, he invited her along to observe and learn. And he'd found her a lovely white Persian kitten with big blue eyes and a bit of a temper. Then he'd told her that the spitting bit of fluff had reminded him of her.

Now, as they cantered across the dunes toward the small oasis, she glanced at her husband and reminded herself that it was important to resist him. Although the reasons were becoming less and less clear. Despite her resolve, Dora found herself falling more and more in love with him each day. She still hadn't figured out how to get him to listen to her out of the office. He wouldn't discuss the problems in their marriage, and he hadn't once apologized for his early behavior or even admitted he'd been in the wrong. They were at an impasse, and she didn't know how to change things.

They rode into the oasis. Date palms lined the fresh spring fed by an underground river. New grass carpeted the bank, all the way down to the water. Dora reined in her horse, then waited for Khalil to dismount. He always helped her to the ground, and she let him. They both knew she was capable of dismounting on her own, but she liked the feel of him next to her, holding her close. It was one of the few times they touched outside of the bedroom.

The day was as clear and bright as always. The rainy season had already passed, and they were heading into the heat of summer. She wondered how bad it would be and how long it would take her to adjust. Despite the problems with Khalil, Dora couldn't imagine living anywhere else. Whatever happened between them, she'd decided that El Bahar was her home, and she didn't plan to leave.

"You're looking serious about something," Khalil said lightly as he removed the thermos from his saddlebag.

"Not really. I was thinking about how much I love my new country. It's very beautiful, a balanced combination of history and future. You're even somewhat progressive about women."

"You think so?" he asked. "I've heard that the palace has a woman working in government. She's responsible for acting as liaison between El Bahar and foreign corporations. Can you imagine such a thing?"

She spread a blanket on the ground. "How incredibly shocking. I've heard the same rumor. I've also heard that she's quite brilliant."

"Really? Everyone I talk to thinks that her husband is the brilliant one."

Dora gave him a mocking glare. "I'm sure that's your favorite rumor of all."

"It is."

She took two mugs from her bags and sat on the blanket. Khalil settled next to her. The sunlight illuminated the left side of his face, and she found herself looking at the faint scar on his cheek.

She'd seen it before, of course. It was one of the first things she'd noticed about him. That and the fact that he was impossibly good-looking. A handsome prince, although in this case, both descriptions were accurate.

"Tell me about your scar," she said impulsively as she reached out and touched the faint, thin line. "Unless you'd rather not talk about it."

Khalil poured coffee and handed her a mug. "There's not much to talk about. I was young and foolish." He shrugged. "I was fifteen and fencing with a friend. We both thought that we were the best ever, perhaps invincible, and it was a competition to determine victor of the world."

"I didn't think people got hurt fencing."

"They're not supposed to. A protective tip covers the point. But as I said, we were young and stupid and didn't bother with precautions. The duel was intense, and he managed to cut me on the face."

He stared out at the horizon. "How strange. I haven't thought of the incident in years, and now it's come up twice in just a few weeks. My grandmother reminded me of it shortly after you arrived."

"Why?"

"Because of you," he said, although his answer made no sense.

"There was a lot of blood," he continued before she could ask more questions. "I started yelling. The king and the fencing master came running. I told them both what my friend had done, and in a burst of uncontrolled anger, I swore I never wanted to see him again. I was rushed to the hospital. I was frightened and in a lot of pain, although I wouldn't admit either to anyone."

Dora touched his arm. "You don't have to talk about this if you don't want to."

"I'm fine," he told her. "In a few hours I'd had stitches and was resting comfortably. I had time to regret my harsh words to my friend, and I told my father that I wanted to see him.''

His mouth twisted into a grim line. ''But a prince had spoken, and a prince was to be obeyed. My friend had been sent over the mountains to stay with family until I recovered and sent for him again. But there was a car accident, and he was killed on the way. I never saw him again.''

Dora stared at him, not sure what she was supposed to say. ''Sometimes I feel as if we've never even lived on the same planet. How am I supposed to relate to your life?''

''You can't. But you can deal with the man who has lived it.'' He turned to face her. ''Is that so difficult for you to imagine?''

''No.''

They were suddenly sitting too close. Or had they always been next to each other and had she just now noticed? The air seemed to grow hotter by the second. Khalil shifted until he had his arm around her, and his mouth was inches from hers.

''Kiss me,'' he demanded.

She stared at him. ''I can't.'' Maybe she'd picked a dumb hill on which to die, but this was the last barrier she had in place against the handsome prince who wanted to steal her soul.

''You won't. There's a difference. Stubborn fool. When you have my children playing around your feet will you still deny me?''

She turned away so he wouldn't see the panic in her eyes. Children. Dear Lord, she had done her best not to think about getting pregnant. At the rate they were making love, it was just a matter of time. Khalil was a vigorous lover who visited her more nights than not. She wasn't on any kind of birth control and as a princess in El Bahar, she couldn't exactly walk into the local drugstore and buy condoms.

She'd thought about going to Fatima, but although she and Khalil's grandmother had made peace, Dora doubted that Fatima would approve of preventing a pregnancy.

Even though they were sitting in the middle of a desert, Dora suddenly felt as if invisible walls had started to close in around her. She was cold and hot at the same time. She didn't know how to handle this situation.

"We should head back," she said quickly, trying to pull away from him.

Khalil didn't release his hold on her. "Not yet. Stay a little while."

She pressed her lips together. In this mood, when he was caring and conciliatory, it was impossible to resist him.

"Sweet Dora, you are my wife. Why is it so difficult to do as I request?" He sighed. "You are stubborn and infuriating, yet I can't imagine going an entire day without seeing you. I have told the king I will no longer travel without you."

Dora stared at him. Unable to help herself, she reached up and touched the thin scar on his left cheek. His eyes were large and dark and filled with an emotion she'd never seen before. Affection perhaps? Vulnerability? Was it possible that Khalil was changing?

She knew what she wanted. In her heart of hearts, she wanted it all—the fantasy and the fairy tale. She wanted her husband to fall in love with her, most likely because she was in love with him. She wanted a real marriage, not this battle of wills they'd somehow created. Yet as much as she wanted to give in, she believed with every beat of her heart that if she didn't stand firm on this issue that he would grow complacent. He had to understand that he couldn't play with her emotions. He had to learn that what he'd done was wrong.

"Kiss me."

His words were a request, not a demand, and she found herself unable to deny him. She wanted to kiss him. She wanted to be close to him, to feel his body next to hers. This was her husband, and it hurt her to deny him. But deny him she must.

Then she again touched the scar on his face. The thin ridge reminded her that Khalil had admitted to making a mistake. Was that his own arrogant, twisted way of telling her there were other words he regretted?

She studied his face, the handsome lines, the set of his mouth. Who was this man she'd married? What did she know of the depths of his soul?

And then she pressed her mouth to his. Not because he'd asked, but because he'd shared a bit of his life with her. Because he'd compromised just a little. And mostly because she needed to feel his hot passion fueling her own.

She slipped her hand into his hair and felt the cool strands slipping against her skin. She leaned into him, wanting to be closer, yet not actually pressing against him. She kept her mouth closed, her kiss chaste, yet she felt the difference in both of them as she gave herself willingly to him.

She rested her free hand on his shoulder, then slowly parted her lips. When he didn't respond, she brushed her tongue against his lower lip and when he opened for her, she entered his mouth. At the first touch of her tongue against his, he shuddered. As if contact was more than he could stand—as if this surrender of hers was more than he could stand.

She braced herself for his assault, but Khalil did not attack, or even try to make love with her. Instead he broke the kiss. When he pulled back he cupped her face and stared at her.

"Thank you," he murmured, his voice low and controlled.

She waited, but there were no smart comments, no claims of victory. Instead he pulled her to her feet and helped her onto her horse. They rode back to the palace in silence. Once there, he swept inside without saying a word.

"I'm not discounting all that your majesty has already done," Dora said patiently. "However, the job isn't complete. We have more work to do."

Fire flashed in her eyes, and color stained her cheeks. She looked passionate and committed, and it was all Khalil could do to stay in his seat and listen quietly. What he wanted was to jump to his feet and publicly claim this woman as his. He wanted to drag her off to his rooms and make love with her for the rest of the afternoon.

But he didn't. For one thing, Dora, his brothers and he were having a working lunch with the king, and Khalil didn't think that any of them would appreciate his impulsiveness. Well, Dora might, but she would never admit it. Another reason to resist was that his most stubborn wife continued to sleep in her own quarters, across the palace from his. Despite that lone kiss the previous week, she had not willingly come to him and initiated their lovemaking. She frustrated him until he was sorry they'd been at peace with their neighbors for so many generations. He was in the mood to go to war.

Instead he sat quietly while his wife argued with his father. It was the king's fault. Givon had been the one to set up the brief tour of the country for Dora. She'd spent three days this week visiting nearby towns and villages, and each night she'd returned home filled with ideas.

"The colleges are open to all," the king said and took a spoonful of sorbet. "Even the women."

"Yes, and how much they appreciate your forward thinking."

Her voice was calm, but Khalil caught the faint note of sarcasm in her tone. She was beautiful when she was inspired, he thought suddenly. How had he not noticed that before? When they'd first met, he'd barely seen her. Then they'd married so quickly, and he'd been angry and confused about all that happened. There was also the matter of her resistance. Yet despite it all, or perhaps because of it, he'd grown to see the real woman who was Dora Khan, princess of El Bahar, and he knew that she was a jewel. That he'd stumbled upon her under what were at the very least unusual circumstances only made him treasure her more.

"King Givon," she said, pushing her dessert aside and leaning forward. "Opening the colleges to women isn't enough. Despite the advances made during your glorious rule, many families still believe it is a waste to educate a woman. They don't bother to send them to more than a half dozen years of school, and most only receive that much because your government has made it the law. There are hundreds of bright and articulate females out there, and their potential is going to waste."

The king raised his bushy, graying eyebrows. "They marry, they produce children. That is not a waste."

"Oh, I agree completely. If you're saying that your people are El Bahar's greatest resource."

Khalil watched as his father considered Dora's words. Khalil saw the trap at once, but he had the advantage of knowing his wife's agile mind. The king was not so fortunate.

"Of course. They are our future."

"If that is your belief, then I don't understand your willingness to ignore and waste nearly fifty percent of the resources available to you. Educated women can still marry and have many children, but uneducated ones can do little to improve technology or teach in the schools, or become doctors and lawyers and entrepreneurs."

She stared at the king. "These women deserve a chance to be their best. Not only for themselves, but for their country. All I'm asking is that you consider preparatory schools for teenage girls. Give them the opportunity to learn what they need so they can attend college."

King Givon glared at her. "Schools mean buildings and teachers. That requires a large financial commitment."

"You'd need scholarships, too," Khalil reminded him. "Very few families could afford to send both sons and daughters to college."

The king frowned. "You want too much."

"It's not possible to have too many dreams, Your Majesty. Especially when those dreams reflect what is best for El Bahar."

"Oh, so now you want to tell me how to run my country?"

Khalil forced back a grin. If the king thought he was going to intimidate Dora, he was in for a shock. Khalil had long since learned that his wife had a mind of her own. He glanced at his two brothers who had wisely stayed out of the discussion. Their gazes moved from Dora to Givon and back. He noted the faint flicker of respect in their eyes when they looked at his wife, and he was proud. He might have chosen her because she was convenient and met many of his criteria, but he wanted to keep her because he could not have found anyone more suited to himself and his world.

Dora smiled at the king. "Your Majesty is a wise and compassionate ruler. I would never presume to tell you how to oversee your country. I'm merely pointing out that there is no point in trying to move forward with the heavy weight of a silly tradition holding El Bahar back."

The king glared at Jamal and Malik. "Have you nothing to say?"

The two brothers exchanged a glance. Malik shrugged. "We don't want to get involved."

"They're afraid," Dora said.

Malik looked at her as if he was going to protest, then he grinned. "Let's just say that Jamal and I have no desire to take you on, Princess Dora. You would be a most formidable enemy."

"And a most advantageous ally," Jamal added.

The king made a low growling sound, then turned to his youngest son. "Have you nothing to say, or are you content to let your wife speak for you?"

"As a man married to one of the bright, articulate women Dora mentioned earlier, in this matter I'm quite comfortable letting my wife speak for us both."

The king did not look pleased with his response. He returned his attention to Dora. "I will consider what you have discussed with me and take it up with members of the inner council. That is not a promise or a commitment, Dora, it is my word that I will not dismiss your ideas. Your heart is in the right place." The king softened his words with a faint smile. "Even if you remain a Western woman filled with foolishness about equality for your gender."

"Who's the fool?" she asked. "She who speaks the words, or the man who listens?"

Givon laughed. "Leave me, all of you. I have work to complete this afternoon."

They rose and left the king's private dining room. Malik and Jamal headed toward their offices, but Khalil put his hand on Dora's arm to stop her.

"Let's go for a walk on the balcony," he said. "I think you probably need to calm down."

"I'm not upset," she told him, but she allowed herself to be led outside onto the balcony.

The summer heat was nearly upon them. Already, midday temperatures climbed to a hundred degrees. They stayed in the shade, but even so they walked slowly so as not to get overly warm.

"I appreciate what you said," Dora told him, slipping her hand into his. "When you told the king that I was bright and articulate and that you didn't mind me speaking for you. That meant a lot to me."

"I told the truth," he said lightly, although he found himself pleased by her praise. "You *are* bright and articulate, and in this matter, I'm quite pleased to have you speak for me."

"Oh, I see. In this matter, but not others."

He stopped and turned so he faced her. "In some matters," he said. "Just as you would be content to let me speak for you in some things, but not others. That is all I meant, and I believe you know that. Why do you want to fight with me?"

She squeezed her eyes shut for a moment, then opened them and exhaled. Some of the stiffness left her body. "You're right, Khalil. I'm being difficult. I guess I'm still frustrated by my conversation with the king. There's so much to be done, and I feel like it's all going to happen so slowly."

"Perhaps, but it will happen. You are committed to my

people and that means more than you can know, to both myself and the king. He *will* listen. My father is a wise man.''

''I know. I'm being a child, wanting what I want, when I want it, which means right now.''

He understood her feelings, for that is exactly how he felt about her. He wanted her on his terms, and he wanted her now.

They started walking again, moving toward their offices. ''There's so much opportunity here,'' she said, again taking his hand. ''I want to roll up my sleeves and get to work.''

''You are.''

While he wanted to continue the conversation, a part of him was distracted by the feel of her fingers laced with his. Ever since the kiss the previous week, there had been more touching between them. She had initiated much of it, and while it gave him hope, it also made him want to have the trouble between them already fixed. But along with being bright and articulate, she was also quite stubborn.

They walked into the main corridor of the office complex and found themselves in the center of bustling activity. Martin walked quickly toward them, saw Dora, stopped and smiled.

''Good afternoon, princess,'' he said, grinning as if he had a delicious secret. ''Did you enjoy your lunch?''

''Very much,'' Dora said, sounding puzzled. ''Thank you for asking.''

''Have you been back to your office yet?'' Martin asked.

Dora frowned. ''No. Why?''

''There's a surprise waiting there.''

Khalil stiffened. A surprise? If one existed, it didn't

have anything to do with him. Had Gerald shown up un-expectedly? A flash of jealousy cut through him like a knife. He and Dora might have some things to work out but he was not about to let his wife return to that eater of camel dung. Besides, he'd made some discreet inquiries shortly after he and Dora had arrived in El Bahar. Gerald had been fired from his job and had been forced to move back home with his parents. The other man didn't know where Dora was, nor had he tried to contact her after that single phone call.

Even though he told himself it was nothing that should bother him, Khalil still urged Dora to hurry. Who else would have prepared a surprise for her?

But when they reached the office, her large room was empty of furniture. Eva met them at the door. Her smile was as broad as Martin's.

"This way, Your Highness," she said, leading them back into the corridor and on to the other side of the office complex. There, near the office for the prime minister and the deputy minister of finance, stood a man securing a name plate on a wide double door.

Khalil read the words. Fierce pride filled him as he watched his wife study the letters. Emotions flashed across her face—first shock, followed by surprise, confusion, comprehension and joy.

*Princess Dora Khan, Deputy Minister of Women's Affairs.*

"I don't understand," Dora said, turning to Khalil. "The king couldn't have done all this since we left lunch. There wasn't enough time."

Eva laughed. "No, Your Highness. He's had it planned for several days. That's why the working lunch lasted so long. He wanted to get your things moved. Oh, and the king said to tell you that he still wants you to act as liaison with Western companies, but that you'll also be busy with the project of your heart, so he's going to ask parliament to grant you a staff of a half dozen or so.''

Dora still looked stunned as she turned her attention to Khalil. ''Did you know about this?''

''No. And I didn't talk to my father about it, either. You've done this one on your own, Dora.''

She flung herself at him and wrapped her arms around him. He held her close. ''Thank you for everything,'' she whispered fiercely.

From the corner of his eyes, Khalil saw Eva disappear into Dora's office, leaving the two of them alone. He hugged his wife and inhaled the sweet scent of her body.

''I told you, I didn't have anything to do with this,'' he said. ''You don't have to thank me.''

She straightened and stared at him. There were tears in her eyes. She impatiently brushed them away. ''Of course I have to. You might not be directly responsible, but you've made all of this possible.'' She raised herself up on tiptoes and kissed him. ''I have to get to work now.''

He watched her disappear behind those wide double doors. Dora had accomplished so much in such a short time—both with his country and with him personally. He couldn't imagine life without her anymore. But as much as he wanted to make this wonderful woman his, he did not know how to make that happen. He knew what she wanted from him, but he wasn't sure he could give it to her. She asked much of him, as both a man and a prince. Could he learn to bend? Did he have a choice? If he didn't, he would lose her.

Khalil found himself trapped by circumstances of his own making. And there wasn't anything he could do but wait and see how it would all play out.

## *Chapter Fifteen*

"You will yield to me, wife, or I will know the reason why," Khalil bellowed as he stood in the center of Dora's bedroom.

His shirttail hung free of his slacks, and his feet were bare. Dora wore little more than her bra, panties and blouse. They'd been in the middle of kissing, when he'd asked her to finish taking off his clothes. But instead of being swept away by passion, she'd found herself slightly distracted and had refused without thinking.

"You know the reason why," Dora told him calmly.

Better to fight about this, she thought, than for him to know the reason that she hadn't been completely involved in their lovemaking. She'd fought against the truth for a long time, and Lord willing, she was going to continue to fight against it. Life was complicated enough without her worrying about any significant changes in the status of her family. She and Khalil had to learn to be a married couple before they could be parents. At least that's what she told herself with more conviction than she felt.

"I do not know anything of the sort," he insisted. "It has been nearly four months. Why won't you admit that you love me?"

His question nearly made her gasp aloud, but she managed to control her reaction. "You want me to love you so that I will do as you wish, but there is more to a marriage than subservience from the woman. I want a partnership. I want us to share and be honest. Those are things you can't seem to understand."

"Of course I understand. I don't want you to be subservient. I want you to admit your feelings."

That she loved him? She couldn't continue to live with Khalil, work with him, ride with him and share the most intimate act possible between a man and a woman *without* loving him, but she would be damned if she would admit it before he did.

She wished it were just a matter of pride. That would be easy for her to overcome. But it wasn't that simple. The truth was, despite loving Khalil, she didn't fully trust him. She needed to know that he cared for her as much as she cared for him. She needed to know that any unborn children would be welcomed and raised by adoring parents as part of a strong family unit. She desperately needed to know that he would never grow tired of her and move on. She wanted to hold the key to his heart as much as he held the key to hers.

"Why don't you admit *your* feelings?" she asked. "You're being stubborn as well. Tell me you love me and that you're sorry and all will be well."

He dismissed her with a wave of his hand. "How much longer do you plan to play this game?"

"Forever, if necessary." She looked at him, then

planted her hands on her hips. "You know my terms, Khalil. You resist them, you deny them and you want them changed, but nothing is different today than it was when I first arrived. You lied to me. You took advantage of the misfortune in my life and told me that you cared for me. You implied that you loved me, then you railroaded me into marriage and brought me here without giving me time to consider other options."

His dark eyes blazed with fire. "I married you. You seem to forget that fact, but it remains the central issue of this discussion. I have honored you by taking you as my bride."

She glared at him. "Oh, and you weren't the least honored by my agreeing to marry you?"

"Of course not," he said. "Look at the life that you had before we met. So small and pitiful. You were nothing, and I gave you the world. I am Prince Khalil Khan—"

She took a single step toward him. "Don't start that. I'm warning you, I'll throw you out of my room right now and never let you back."

She had to grit her teeth to keep from crying out. The wound from his thoughtless words went deep, all the way down to her heart. Nothing? Is that what she'd been to him? Had he really thought so little of her when they were first married? She closed her eyes and forced herself to breathe slowly. She knew the answer to the question. It was as obvious as his quick and easy response. Yes, he *had* thought nothing of her or of their marriage. He'd been in a difficult situation, for reasons that had never made sense to her. She'd been slightly appropriate and very available. End of story.

Something warm stroked her cheek. She opened her eyes and saw that her husband had moved closer. He cupped her jaw. "I spoke hastily," he told her, smiling faintly and with what she wanted to believe was affection. "At the time I didn't know you enough to be honored by the thought of you as my wife, but I have learned. You are a great woman, and I am fortunate to have you in my life."

She wanted to give in to him. She wanted to take off the rest of her clothes and have him do the same, then stretch out with him on the big bed and make love until morning. She wanted to hear words of love and have him hold her close, then find the courage to tell him what she thought might have happened...that their lovemaking could have produced a child who was, at this very moment, growing inside of her.

But she did none of those things. Because Khalil was a stubborn man. Nearly as stubborn as herself, she thought, trying to find a crumb of humor in the situation.

"Tell me you were wrong," she murmured, wrapping her arms around him. "Tell me you're sorry. Tell me that you care."

He pushed her away. "You cry after the moon. You still want your dreams. I am Khalil Khan, prince of El Bahar, and I will not be dictated to by a woman. Accept what we have between us, and be grateful."

She straightened her spine. She was sick of hearing him announce his name and title as if those words had the power to change the tides.

"That may be true, Prince Khalil, but you are forgetting one very important fact."

He raised his eyebrows expectantly. "What is that?"

"I am Dora Khan, *princess* of El Bahar, and I do not sleep with liars."

With that, she walked to the front door of her suite and held it open. Khalil moved slowly toward her.

"Is this what we've come to?" he asked. "A battle of wills."

"It's always been a battle of wills. The only difference is this is the first time you haven't won."

He glared at her. "You will not win this one. Don't push me too far, wife, or you *will* be sorry."

She thought of all her hopes and dreams. How she'd come so far in some areas and not made any progress in others. "I already am, Khalil. You think I turn away from you out of stubbornness or a desire to punish, but the truth is the pain in my heart drives me."

Then, because she couldn't think of anything else to say, she gently closed the door, shutting out her husband and leaving herself very much alone.

Khalil stood in the hallway. He wanted to rage against circumstances or fate or whatever it was that had brought him to this place. He did not deserve to be shut out from the bed of his wife. Didn't she understand that?

He glared at the shut door and thought about ordering her to let him back in. The problem was Dora might choose to ignore him. She could be stubborn that way. Actually she could be stubborn in many ways. She was infuriating. She was also bright and good at her new job. She saw the possibilities in El Bahar that no one had seen before.

If only she would give in on this one simple matter. How dare she expect him to apologize for what he'd done? It wasn't as if she'd had such a great life and he'd taken her from it. She'd been alone, jobless, abandoned by her fiancé. She'd been...

The thought ended, and a new one began. It was most disquieting, so he started walking to distract himself. He hurried down the familiar corridors until he came to his own rooms. But instead of entering, he stood there thinking.

Dora had been a person, he thought at last. Someone with rights and feelings, and there was the smallest possibility he'd been wrong to take advantage of her. Even if she was just a woman.

But to admit that he loved her? Preposterous. He opened the door to his suite and stepped inside. The darkness seemed to surround him. He still ached for her. They'd begun to build the fire but had not had time to quench the hunger with flames. His body was ready to take her to that place of perfect paradise. His arms needed to hold her close, his lips longed to utter her name.

She wanted words of love and foolish apologies. He offered a kingdom—money and power. They battled to be the victor. His grandmother had told him to woo her; his pride said that Dora must surrender first. One of them would have to bend, he thought sadly. If they didn't, they were destined to fail.


The party was going strong when Dora arrived. She stood in a side entrance to the ballroom and admired the beautiful decorations and the glittering crowd. King Givon hosted a "small, intimate" birthday celebration for his good friend and prime minister, Aleser. However, small and intimate in the royal world was different from small and intimate in Dora's experience. There were more than a hundred people in the room.

Dora drew in a deep breath and tried to relax. She felt fine, and she looked good. At least that's what she'd told herself as she'd dressed an hour before.

Since arriving in El Bahar, she'd started letting her hair grow. Now she wore it swept up in an elegant French twist. A few weeks before she and Khalil had gone to

Paris for business meetings. Fatima had given Dora the name of an exclusive salon, which had pampered her with a manicure and facial. Afterward, a gifted artist had taught her the best way to apply makeup. All the horseback riding and the long distances between rooms in the palace had helped Dora drop ten pounds since arriving. While she would never be model perfect, she was an attractive, vital woman. Unfortunately she cowered in the shadowed doorway like a frightened schoolchild. If only she'd been able to walk in with Khalil.

Dora sighed. While her husband had been greeting guests, she'd been throwing up in her bathroom. So much for morning sickness occurring in the morning. Her attacks were infrequent, but they generally came in waves, striking every few hours, then disappearing for a day or two. Still not sure how to tell Khalil the truth about her pregnancy, she'd sent him away, telling him that she'd found a stain on her dress and had to change. The price of her lie was that she would be forced to enter the party on her own.

She took a step into the well-dressed crowd and moved toward the bar. There she ordered sparkling water poured into a wineglass, then plastered a smile on her face and prepared to plunge into the insanity.

"Your Highness," a familiar voice said from behind her.

Dora turned and saw Martin Wingbird hurrying toward her. A tall, stately man walked briskly behind him. She paused.

"Good evening, Martin."

"Your Highness." Martin bowed, then glanced at his companion. "Princess Dora Khan, may I please present Lord Andrew Hall. He's heard about your plans to increase opportunities for young women to attend college and would like to speak to you about that.''

Lord Hall took her offered hand and bowed low over her fingers. ''Your Highness, I hesitated to disrupt a party to discuss business, but I'm only in El Bahar for a short visit.'' He straightened. ''My late wife was a great advocate of female education, as she called it.'' He smiled, but his deep blue eyes remained sad. ''In honor of her, I have dedicated my life to that cause. After hearing about your campaign and your success in convincing the king of the need to educate women, I would like to talk about offering scholarships to worthy female students so that they could attend British universities.''

Dora studied the thin man. His white hair was thick and wavy, his skin permanently tanned. ''How on earth did you hear about my program?''

''News travels quickly, Your Highness. You are a highly visible and respected member of the royal family. People watch and talk.''

Dora laughed. ''I suppose I have to believe you, but I'm still having trouble adjusting to all this.'' She waved to take in both the party and the palace. ''Lord Hall, I would be most delighted to discuss the scholarships with you. Will you still be in El Bahar tomorrow?''

''Business keeps me here for three days.''

''Good.'' She looked at Martin. ''Make an appointment for Lord Hall.'' She returned her attention to the older man. ''I look forward to our discussion.''

''As do I.'' He nodded and moved away.

Dora sipped at her sparkling water. Life was certainly different these days. Just six months ago, she couldn't have imagined a world such as this.

She circled the room, greeting people she knew, introducing herself to others. Small talk wasn't her favorite, but practice made her better. She kept looking for Khalil, wondering where he was and what he was doing. Finally she caught a glimpse of something familiar, and she stopped in her tracks.

Dora stood near a small alcove, one of many that lined the ballroom. Behind her music played and people laughed and talked, but in front of her was relative silence. She waited, then caught the movement again. It was no more than a swirl of fabric from a woman's dress and the gesture of one slender arm. Yet she sensed something familiar...something dangerous.

Quietly Dora moved forward until she could see the two people standing in shadow. She recognized the man immediately—despite looking somewhat like his brothers, she would never mistake Khalil for anyone else. It took her a minute to place the woman. Not because she didn't remember her, but because of the way the light and shadows played on her face.

Amber. The stunningly beautiful woman who had been engaged to Khalil. The woman who was a temptress in clinging red silk that outlined a perfect body. Thick, black hair piled high on her head, leaving her neck looking slender and delicate.

Dora stood just outside of their sight and fought against the waves of pain and hurt that crashed through her. Despite the pretty dress, the jewelry, the makeup, she was a pathetic parody of that beautiful young woman. Amber wore red silk, Dora blue. But the styles were similar enough to cause comment—ribbed column styles that accentuated bosom, exposed shoulders. Amber's dress clung all the way to her knees, emphasizing her amazing curves, while Dora's gown had been softened with folds of fabric so that her still-heavy hips would not be highlighted.

Amber was all things more, Dora thought miserably,

wanting to back up but frozen in place. Her own hair had been put up, but she didn't have the thick length to add height and volume. Her own earrings were lovely diamonds, but they paled in comparison to the jewels glittering on Amber's ears and around her neck. She felt like an ugly parody of the younger woman's beauty.

All her confidence, all her happiness, evaporated like a bowl of water left out in the desert sun. Khalil had been right, she was nothing.

Defeat weighed heavily on her. She forced herself to turn so that she could leave and escape to her room to lick her wounds. At that moment, the music ended and relative quiet settled over the ballroom. While others were too far away to hear what was said in the private alcove, Dora was not.

"I want you, Khalil," Amber purred in her sultry tones. "I am your destiny, not that cow of a wife. What were you thinking, taking her when you could have had me? I know you don't love her. I'm willing to admit I was wrong. I want to be with you. I want to have your sons."

It was too much, Dora thought as tears blinded her. She hurried away before she made a sound and betrayed her presence to the lovers.

Up ahead she spotted a side door and made for it. Pain ripped through her. Pain and disappointment—for all that should have been but never would be. She'd lost before she'd begun. How on earth was she supposed to compete with a woman like Amber? No wonder her husband wouldn't admit to caring about her—he didn't. He loved another and she, Dora, was only in the way. She'd been fooling herself to think Khalil would ever love her.

A sob ripped through her. She opened the door and stepped into the night. But instead of soothing her, the faintly sweet scented air turned her stomach. She rushed to the edge of the balcony and threw up into a potted plant. She'd thought she'd hit rock bottom before when Gerald had rejected her, but this was far worse.

"It can't be all that bad," a soft voice murmured as a delicate handkerchief was pressed into her hand.

Dora took it gratefully, then wiped her mouth. She looked up and saw Fatima standing next to her.

"If you would stop hiding from the truth, child, so much would be better."

Dora tried to force a smile, but she couldn't. "It's not what you think."

Fatima, beautiful as always in her favorite Chanel, leaned close and patted Dora's hand. "I know more than you suspect. I see many things that others do not, and what I don't see, my spies tell me."

Dora opened her mouth, then closed it. Fatima had spies? Then she did smile. Why not? The world was completely mad, and she was trapped in El Bahar.

"I can't leave him," she said, not completely aware she was speaking aloud. "Not just because I love him. If it was only that, I could probably tear myself away."

"I doubt you could, but we can pretend, for the sake of discussion," Fatima said kindly. She leaned against the railing and stared up at the sky. "Look at the lovely stars. So many and so bright." She sighed. "Of course now that you're pregnant, you're trapped. You know that El Baharian law forbids a woman to leave her husband while she's pregnant."

Dora knew all too well. "Unless the husband had been abusing her or their other children. Yes, I've become most familiar with El Baharian law in the past few months."

Dora touched her stomach. Life grew within. Soon that life would be visible to all. Then what?

"How many people know I'm pregnant?" she asked.

Fatima laughed. ''We're dealing with men, my dear. They'll know when you tell them, not before.''

That was something. She had time. But for what? ''Nothing is going to change.''

The night air surrounded them in soft darkness. The sounds of the party were faint beyond the glass doors. Out here, on a small balcony off to the side, they were alone. Dora wished they could stay here forever, that she might never have to go back and face her husband.

''What do you want to be different?'' Fatima asked.

''Everything,'' Dora sighed. ''Loving Khalil is difficult enough, but having his child will tie me to him forever.'' El Baharian law would allow her to leave once the child was born, but to what end? The royal family would not allow her to take her baby with her, and she doubted if Khalil would agree to joint custody. Besides, she didn't want to leave. What she wanted was her husband to love her.

''Not everything,'' Fatima corrected. ''It is a matter of priorities. If you don't mind my saying so, you've gone about things all wrong.''

Dora glanced at her. ''In what way?''

''You must earn what you most desire.'' Fatima turned to face her. ''You are pregnant with Khalil's firstborn. That gives you power no other woman possesses, but you must be wise when you use that power. Far better for you to win your husband on your own.''

Tears filled her eyes. ''So it's obvious to everyone that Khalil doesn't love me.''

Fatima touched her bare arm. ''What is obvious is that you two began your marriage for reasons other than love. Such is the way of many royal matches. Only the very lucky, or the determined, find love later. Is that what you want? Khalil's love?''

Dora nodded, then swiped at the tears on her face. "I desperately need that. I can't live half a life anymore. I've done it that way for too long." She sniffed. "But it's too late. He's in love with Amber, and there's no way I can compete with her. She's younger, she's more beautiful."

Fatima dismissed the information with a wave of her hand. "She's nothing. You're the princess…you're already his wife. Amber is not all you believe her to be. She is like a magician's smoke. Very impressive during the performance, but nothing remains afterward."

The older woman stared intently. Dark eyes seemed to see into Dora's soul. "Khalil went to a lot of trouble to marry you. He turned his back on his betrothed and the traditions of his family. He risked his father's anger. Have you ever wondered why?"

Dora tried to remember what Khalil had said about that. "He didn't think Amber would be a good mother." She rubbed her temples, which had begun to ache. "Except she's so lovely."

"What is beauty? True loveliness comes from a good heart, not long legs or a pretty face." She straightened her shoulders. "When I married my husband, the harem wasn't as it is today. All those years ago, it was filled with beautiful women from all over the world. I was his wife, but he wasn't interested in me. Who wants plain bread when there are trays of sweets to explore?"

Dora didn't know what to say. Women in the harem? At least she didn't have to compete with that. "What did you do?"

"I decided that possession of his name was not enough. I had to earn his heart. You must do the same."

Oh, sure, something simple, she thought glumly. "How am I supposed to do that?"

Fatima smiled. "Give him what he most desires and in a way no other woman can. Then you will have all that you most long for in your life."

## Chapter Sixteen

"Give him what he most desires...you will have all that you most long for in your life," Dora muttered when Fatima had left her alone on the balcony. "Oh, sure. Words to live by. But what do they mean?"

Although she spoke the question aloud, no answer appeared to her. The silence itself seemed to mock her, and she had to fight against the pressure of more tears. She didn't want to cry anymore, she thought. She didn't want to be unhappy. She had to find a way to make her marriage work, or she had to leave. She was tired of her games with Khalil.

But where did she begin? How did she change herself, or get her most stubborn husband to see the truth? Was Fatima correct and could she, Dora, give Khalil his heart's desire? Did she know his heart well enough to understand what he might want?

Too many questions and no answers. What she needed

was to be in her husband's company. Only his smile, his light touch on her arm, would restore her good humor.

But before she could leave the balcony, a woman appeared out of the shadows. "Ah, Princess Dora, how lovely to see you again."

Dora froze. The ever-stunning Amber stood in front of her. The young woman had destroyed all of Dora's illusions, not to mention her wedding day. She didn't want to hear any more of her hurtful words. What she really wanted was to bolt for cover, but she would be damned if she would let this El Baharian heartbreaker see that she had her running scared.

"Amber. Very nice to see you again." She gave a regal bow. "Are you enjoying the party?"

"Of course. My father is happy to have his family around him to celebrate this day." Amber pouted slightly. "He's been difficult about me being gone so much, but it's impossible for me to stay long in El Bahar. So painful."

Dora supposed she should be more sympathetic, but she wasn't in the mood. Nor did she trust Amber. "I would guess that being around your former fiancé and his new wife would be difficult. How nice that you can afford to travel. It distracts as well as broadens the mind."

Amber's delicate eyebrows drew together. "Don't sound so confident, *Your Highness*. Things are not as they appear."

"Aren't they?" Dora made a great show of glancing at her wedding ring. "And here I thought *I* was the one he'd married."

"You might have his name and his ring, but you don't have his heart. That belongs to me."

Dora didn't have a quick response for that one. While she wasn't sure that Amber knew anything about anyone's heart, Dora knew that she didn't have possession of Khalil's heart, either.

Amber took a step closer. "We're still lovers. He still visits me when he can."

Dora wanted to deny the words. Her husband came to *her* bed more often than not. He was vigorous and passionate, and she didn't believe for a single moment that he was with another woman. Khalil had many flaws, but deception wasn't one of them.

Or was it, a little voice in her head whispered. What about the lies he told at the beginning of their relationship? What about his stubborn refusal to admit that he was wrong and that he'd hurt her?

"I don't know when he'd have the time," Dora said coolly, refusing to let the other woman know that she was trembling from both fear and pain.

"Of course you wouldn't know," Amber scoffed. "You sleep alone in your chamber on the far side of the palace. You have no way of knowing how often I've crept into his bed or he into mine." She took another step closer and clutched Dora's arm. "He's already had me this night. You can plan on spending *your* evening alone."

Dora jerked free. She refused to believe these stories, she told herself, even as the hurt ripped through her. "You're lying. I will tell Khalil of your lies, and you will be banished from the palace."

Amber laughed. "My father is prime minister of El Bahar and the king's closest friend. My family has been close to the royal family for generations. Don't think that a few words and a ring are going to come between me and the man I love. Go to him, tell him what I said, if you dare. Find out how little you matter. You are nothing."

"I am his wife."

"For now."

Dora squared her shoulders. "You are a spoiled child, Amber. In time you will learn that being a man's wife gives a woman more power than it would appear. You may be younger and beautiful, but I will win this battle."

Amber shrugged. "We'll see. And if he doesn't join you in your bed this night, we'll both know that I'm telling the truth."

Dora thought about calling the other woman a bitch, but decided it was too childish. Instead she returned to the glittering ballroom with the intent of finding her husband.

But once inside, the agony of her encounter with the younger woman stole her breath and made her legs tremble. She was going to be sick, she thought as she frantically tried to retrace her steps. Only this time it wouldn't be because of the baby. Oh, dear God, what if Amber was telling the truth?

Dora could feel herself losing control. Tears threatened and with them, agonized sobs. She didn't want to lose Khalil—not when they'd come so far. She loved him. Perhaps she'd loved him from the very beginning, she wasn't sure. She only knew that without him, her world would be smaller and meaner than it had ever been in the past.

A shadow fell over her. She looked up and saw her husband standing in front of her. "You look ill," Khalil said. "Do you not feel well?"

She opened her mouth to explain, then closed it. What was there to say? Did she dare repeat Amber's lies? Except there was a small chance that they weren't lies. And if that woman spoke the truth then she, Dora, would be lost forever.

"I think I'm just tired," Dora said weakly. "I need to go to my room."

Khalil wrapped a sheltering arm around her and led her away. When they'd entered her chamber, he turned on the lights, then gently helped her undress. Finally he eased her into bed.

"I'll make your excuses to the king," he said, his voice kind, his expression concerned. "Sleep and feel better in the morning. I won't disturb you this evening."

She told herself he was just being considerate; she told herself it had everything to do with his perception of her being sick and nothing to do with Amber...but she wasn't sure.

"I don't feel that ill," she murmured. "Perhaps after the party..."

He shook his head. "You often accuse me of being insensitive, so I won't give you ammunition. If you're not well, I refuse to insist." He gave her a sad smile. "It is not in you to be won over this night, sweet Dora."

He pressed a kiss to her forehead, then left her alone.

She stared after him, willing him to return to her. This wasn't happening, she told herself, listening to the silence and wondering if that emptiness was going to fill her world for the rest of her life. Amber couldn't be correct, could she?

Dora sat up and pulled her knees to her chest. Had she come so far only to lose it all in the end, or had the prize never been hers?

She'd been a fool. Khalil had once accused her of being a nobody, and he was correct. She was just a glorified secretary who had happened to snag the attention of a wealthy prince. Not because she was beautiful, or witty, or smart, but because she was available. A virgin with childbearing hips. Talk about a claim to fame.

The first tears fell slowly, then faster and faster. Great sobs robbed her of breath. She clutched her knees, pulling them close to her chest as if she could hold in the last drops of happiness that had been hers. But there was no more happiness…just pain and suffering. If only things had been different.

She cried for what felt like hours, then she brushed her face and told herself to figure out a way to let it all go. The relationship was over, she thought as her heart broke. All her dreams, her plans for the future. Khalil didn't love her, didn't even want her. She didn't know if he'd really been making love with Amber or not, but Dora knew that the young woman in question was determined to win Khalil. Dora had no way to stop her. And if not this stunning creature, then surely another would claim Khalil. He was a prize, the kind of man any woman would desire.

*Give him what he most desires.*

Fatima's words returned to her, echoing inside her head. She listened, then turned them over, but they didn't make any more sense now than they had before. What could she possibly give Khalil? He was a handsome, rich prince, and she was a nobody.

Frustrated, Dora threw back the covers and pushed to her feet. She stormed across the room, heading for the balcony. The great emptiness inside of her grew until it threatened to swallow her. She was trapped in a sham of a marriage. She had no way out, no hope, no—

A slip of movement caught her attention, and she spun toward the shadow. There was little light in the bedroom, but Khalil had left on a floor lamp in the parlor. As she stared into the darkness, Dora realized that what had caught her eye was merely her own reflection in the mirror at her dresser. Her pale gown had shimmered slightly.

She paused to stare at herself, then reached up to brush her cheek. How different she looked, she thought with some surprise. Her time in El Bahar had changed her appearance, or maybe it was just her new life that affected her. Gone were the shyly lowered eyes, the deferential tilt of her head. Instead she stood tall, with an air of confidence about her. She'd slimmed down, and while she would never be fashionably thin, her top and bottom were now the same size. Her longer hair flattered her face, softening her features and making her look more approachable.

Sometime in the past few months, the small mouse had been transformed into a more self-sufficient creature. She didn't see herself as the desert wildcat Khalil liked to call her, but she'd made definite improvements.

She walked over to her desk, to the stacks of folders there. Sometimes she worked in the evenings. There was so much to do, and it all took time. Meetings filled her schedule, and when she wasn't busy with that, there were speeches to write, phone calls to make, not to mention her time with Khalil. She'd come a long way from the lonely virgin who ached to belong to someone.

Dora glanced around the spacious room, then clicked on the desk lamp so she could see more clearly. The luxurious furnishings no longer intimidated her. In fact, very little intimidated her. Even Amber's harsh assessments of her life and her relationship with Khalil had wounded, but not destroyed. She was no longer Dora Nelson, doormat, she was Dora Khan, princess of El Bahar.

In a blinding flash of insight she could neither explain nor describe, she understood what Fatima had been talking about. She understood the one thing she could give to Khalil that he most desired. Her love.

She smiled as she shook her head. How simple. Why didn't she see it before? Khalil wasn't interested in an affair with Amber, and he didn't want a showpiece for a wife. He needed and wanted an equal partner—someone who would match him in intelligence and drive, not to mention vision for El Bahar. She was all those things, not Amber. And even if the other woman was younger and prettier, Dora refused to believe their lovemaking could be any more satisfying than what she and Khalil shared. When he took her in his arms, she felt the magic as their intimacy bound them together in a biological and spiritual union that could not be destroyed.

Except...except he'd never once admitted he was wrong. He'd never apologized for what he did back when he seduced her and married her, and he'd never acknowledged his feelings. He'd never told her he loved her.

She sank onto the chair in front of the desk and rested her hand on the pile of papers there. It was a question of stubbornness and wills, she thought. Who would give in first? And if no one gave in, who would win?

"If I give in on this, I..."

Dora pressed her lips together. If she gave in, then what? Would Khalil suddenly walk all over her? Would she cease to be a deputy minister? Or would she achieve her heart's desire?

"But I want him to be the one to bend," she said aloud. "I want him..." She pressed her lips together. "I want him to love me back."

She thought of how he'd persevered, coming to her room night after night and seducing her until she consented to make love with him. She thought of how she frustrated him by refusing to live in his quarters, yet he never displayed his irritation when they worked together. She thought of his pride when she'd been made deputy minister and how he was content to watch her take on the king when her ideas differed from Givon's. On more than one occasion, he'd allowed her to speak for them both.

She thought of his attempts to woo her and how they

spent evenings alone, just the two of them, reading or talking. She thought of the places he wanted to show her. She thought of how he teased her that he would only allow her to give him sons, yet how he liked to talk about having at least one daughter, or even two.

These were not the actions of a man who didn't care, or even those of a man who had *settled*. Perhaps she had not been his chosen bride, but she was now his only wife. He had yielded in many ways. Was she going to risk it all to have him answer her demands?

She curled her fingers into her palm and as she did so, she felt something thick and hard under the papers. At first she wasn't sure what it was, but as she cleared away the sheets, she smiled as she saw the ceremonial dagger that a visiting dignitary had given her the previous week. Not knowing what else to do with it, she'd been using it to open letters.

Now she stared at the gleaming blade and the gold handle. She touched the cool metal. How on earth was she going to talk to Khalil about their relationship? They needed to change the status quo, but she hated to give in nearly as much as he did.

As she traced the blunt side of the blade, an idea formed. It was outrageous and ridiculous, and it just might work. A quick glance at the clock told her that the party should be over by now. Dora grinned as she rose to her feet. There was no time like the present. And if she was wrong about Khalil and he was currently with Amber, then she was better off knowing before she made a complete fool out of herself.

Less than a half hour later, she moved quietly through the halls of the palace. She'd dressed in one of her most elegant gowns, a low-cut designer original that exposed more cleavage than she usually liked—but tonight she needed to be armed in more ways than one. She held the dagger in her right hand, pressing it flat against her body. She doubted anyone would notice the weapon.

Fortunately she made her way to Khalil's chamber without being seen. Once there, she let herself inside and quietly locked the door behind her. Then she walked toward him.

Her husband was alone. She took in that information with a brief glance around the room. He sat at his desk, which faced the ocean. So far he hadn't noticed her presence.

She studied him. The French doors were closed, but he hadn't drawn the shutters, so the lamps in the room made the windows reflect like mirrors. She could clearly see the dark lock of hair that fell across his forehead. He'd discarded his tuxedo jacket and tie and tossed them across the sofa. His shirt was unbuttoned, and his sleeves were rolled to his elbows.

He was the picture of masculine casualness, and his male beauty took her breath away. How she wanted him, she thought as the longing swept through her. Not just in her bed, but in her life. She wanted to grow old with this man. As far as she could tell, there was only one way to find a compromise between what she wanted and what he was able to give. Dear Lord, please let her be right.

She took a step toward him, then another. Her heart pounded so hard, she thought she might faint. When she was six feet behind him, Khalil finally looked up and caught her reflection in the mirror.

"Dora, what are you doing here? Are you all right?"

She watched his face, noting the transformation from delight at her unexpected appearance, to concern. Then she moved up behind him and held the dagger to his throat.

He didn't even have the courtesy to look surprised, she thought in disgust as Khalil simply set down his pen and met her gaze in the window.

"If you sought to gain my attention," he said calmly, "you have done so."

She pressed the blade against his skin. "If I ever find you've been unfaithful to me, I will cut you, Khalil, but it won't be across the throat."

"I see. Thank you for telling me in advance. However, I'm not concerned. I have no desire to be with any woman save my wildcat of a wife."

She watched as a slight smile pulled at the corners of his mouth. "Don't for a moment think I'm bluffing," she informed him. "I will do it. You are my husband and the possessor of my heart. As such you owe me respect and honor."

His smile disappeared as if it had never been. In one quick movement he grasped her wrist and pulled it away, then spun in his seat until he faced her. When he rose to his feet, he pulled the dagger free and tossed it to the ground where it skittered against the tile and slid into the corner.

"What did you say?" he asked, his gaze intense.

She stared at his face noting the tightening of the muscles around his mouth and the light of some new fire in his eyes.

"Tell me," he insisted. "Tell me again that I am the possessor of your heart."

This wasn't exactly the turn she'd expected for their conversation, and his scrutiny made her a little nervous. "You heard me the first time." She wiggled to free herself, but his hold on her wrists only tightened. "Let me go."

"Never," he said fiercely and swept her up in his arms.

He carried her across the room and lowered her onto the bed, then settled next to her. "I will never let you go, wife of mine." He stroked her face, then brushed his thumb across her lips. "For you are mine, aren't you?"

"Yes," she whispered, unable to deny the truth. "I love you with all my heart." She glared at him. "But don't think that's going to change things between us, because you love me, too. I want a real marriage. I want us to live together like man and wife, and I want you to swear you're never going to sleep with anyone else, especially Amber."

At the mention of the younger woman, some of the light faded from Khalil's eyes. He drew her close and wrapped his arms around her, urging her to rest her head on his shoulder.

"I should have known she would make trouble," he murmured. "I should have told you the truth about her, but I was ashamed."

Dora looked at him. "I don't understand. You were engaged to her."

"Yes, but it was an arranged match, and one I was frantic to avoid. I never wanted to have anything to do with her. She disgusts me. For several years Amber has been something of a hedonist. She finds sport in hopping from bed to bed. I didn't want to tell the truth about her because of her father."

Dora had learned enough of El Baharian law and custom to understand that. "Aleser is a good leader for the country," she said. "If you told him about his daughter, he would be forced to resign."

Khalil nodded. "When we were in New York, Amber came to see me. She reminded me that we were engaged and insisted we would be married. I felt trapped."

So many things fell into place, Dora thought. Khalil's

need to find a solution to a difficult problem. Why the other woman had been so cruel.

"And there I was," she said. "A tolerable answer."

He wrapped his arms around her and rolled until she rested on top of him. "Far more than tolerable," he said, brushing her mouth with his. "You are the light of my life."

"You love me," she said.

He sighed. "Yes, Dora. I love you."

She smiled. "Oh, Khalil, we've both been so very stubborn. It makes me sad."

"It should. The situation was your fault entirely. If only you'd been a cooperative, sensible woman we could have—"

She pushed away from him and tried to scramble off the bed. He held her fast.

"Where do you think you're going?" he asked, hauling her up against him.

She pushed again, but couldn't make any progress. The man was too strong. "The dagger is still in the room," she said, glaring at him. "I think I'll use it on you."

He laughed. "Never. You love me too much."

"I know. I hate that."

"No, you don't."

She relaxed against him. "No, I don't," she agreed.

He stroked her hair, then kissed the top of her head. "Have you loved me long?" he asked.

His voice sounded casual, but Dora heard an undercurrent she couldn't explain. She looked at him. Darkness filled his eyes, something that, had it been anyone but Khalil, she would have labeled as uncertainty.

"Yes," she told him. "Almost from the beginning."

"Then how could you have turned away from me all

those times I came to your room. Why didn't you want to make love?''

He asked the question not as a prince, but as a man. A man who has been brought to his knees before a woman. Her heart ached for him. ''Every time I struggled against my desire for you. I wanted you desperately. I always want you.''

He kissed her deeply. ''As I always want you. The reason I didn't come to you tonight was because you seemed to feel ill.''

''I know.'' She knew so much more now. Amber would never come between them again.

Khalil sat up and pulled off his shirt. He quickly slipped off his shoes, socks, slacks and briefs, then stretched out naked on the bed.

''You have much to answer for,'' he said imperiously. ''You have denied your husband his proper place in your bed, as well as your heart. The punishment for your actions will be severe.'' He motioned to his arousal. ''You may begin atoning for your sins by servicing me this evening.''

''Oh, may I?'' Dora asked, not sure she could believe he'd actually said that. Tell a man you love him and he assumes he owns the world.

''I would not deny you your opportunity to please me.''

''How gracious,'' she murmured and rose to her feet.

So Khalil thought he would get the best of her, did he? She hid a smile. Two could play at this game.

Dora slowly slipped off her dress, then her stockings. She unfastened her bra and let the straps slide down her arms before releasing the garment. When she'd pulled off her panties, she knelt over her husband and lowered herself until her erect nipples nearly brushed his mouth.

"Tell me what you want, Prince Khalil, and I will do your bidding."

His eyes glazed over slightly as he reached up and pulled her closer. Then he licked her nipple and made them both moan. She shuddered. Already she was wet. She could feel the heat and the pressure between her legs, and he hadn't even entered her. She was aroused and ready just by being close to him.

"I want you," he said, gazing at her. "I love you. Promise you'll come live with me here."

"There's nowhere else I'd rather be. Anything else?"

He thought for a moment. "Promise that you'll always love me."

Her feelings welled up inside of her, filling her with a sense of rightness she'd never known. "Forever, husband."

"Which is nearly as long as I will love you."

"Is that everything?" she asked. "Do you have more desires?"

"Several." He grinned. "You may begin satisfying them by making love with me. Lower yourself onto me."

"Yes, Your Highness."

She did as he requested, sliding her waiting heat over him, taking him inside, deeper and deeper. He groaned.

"Dora," he gasped as his eyes sank closed. "I've missed you."

She didn't bother pointing out that it had only been two nights since they'd last made love. Instead she tightened her muscles around him until he was tense and ready. He arched into her, holding her over him, moving her hips until she rode him up and down in a rhythm designed to take them both over the edge.

She found it difficult to concentrate, but she forced herself back from the edge long enough to speak his name.

"What, love?" he asked.

She held her hips still, then lowered them again, at the same time she brushed his lips with hers. "I'm pregnant."

His eyes widened, and he opened his mouth to speak, but it was too late. His shock had allowed passion to take him unaware, thrusting him into paradise. He gave a strangled groan, a half laugh, then drew her close.

She knew then that she had won. Not just their teasing game, but the love of this wonderful man. What had started out as a marriage of convenience and duty had instead turned into the miracle that occurs between the most fortunate of men and women. She and Khalil were among those lucky enough to find a match that would last longer than a mere lifetime...one that was destined to be written in the clear beauty of the El Baharian sky.

\*     \*     \*     \*     \*

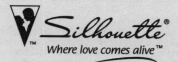

If you enjoyed what you just read,
then we've got an offer you can't resist!

# Take 2 bestselling love stories FREE!

# Plus get a FREE surprise gift!